MURDERER'S
VANITY

AN AMOS LEE MAPPIN MYSTERY

MURDERER'S VANITY

AN AMOS LEE MAPPIN MYSTERY

HULBERT FOOTNER

COACHWHIP PUBLICATIONS

Greenville, Ohio

CONTENTS

CHAPTER ONE

TYRRELL BLAIR THE PUBLISHER was a famous host. Since early manhood it had been his ambition to have people say that he gave the best dinners in New York, and in the end he realized it. Whether in his own home or in a restaurant, he insisted on inspecting the food before it was cooked, and indeed he frequently interfered in the cooking too. It was his boast that the most famous chefs in the world were among his personal friends. There was never anything spectacular or bizarre about Blair's dinners; the focus was exclusively upon food perfectly cooked and washed down by perfect vintages.

Amos Lee Mappin as he ate it, guessed that this particular dinner, simple as it was, had cost hours of planning and preparation. It was the classical Maryland dinner; Chincoteague oysters, terrapin stew, fried chicken with corn fritters that swooned on the tongue; no sweet, because Blair said that sweets spoiled the palate for wine, but a salad and an assortment of cheeses. With the successive courses came an Amontillado of distinguished lineage, a Montrachet that Titania might have sipped by moonlight, a Romanée Conti ("Not exactly de rigueur with chicken," explained their host, "but for the sake of variety!") and a marvelous champagne. From the bottles of the last-named the labels had been removed. "An importation of my own," said Blair with a wave of the hand.

Lee Mappin loved to dine out, but limited himself to three nights a week in order not to dull the edge of his pleasure. Being a gourmet too, in his own quiet way, he could always be had for one of Blair's dinners. At this one he was the guest of honor, the occasion being the publication that day by the firm of Blair and Middlebrook of Amos Lee Mappin's latest studies in crime, "Murder and Fantasy." Lee thought it a little silly to give a formal dinner for such a purpose, but of course he was not going to stand in the way of promoting his own book. Among the guests were Lewis Gannett, Harry Hansen, John Chamberlain and other distinguished reviewers. It was not easy to capture these birds for dinner.

Lee himself at all times was much sought after as a dinner guest. Nature had not done much for him outwardly; he was the smallest man at the table, besides being over-plump, and shiningly bald. But notwithstanding these physical disabilities he had a curious air of distinction. He was known to have a pretty wit all the more effective because his manner was so mild and disarming. His quiet voice was listened to with closer attention than many a bigger man's roar.

In addition to good food Lee loved to watch the play of human expression around a dinner table; to note the impact of contrasting personalities. This, he claimed, was the purest pleasure known to man. To make it perfect, there must be beautiful women's faces included; the average of good looks around this table was high. On Lee's left sat Mary Blair, a distinguished, dark-haired beauty. Some thought her cold and inexpressive, but when you knew her better there was the suggestion of an inner warmth, very alluring. She was Tyrrell Blair's third wife. It was occasionally the publisher's humor to invite all three of his wives to lunch in a fashionable restaurant, and show them off to the amused spectators. Something of the Turk about Blair, thought Lee. Lee got along excellently well with Mary Blair. She had once confided in him that he was one of the few people she was not afraid of.

Later in the evening Lee was to broadcast. "Will this be your first time on the air?" asked Mary.

"My very first."

"Are you nervous?" Her way of lowering her voice as if to single him out privately was charming. "I hope it's not interfering with your appetite."

"For terrapin?" said Lee. "Watch me! . . . Why should I be nervous? The script has been prepared beforehand; all I have to do is read it to Mike."

From the other side of Lee, Peggy Deshon broke in: "I was on the air last week. All the preparations were so solemn I was terrified at first, and then it roused the devil in me. You know, like a child is tempted to be naughty in church. I wanted to swear into the mike just to see what would happen. But I didn't."

They laughed. "You wouldn't have got far," said Lee. "I am told that the man at the controls is ready for anything."

Peggy Deshon was the wife of the clever Rafe Deshon, who managed Tyrrell Blair's promotion and publicity. She was a perfect flower of modern New York, the darling of the paragraphers, and quite as clever in her way as her husband. At the dinner table a man could not have asked for a better partner, Lee thought, though she might prove a little unrestful by the fireside—but he absolutely could not imagine Peggy sitting by the fire.

Looking around the table, Lee saw that his two secretaries, Fanny Parran and Judy Bowles, for whom he had obtained invitations, were doing their full share to keep up the average of beauty. No prettier girls anywhere, he thought, the one as blond and fluffy as the other was dark and statuesque. But Fanny's fluffiness was deceptive, as many a brash young man had discovered.

The faces of the men at the table, while less pleasing to the eye, were full of character. At the head, Tyrrell Blair, a big man, full-blooded, supremely confident, fifty years and some but as yet showing few signs of decay. The fact that he had been accustomed since boyhood to the world's best, had given him a kind of kingly air—though palace-born kings seldom show it. His affairs with women were notorious; in his regal way he disdained concealment; the charmer of the moment was seated beside him now; his wife did not appear to resent it. Like other modern couples they were accustomed to go their separate ways. Blair could seldom be lured away from New York, but Mary spent long periods at their other houses in Florida, Old Westbury, or Bar Harbor.

Blair was announcing in his fruity voice: "I could sell the worst book ever written!"

Smiling to himself, Lee thought: Not the most tactful remark in the world. Luckily my skin is not as thin as some authors'. He saw Rafe Deshon glance at his employer dryly. Evidently Rafe was saying to himself: You mean I could sell the book for you.

Rafe Deshon, was a perpetually interesting study to Lee, who could not quite get his number. Rafe had everything; good looks, brains, and wit. Lee had never seen Rafe do the wrong thing or get in his own light. Rafe was considered the mainspring of the Blair company, the man who really made the works go, while the senior partner amused himself. His salary was said to be $50,000 a year. In addition, Rafe conducted a column in the town's most popular weekly and was one of the most run-after young men between Madison Square and the Plaza. All he seemed to lack was a heart.

Among the other men at the table was Fanny Parran's red-headed journalist, Tom Cottar, who, disregarding Blair's arrangements had contrived to get a seat beside his girl. Lee liked this homely, impudent lad, and was a little jealous of him, because Tom so conspicuously had what Lee had always felt that he lacked, an attraction for women. True, nowadays the ladies crowded around Lee, but that was because he had become famous, and it gave him little satisfaction as a man. Tom and Fanny were disputing in low voices. They could never agree about anything under the sun.

Next to Judy sat Boris Fanton, the preferred radio announcer of the moment, a dark, handsome man with passionate eyes. Lee distrusted emotional men. The fellow possessed a beautiful deep voice to which millions of ladies had succumbed on the air. He and Judy had become very friendly during the last few weeks, and Lee did not like it. There were said to be marital complications in Fanton's past which had never been cleared up; moreover, there was a look of bad temper about him. In a lull of the conversation Lee heard him saying to Judy:

"I insist on editing my scripts. You see there is always an awkward way to speak a thing and an easy natural way, and writers don't know the difference."

Conceited puppy! thought Lee.

Since they were celebrating the publication of a book by Lee Mappin, the conversation inevitably got around to the subject of crime. Somebody asked the question:

"Why is crime so popular?"

There were several answers. One said: "Because we lead such dull lives."

Another: "Because we all have suppressed criminal instincts."

"If that is so, why does the detective always come out on top in crime novels?"

"Maybe the public would enjoy it more if the criminal came out on top, but the publishers don't dare issue such books."

"I will publish any book ever written if it has blood in it!" cried Blair, striking the table.

While the others lighted cigarettes, Lee took a pinch of snuff. "In my books," he said mildly, "which are accounts of real crimes, the detectives don't always come out on top. But of course my books don't sell like novels."

"Lee's books sell better than novels," cried Rafe for the benefit of the assembled reviewers.

At ten minutes past nine Fanton, with a glance at his watch, stood up. "If you will excuse us now," he said in his deep, thrilling voice. "We have to go over the script, you know, for the timing."

Lee and Rafe Deshon got up. "Good luck, Lee!" cried the other guests. "Don't drop your script on the floor . . . Don't lose your place . . . For God's sake don't sneeze!"

The dinner was being held in a private room of the Louis XVI Restaurant in the R.C.A. Building, consequently the three men had only to take an elevator to the appointed studio. Blair had installed a big radio cabinet in the dinner room so that the other guests could hear Lee's talk.

Above in the studio, Lee looked around with interest. Like everything connected with the show business, the long room exhibited an orderly disorder. All the strange and varied properties required by the acts using that room were scattered around, together with weird electrical gadgets that he could not guess the use of. It was an extraordinary litter of incongruous objects, but he knew that nothing was unnecessary, nor would anything be mislaid.

Fanton had three clean scripts, one for each of them. "This incorporates all the changes we agreed on this afternoon," he said.

Deshon was supposed to be interviewing Lee. They sat down opposite each other at a small table, each with a microphone hanging before him. Fanton, standing nearby, read his script from a lectern. Alongside the table stretched a large plate glass window, but Lee paid no attention to it since all was dark on the other side.

Lee was warned not to rattle the pages of his script during the broadcast. "The best way is to let each page flutter to the floor as you finish it," said Fanton.

The announcer glanced at the studio clock and began to read. Nature had given him a fine speaking voice, and the voice had procured him a well-paid job. Unfortunately, Lee noted, he had now fallen in love with it; he caressed it, he played on it like an organ. He won't last long, thought Lee. After Fanton, Rafe took up the story, and finally Lee got his cue.

While Lee was speaking a great sound filled the room like the voice of God. "You don't need to speak so fast, Mr. Mappin. We are giving you all the time you want."

Lee looked around him wildly and at last found the little control room on the other side of the plate glass, where a young man was seated before his instruments. This one he suspected, was the real boss of the proceedings.

When the rehearsal was over Lee said in his mild way; "There is a change in the script that I was not consulted about."

"What's that, Mr. Mappin?"

"You make me get off the old gag here that murder will out. In my original script I said the exact opposite. Did you edit me, Mr. Fanton?"

"No," said the announcer a little sullenly. "That was done upstairs."

"But why? In my books I have said over and over that of course there are murders which never come to light."

"They considered up-stairs that it would be against the public interest to broadcast such an idea."

Lee tapped his snuff box and took a pinch. "How solicitous of them! However, these are supposed to be my ideas, aren't they?"

"What do you want to do about it?" asked Rafe Deshon.

"God forbid that I should go against the public interest," said Lee dryly. "I suggest that we cut out the whole section dealing with the prevalence of murder, pages six and seven."

"You can't do that," said Fanton excitedly. "We'd be a couple of minutes short."

"Then I'll write in something else."

"There's no time. We're on the air in forty-five seconds. And you're not allowed to ad lib."

Lee ran up his eyebrows. "Not allowed?"

Fanton glanced at the studio clock. "Get ready."

One cannot keep millions waiting. Rafe Deshon was biting his fingers in anxiety. "What am I to do when I get to page six?" he demanded.

Lee was a good-natured man. "Oh, let it go," be said. "It's not of world-shaking importance . . . next time—if there is a next time, I will take care that my ideas are not tampered with."

Afterwards when he remembered his easy acquiescence, Lee thought: It's a good thing we can't foresee the consequences of our careless acts or we'd be afraid to do or say anything.

Meanwhile when the red second hand of the clock pointed to 60, a little sign flashed in fiery letters: "You are on the air!" Fanton turned on his mellifluous voice. Following him, Rafe Deshon's voice by contrast was crisp and telling. Rafe was an old hand at this, and Lee noted with what accuracy he attuned his effects to the ear. When it was Lee's turn to speak, a little thrill of excitement possessed him. He tried to visualize the listening audience of millions but was quite unable to do so. During Lee's talk Rafe punctuated it with little chuckles of appreciative amusement into his mike; but Fanton, when he was not speaking himself, was merely bored.

CHAPTER TWO

Amos Lee Mappin rented a suite in a handsome old dwelling on lower Madison Avenue which had been converted into offices. Since he insisted on maintaining the status of an amateur, he had no absolute need for an office, but he could afford it, and he said that the act of going to the office kept him at work. Moreover, at the office he could make appointments to meet all sorts of queer characters that he did not care to bring home. The secret of his private address was carefully guarded.

The office suite consisted of a large room on the second floor with three windows looking down on the avenue and two smaller rooms in the rear, all furnished in plain and businesslike fashion. There was no elevator in the building. The front room was the daily habitat of the blond Fanny Parran and the dark-haired Judy Bowles who served Lee in the triple capacity of secretaries, research workers, and, when he happened to be actually engaged in an investigation, as operatives. The small room which Lee used for a private office had its own door on the corridor, to enable him to slip out unseen should there be an unwelcome caller in front. The building was kept in order by a respectable couple who lived in the basement.

Lee's mail was very heavy owing to the amount of publicity he had received. He made a point of answering every letter, however trifling, because it pleased him to think of the innocent pleasure he conveyed by this means, even if his answer was only a form. The broadcast produced an increased number of letters. Skimming over them on the following morning, Lee thought: What a lot of

people there are in the world with time on their hands! One letter
Fanny had not ventured to open since it was marked: "Private and
Confidential." It was in a plain envelope, the address typewritten;
it had been posted late the night before in the General Post Office,
New York. Lee opened it and read:

> Lee Mappin:
> I have just been listening to your broadcast, and I
> must say I was surprised and disgusted to hear a man
> who claims to be as intelligent as you do, putting out
> the old dope to the effect that "Murder will out." You
> ought to know better. A few minutes thought (if you
> are capable of thinking, which I doubt) would con-
> vince you that for every murder that is discovered,
> there must be ten which never come to light. When
> you consider the mental calibre of detectives (and I
> include you) the wonder is that murder is ever found
> out. It is only the congenital fools among murderers
> that are caught; those who are incapable of planning
> a good crime, and those weaklings who lose their
> heads and give themselves away afterwards.
>
> For some time past I have been preparing to com-
> mit a murder, and my plans are almost ripe. I am in
> no hurry because I enjoy the preliminaries. Murder
> provides the keenest thrill a man is capable of feel-
> ing. It is ten times more fascinating than a play on
> the stage to watch the unsuspecting fly buzzing
> closer and closer to the web you have stretched for
> him. Do not try to laugh this off by telling yourself I
> am mad. Never in my life has my brain functioned
> better. I never before had such an incentive to clear
> thinking. And it isn't merely a stunt crime, under-
> taken to prove my ideas. I hate the person who has
> injured me and, what is worse, threatens to make a
> fool of me, publicly. I'm not going to wait for that.
> My hatred is like a fire in my breast. God! how sweet

it will be to kill! Nor will I ever feel remorse. I never was sorry for anything I did. As long as I live I'll hug the thought of my crime.

So there's a problem for you, Mr. Crime-detector! You think yourself very clever, but I am cleverer. I work calmly; I provide for everything. You will never be able to come close to me. My only regret is that nobody can ever know how perfect a murder I have planned. I'll let you know when I pull it off, and will keep you informed from time to time how close you are getting, and in that way I will enjoy a kind of vicarious satisfaction.

                                        Yours,
                                        X.

Lee, frowning, read this over a second time. He told himself he was a fool to let it irritate him because it was obvious that the writer had set out with just that intention. Yet he couldn't help feeling irritated. Somebody was pulling his leg he was sure, and if he took it seriously, the writer would give him the big laugh directly. The only thing to do was to ignore it as he had ignored all anonymous letters . . . Yet there was something about this one that disturbed him deeply: was it a ring of genuineness? The writer's cry of hatred sounded real. But even suppose there *was* something in it, what could he do? His hands were tied; the letter conveyed no clue.

It had been typewritten on a sheet of inexpensive white paper with a smooth finish. The paper had for a watermark the word Cronicon with U.S.A. beneath. He made a memo of it. The spacing of the words was irregular and there were some erasures, suggesting that it had not been written by an expert typist. There were no mistakes in spelling and the language was that of a person of some culture. Lee got out his magnifying glass. The letter had been typed with a fresh ribbon, he could see, and the machine was a fairly new one. There were some infinitesimal peculiarities in the type that might perhaps be identified—but first he would have to find the machine, he told himself grimly.

In the end, still feeling exasperated and disturbed, he filed the letter away among his literary curiosities without showing it to anybody. He had an engagement to lunch at the Colony with Rafe Deshon. Rafe turned up looking like the glass of fashion and the mold of form. There was a slight stir when the pair of them entered the restaurant a few minutes later, and many of the marvelously-hatted women turned their heads.

"You are famous to-day," whispered Rafe. "After the broadcast."

"Nonsense," said Lee. "It is your blond head they are looking at, not my bald one."

"Nothing to it," said Rafe. "I'm only the promoter, the introducer. They never look at me, but only to see who I'm bringing."

Lee's roly-poly little figure was not imposing, but it had distinction. He could never have been dismissed as a nonentity; the grey eyes behind the brightly polished glasses were too keen. His style of dress was all his own; he had gone early nineteenth century so far as he could without attracting too much attention; narrow trousers, white waistcoat, a black satin cravat which suggested a stock, and so on. It suited him and he knew it. Whenever he was embarrassed or wished to gain a moment's time before speaking, he took snuff.

They were shown to a table. Rafe was full of last night's broadcast. The station, it seemed, was inundated with telephone calls and letters; Lee's debut on the air was considered a great success. Already one of the leading agents had made an offer for Lee to give a weekly broadcast on crime at a flattering figure. A sponsor had come forward, and time was available on a coast-to-coast network.

Lee thinking of the annoyance that had resulted from his first broadcast, said: "I won't do it!'

Rafe said: "As a public figure, you can hardly avoid it."

"I don't want to be a public figure," said Lee. "I'm happier when I'm working in the dark like a mole."

"It's not my fault if the public insists on beating a path to your door."

"I can refuse to answer the bell," said Lee.

"Think how it would promote your book. You could plug it week after week."

"Absolutely, no," said Lee. "That's one of the things that's the matter with the world. Too much plugging!"

Rafe was too wise to pursue the matter further. Lee was well aware that he would bring it up again.

Upon returning to the office he found that Fanny and Judy were holding an impromptu reception. Seven or eight bright young men were clustering around the girls' desks, the red-headed Tom Cottar among them, and a good time was being had by all. On the outskirts of the group hovered Jim Costin, the janitor of the building—or, it would be more proper to say, the janitor's husband, since Costin had never been seen to do a tap of work around the house.

This Costin was a travesty of a gentleman in seedy attire. A man of some education, he was completely dependent on his wife, a grim silent woman who worked hard to keep her children decently clad. Costin claimed to be writing a book and spent most of his daytime hours in the reading-room of the public library. Fanny, who often visited the library for research, reported that he sat there idly turning pages of old illustrated weeklies, or enjoying a snooze when he could escape the notice of the attendants. When they happened to meet, Costin addressed Lee familiarly, as one author to another. It amused Lee to draw him out. At the moment Lee marked how Costin was listening to the talk of the reporters with an attentive ear. He really had no business to be in the room, and at Lee's entrance he quietly slunk out. The reporters were waiting for Lee. Tom Cottar was constituted their spokesman, and he said:

"Mr. Mappin, we understand you received a letter from a crank this morning, announcing that he was about to commit a murder."

Lee concealed his surprise and annoyance. "Oh, *that!*" he said with a laugh. "I don't take any stock in anonymous letters. Do you want to see it?"

"Only for the purposes of comparison, sir. We've all received copies."

"The deuce you have!" said Lee. "Well, anyhow, that relieves my mind."

"How come, Mr. Mappin?"

"Well, I thought there might be something in it, and I was a little worried. But if it's newspaper publicity the writer is after, that proves he's only suffering from an inflamed ego."

"I don't know," said Tom. "Somehow this doesn't sound like the usual crank letter. There is real feeling in it."

This, which coincided with Lee's own inward opinion, induced a fresh spurt of irritation in him. He was careful to hide it from these wise young guys.

One asked; "Have you any idea who wrote it, Mr. Mappin?"

"Not the slightest."

"What are you going to do about it?"

Lee looked surprised. "Do about it? Why, nothing."

"Oh, you can't do that, Mr. Mappin. Not after it's been noticed in the press."

"Why can't I?"

"All your fans will expect you to take action; to show up the writer."

"That would be attaching too much importance to him. He is either a harmless lunatic or a practical joker. I have more important things to attend to. I rather incline to the practical joker theory. I wouldn't put it past one of you fellows; perhaps my young friend Tom here wrote it, just for the sake of the story."

"I wish I *had* thought of it," said Tom grinning. "There's a good story in it. But I didn't."

"Or my ingenious promoter, Rafe Deshon," said Lee. "You'd better be careful or you'll be giving him free publicity."

"The publicity won't be any good to you unless you take some action," said Tom.

Lee shook his head. "You've had your fun with me now, boys. If you'll excuse me . . ."

"Analyse the letter for us," one pleaded. "You're a psychologist. What can you tell about the writer from his letter?"

Lee reflected that the letter-writer would be sure to read what he might say. If he could sting the man into writing again, perhaps in his second letter he would betray himself. "Okay," he said, picking up the letter with a smile, "let's see what this tells us."

After studying it for a moment, he went on: "In an anonymous letter the submerged personality comes to the surface, and generally it's not a pretty sight. This is no exception. The man, you see, insults me crudely because he feels safe in doing so. He would never dare tell me to my face that I am a fool."

"You speak of him as a man," put in Tom, "but can you be sure that the letter wasn't written by a woman?"

"Absolutely. The language, the form of expression is masculine. We all know these frustrated egoists. Their names decorate the walls of public toilets. It will give him an exquisite pleasure to read his letter in to-night's papers. He is a neurotic; one of the feeble creatures who compensate for their weakness by indulging in fantasies, daydreams of murder and so on. They are not dangerous. Such a man should not be treated as a criminal, but sent to a psychoanalyst."

Tom Cottar lingered behind the others for a moment. "But Pop," he protested, "there is more in this . . ."

Lee's eyes gleamed behind his glasses. "Write what I gave you," he said, "or nothing."

"Okay, Pop."

Not that he expected anything to come of it, but just as a precaution, Lee called up his friend Inspector Loasby at Headquarters and suggested that he have the General Post Office watched that night. Loasby promised to have it done. Men were to be stationed in the corridors where the letter chutes were, and other men inside at the bottom of the chutes. If a letter dropped addressed to Amos Lee Mappin the man inside was to blow a whistle.

Nothing came of it, but next morning Lee received another letter in the first mail. This one had been posted at Station W. on the upper West Side. The newspaper interview had had the effect that Lee designed; the letter-writer was angry.

Lee Mappin:
I always suspected you were a false alarm and now I know it. You made a pitiful exhibition of yourself in the papers this evening. The whole town is laughing at you. You are nothing but a balloon all blown up

by publicity, and at a prick you collapse. You call yourself a psychologist and when you are asked to analyse the character of the writer of my first letter, being completely up in the air all you can answer is that I am a writer on the walls of toilets. You know more about toilet writing than I do. You call me a neurotic, a day-dreamer. As a matter of fact I'm the exact opposite. I'm considered . . . (Here two words were blacked out.) I feel quite safe now. You will never catch up with me, and neither will your friends the police that you have called in to help you. I suppose I ought to be glad you're so dumb, but in reality I'm disappointed. I anticipated engaging in a battle of wits with you, but now I see you haven't any wits to match me with.

Mind, I have warned you that I am about to commit a murder, and I now repeat the warning. If you fail to stop me, the blood of the victim will be on your head. You can't get out of that.

X.

Lee read this with a grim smile. This letter showed more mistakes in typing, due no doubt to having been written in the haste of anger. It was all very well to make the man sore, but it didn't get him much forrader. The writer's anger ruled out the practical joker theory. There would be no call for a joker to get angry. Only two alternatives remained; either the letter-writer was mad, or he was really a potential murderer. Lee studied the letter for indications of madness. The preposterous assertion in the last paragraph showed a warped mind perhaps, but scarcely insane. Many little things that he could not define in his conscious mind, strengthened Lee's feeling that the writer of these letters actually meant to kill. It was overweening vanity that forced him to confess the gruesome secret in advance to Lee.

Lee jumped up and paced the little room gritting his teeth. What a truly horrible position he would be in if a murder was committed and he, while knowing about it, was unable to prevent it. This man must be acquainted with me, he thought, he has so unerringly picked out the weak joint in my armor.

Copies of the second letter as of the first were sent to the various newspapers. The editors decided that it was too scurrilous to run. However, they sent the boys around to Lee's office to ask if he had anything to say about it.

"Not a word!" said Lee. "The cruelest punishment we can inflict on this bird is to refuse him any space."

The reporters agreed. Tom Cottar with his uncanny perspicuity, said:

"This letter sounds almost as if the man knew you, Pop."

"Oh, no!" said Lee quickly.

"Then how do you account for the personal hatred that it reveals?"

"I've met with that before," said Lee. "It always surprises me because I look on myself as a very inoffensive person. I explain it this way: (a) the man is an egomaniac, therefore (b) he prizes publicity above everything else in the world and (c) he is bitterly envious because so much publicity is thrust on me unasked."

When the boys left him Lee sent a copy of the latest letter down to Inspector Loasby. He kept the originals in his office safe.

On the following morning, letter number three arrived. This had been posted at another branch post office, Station D.

> Lee Mappin:
> To-day I purchased the weapon. It's a common kitchen knife with a six inch blade. I invite you to trace the purchase. A knife just like it can be bought for a few cents in any one of ten thousand stores in the Greater New York area. I have sharpened it to a point like a rapier. The quality of the steel is wretched of course, but it will serve for one stroke. I have been studying anatomical charts to make certain that one blow is sufficient. I know the exact spot to strike either in the breast or in the back. A gun would be cleaner and more certain, but a gun makes

too much noise. When I plant my knife nothing will
be heard but a low, choked cry. Moreover, I require
the knife for another purpose afterwards.

X.

CHAPTER THREE

WHILE LEE WAS DEALING with this private anxiety he was involved in his publisher's intensive campaign for the promotion of his book For an entire afternoon he was forced to sit at a table in the aisle of a crowded, stuffy, department store autographing copies of "Murder and Fantasy." The intending purchasers stared at him as if he were some grotesque animal in a menagerie. They asked him inane questions to which he was forced to make equally inane answers. If he answered intelligently he wasn't understood. All this was very trying to his dignity, but he had to put up with it, because, having quarreled with his publishers' indifference to his work in the past, he could not very well object to their present measures.

On the morning following this ordeal Lee received another of X's letters. It said: "I bought a copy of "Murder and Fantasy" from you yesterday. So you've taken to peddling your own wares! Nice work! You show a certain amount of industry in digging up the details of past crimes from old newspaper files, but there isn't an original thought from the first page to the last. You're nothing but a literary parasite. Of course I knew this before I bought the book, but I wanted to have a good look at you close to. I was not impressed."

Lee could afford to smile at this. The crude malice reminded him of the comic valentines of his youth. They too, were sent anonymously. He strongly doubted that the writer had bought a book of him, because he had a persistent hunch that the letters came from somebody that he knew personally. He called up the faces of the day before as well as he could. The great majority had been women, but there were a dozen or so of men. He could not bring to mind a single face. Well, I can't remember everything, he told himself.

The letter went on: "You ought to tell your friend Loasby he might as well call off his men from the branch post-offices. While they are loafing and watching the letter slots, the crooks are making hay elsewhere. I shan't use the post-offices again. After all, there's a letter box on the nearest corner."

Every day during this time there was some sort of social show where Rafe Deshon said it was absolutely necessary for Lee to show himself; a reception to a visiting celebrity; a first night at the theatre; a public dinner. In particular Lee detested the public dinners. Though he and Rafe had been thrown much together for some time past, Lee had never cared greatly for the publicity director. Rafe, handsome, smiling, overflowing with ingenious new ideas for publicity, seemed a little too good to be true. It was not blood that ran in his veins but advertising copy.

When Rafe released Lee, Peggy was generally there to take him in charge. Peggy would show him off at the smartest nightclubs where she reigned like a Dresden china queen. When Lee objected that the Monte Carlo was not exactly his style, she rejoined smartly:

"Nonsense, Lee! You're a celebrity and you look the part. You have what it takes to succeed in New York!"

"When I consider how my dancing pumps hurt it hardly seems worth while."

"Everybody's feet hurt after two in the morning."

"Don't you get tired of doing the same thing every night?" he asked.

"I can't afford to get tired. It is in three or four places in New York like this that all the stones of publicity are dropped. From here the ripples are spread to the furthest edges of the country by the syndicated articles of the society reporters. Reputations are made and unmade here."

"What a bore it is to keep up a reputation!" said Lee.

Peggy's eyes narrowed. "I must be first or nowhere," she said.

One night Rafe and Peggy gave a small dinner to bring Lee in contact with the most powerful personality in radio. The radio offer had been increased and Lee was gradually being maneuvered into a position where he would have to accept it. The Deshons did not live in an apartment but in a recherché little house in the Sutton Place neighborhood. The furnishings of this house expressed the day after to-morrow in modernity. Every time Lee went there it appeared to have been done over. That was because when other women displayed anything Peggy had, Peggy threw hers out. Lee had been told that these amazing pieces of furniture and works of art cost the Deshons nothing because everything in Peggy's house was sure to be written up in the press.

Luckily for Lee's digestion the food was conventional.

As always he was amazed by the play of smiling camaraderie across the dinner table between Peggy and her husband. How were they able to keep it up? he asked himself. What were they like alone together? They put on a perfect show, yet he had a feeling that some place, some time, somebody had to pay for this excessive vivacity. To-night while he was in the house the veneer cracked for a moment, and he had a startling glimpse of what lay beneath.

It was after dinner and the guests were departing. Rafe and Peggy were downstairs seeing them off while Lee waited in the drawing-room at the back of the house above. He and Peggy were going on to a nightclub. For her drawing-room Peggy favored a French wallpaper at the moment with a design of big rosy flamingoes against a tropical swamp. Lee found it a little nightmarish and walked to the open French window. Outside there was a balcony. The night air was delicious in his face and the view over a short back yard to the East river twinkling with lights, very soothing.

But he heard voices close to the dining room windows under the balcony which murdered peace; low, terrible voices curdling with bitterness.

"I hate you! Oh God! how I hate you! It keeps me awake at night!" This was Rafe.

And Peggy: "That's because I've got your number, you poor four-flusher, you nothing-at-all! You know how I despise you and you can't bear it!"

"Be quiet! A man can stand only so much. Don't push me over the line!"

"You can't divorce me! You can't divorce me!" Peggy's voice hissed like snakes. "I'm necessary to you."

"No, but I could kill you!" said Rafe.

Peggy's answer was a silvery laugh. Peggy's laugh was famous and she lost no opportunity of letting it be heard.

A few moments afterwards the couple entered the drawing-room wreathed in happy smiles. Lee could scarcely believe his eyes. Peggy slipped her hand under her husband's arm.

"What have you got to do tonight, Ruffian?"

He patted her fingers. "Plenty, beautiful. First to the *Herald-Tribune* to make sure that a story I gave them is in print. I'll have to drink with some of the fellows there. Then to the Lambs to see a theatrical manager. He's not fit for human society until one o'clock. It'll take me a couple of hours to wangle what I want out of him. Then home to snatch forty winks. Got a big day at the office to-morrow."

"Wouldn't it be wonderful to spend an evening together for once," said Peggy.

Lee hoped they would not feel it necessary to stage a kiss for him. However they did not. Rafe departed.

A few minutes later Peggy and Lee were on their way in a taxicab to one of the town's most gilded spots. Peggy was chattering in her usual flip fashion. It gave Lee a bad taste in his mouth. Since these people called themselves his intimate friends, he felt justified in asking bluntly:

"Peggy, what's the trouble between you and Rafe?"

She laughed. "What on earth gave you that idea, Lee? Why we're considered the perfect modern couple."

"While I was waiting for you," said Lee, "I went out on the balcony. I couldn't help hearing you and Rafe in the dining-room."

"Oh, *that!*" she said. "Just a little husband and wife stuff behind the scenes. We all do it." Lee said nothing. She felt impelled to explain further. "We get along as well as most couples in this cock-eyed world. Better than most I guess, because we have a strong community of interest. I play Rafe's game and he plays mine. That creates a stronger bond than love, Lee."

"Maybe," said Lee. "But it must be pretty horrible to go on living with somebody you dislike."

"I don't let myself think about it," she said carelessly. "Rafe sticks to his part of the house and I to mine."

"Are you in love with somebody else?"

"No . . . Yes! It depends on what you mean. There is only one man in the world that I want, and he has no eyes for me. So I amuse myself with the others—plenty of others; always taking care never to let it get too serious."

"Who is the man?"

"Not going to tell you. You're too sharp anyhow. You can find out if you're sufficiently interested."

"And Rafe?"

She laughed. "You surely didn't believe that stuff about seeing a man at the Herald-Tribune and a theatrical manager at the Lambs' Club. He's gone to the tough girl friend; I heard him making the date. You should see her, Lee. A horse of a woman with a voice like a foghorn. He can have her. Honestly I don't care. But what makes me mad is that he won't allow me to be equally free. Am I supposed to live like a nun? Is it fair?"

"There's no fairness in marriage."

They were drawing up to the curb in front of their night club. Lee ordered the chauffeur to drive on up to Eighty-first Street and return.

"We should have gone in," said Peggy a little sullenly. "I don't like heart-to-heart talks. I prefer not to think at all."

"Can you live without thinking?"

"Sure! I make a rattle to keep the bogey-man away."

"What is the game you are playing, Peggy?"

"Why, to get on in the world, to be somebody, to lead! Don't think I'm kidded by this crazy life. I didn't make the world. I have to take it as I find it. I'm after something solid. Publicity makes names and names rule. I was born a have-not and I'm going to be a have. I can't get what I want without Rafe, but I can get it through him. So I use him. It's almost in my hand. Soon now Rafe will control the firm of Blair and Middlebrook while old Tyrrell gorges himself into an apoplexy. Then I can sit back and thumb my nose at the mob. When you tell them to go to hell they bow down to you more than ever."

"Good God, my dear, this is horrible!" said Lee.

"Not horrible but only honest. You're a sentimentalist, Lee."

"Well, I'm rather glad of it."

"The day of sentiment is over. It's a bad world, and you have to fight it with its own weapons."

"You can't live like this. Nobody can. In refusing to think and in suppressing all your feelings you're doing violence to the human nature in you. Believe me, nature has unexpected and horrible ways of getting back at you."

She laughed. "You think I may crack up, eh? Not I!"

Lee took another line. "Who is Rafe jealous of?"

"Of the man I told you about. Because he is a man, every inch of him, he's *real*; and Rafe in his heart knows he's only a sham man. So he hates him. What can I do about it? I can't give the other man up because I never had him!"

"You see," said Lee softly, "it is foolish to deny reality; you are at the mercy of reality."

Her voice began to shake. "For God's sake, Lee, don't fish up things from the bottom! What good does it do? We're all on the toboggan. Let her slide!"

She was staring straight ahead of her. The cab was passing a street light. Lee took her chin between thumb and forefinger and turned her face so that the light shone in it. Her eyes were brilliant and dry.

She laughed. "I'm not going to drizzle. A modern woman can't afford it. And I'm going to win!"

"All right," said Lee. "Just the same I advise you not to taunt Rafe. He might spoil your game."

She laughed. "Did he threaten to kill me in the dining room? I'm so accustomed to that, it doesn't register any more. You take him too seriously, Lee. He hasn't got the guts to do it. You take us all too seriously. Nobody has any strong feelings nowadays; we're just actors putting on a sorry show!"

"You're sick," said Lee, "and don't know it."

Peggy laughed. "A couple of glasses of champagne will cure me!"

When they entered El Zingara the major-domo and the captain of waiters bowed before them, the proprietor himself, an important figure in the New York scene, hastened to greet them. A table amongst the elect in the front of the room had been saved. As they moved toward it there were cries of welcome to Peggy from every side. Many came pressing up for a closer greeting. To Peggy it was more intoxicating than wine. She was in her own element here.

As they sat with their backs against the wall and a little table in front of them, there were always two or three leaning over trying to engage Peggy's attention. The red-headed Tom Cottar came by. The corners of Tom's lips were permanently turned up in a mocking grin.

"Hi, Beautiful!"

"Hi, Red!"

Peggy's greeting matched Tom's in mockery, but Lee felt a wariness drawing over her. Was this the man? he asked himself, measuring Tom. Tom was a stalwart, virile fellow, but his face was not much to look at. A handsome face is a positive disadvantage to a man, Lee thought. Peggy was waiting for Tom to ask her to dance, but he passed on to another woman at another table. Peggy drained her glass and pushed it toward Lee to be refilled.

ON THE FOLLOWING DAY there was an immense cocktail party at the Tyrrell Blairs. Though it was so large an affair, the list of guests was made up with the greatest care because this was to be a party that established social ratings. If you were not there you were nowhere. Rafe and Peggy Deshon checked the list since Mary Blair could not be induced to attach sufficient importance to such matters. It was useless for Lee to try to get out of attending the party. Rafe said: "If you don't show yourself everybody will say you're going to give your next book to another publisher."

"But as long as I'm not going to," objected Lee.

"The firm's credit would suffer in the meantime."

The Blair penthouse was a three-story affair topping one of the most conspicuous buildings overlooking the East river. It had everything including a yacht landing in the basement. This was no good to Blair who protested that he hated the water and had never owned even a row boat. When Lee arrived at six o'clock the immense rooms were already thronged. All the sharp-eyed guests were engaged in making mental notes of who was there. It was a fair May day and outside the French windows the aerial gardens were at their loveliest. Few persons however left the rooms for fear of missing something. Lee went out and looking on the amazing city from among the perfumed flowers thought: After this, what?

Tyrrell Blair sent for him. Standing in front of the renaissance chimneypiece in the lofty sala Blair dominated the whole crowd with his tall heavy figure and strong voice. Blair with his feats of eating and drinking, his affairs with women, was becoming a legend even while he was alive. He kept Lee beside him, introducing him to all as: "My cleverest author.

Lee smiled inwardly at the proprietary air.

"Lee's a psychologist and a philosopher," announced Blair, "A dangerous combination! He knows what makes the wheels go round in all of us."

Lee, while he smiled and said what was expected of him, thought ruefully that if he was a philosopher, this was no place for him. Getting away as soon as he was able he went in search of Mary Blair.

She was holding court in another room. A tall figure in soft blue draperies the color of her deep eyes. She was going through the motions of a gracious hostess, but Lee guessed from her slightly distrait expression, that her feeling about the show was similar to his own: Why all this clamor when stillness is so sweet? Mary was by nature a still woman. Other women were inclined to despise her because she did not rebel against her husband's flagrant infidelities; Lee would not allow himself to despise a quiet person. You never knew!

As he approached, Mary gave him a special smile. He joined in the talk around her. When an opportunity presented itself, he said:

"Will you come with me for five minutes? I want to show you something in your own place that you may not have seen."

She excused herself from the others, and they passed out into the lofty garden. It was not crowded here. A few people leaned on the parapet, gazing at the miraculous city; others lay in wicker chairs outside the windows. The garden was constructed on two levels, so that those in the chairs looked over the heads of those at the parapet.

"This is wonderful," said Lee.

"Wonderful for what it is," said Mary. "I prefer my garden on the ground."

He took her to the south side and made her sit in a certain chair. He had discovered that looking from this spot you saw the stark grey bulk of the R.C.A. Building like a gigantic sarcophagus enframed between two branches of flowering lilac. From the chair level nothing else was visible but clear sky.

"A study in contrast," said Lee. "Death and springtime."

"A forced Springtime," murmured Mary.

"You should have it photographed to-morrow morning when the sun is right," said Lee; "before the lilacs fade."

"Why?" she said indifferently. "I have no desire to preserve it."

He looked at her quickly.

"I want to forget all this as quickly as possible," she said with a secret smile. "And I shall, too."

This sounded like the beginning of rebellion. He felt that it would interrupt her delicate confidences to ask a question, and so he held his tongue.

"You must think I am daft," she went on, smiling. "I always feel a little daft when I am with you. That is because I have to keep such a close guard on myself all the time in there." She inclined her head towards the windows.

"Let's be daft," said Lee.

"Lee, what do you want most of life?" she asked irrelevantly.

"One must choose what is within one's grasp; for me a little wisdom."

"Wisdom!" she said scornfully.

"What do you want, Mary?"

"Happiness!" Her breath caught on the word, and it was easy to see that she had a special happiness in mind. "I'm willing to pay," she added. "I have faced that out."

"You are entitled to it," he said.

She laughed softly. "Isn't it funny, when you and I are together we always talk in half hints."

"But we do not misunderstand each other," said Lee.

"We are never alone together for more than a minute or two. Wouldn't it be nice if . . ."

She was interrupted by a heavy voice behind her saying: "Here you are, you two!" Concealment drew over Mary's face like a film of wax. Lee turned around with a bland smile. "I brought Mary out to show her a curious effect. You can only see it when you sit here. Look! Death and Springtime."

"Death?"

"The top of the R.C.A. Building looks like a gigantic coffin."

"That's wonderful, Lee. To-morrow I'll send up my best photographer to take it in color . . . Come on in. A lot of new people have arrived. You are my star attraction, you know."

As they followed Blair through a window, Lee murmured to Mary: "How about having tea with me some afternoon?

"I'd love it."

"Sunday?"

"Not Sunday."

"Monday?"

"No; Tuesday. Call for me at four on Tuesday."

The next item on Rafe Deshon's calendar of engagements for Lee was a private view at the Whitney Galleries of Art. Many of the same people were present but this was a rather more bohemian gathering because the artists were included. Rafe and Lee met an eminent personality upon entering and while the former was engaged in flattering him, Lee slipped away. Avoiding the receiving line, he found a seat where he could amuse himself by looking at people looking at art.

Judy Bowles was at the show, and he presently picked her out across the room, standing with her back to him while she gazed at a picture. Beside her stood a young man. They made a fine complement to each other because he was as blond as Judy was dark, and for a moment or two Lee hoped that his girl had shipped the radio announcer. But he could not be sure that these two were together, because he did not see them speaking. The young man was a superb physical specimen; tall, broad-shouldered, with a firm stance. Lee was particularly struck with the good shape of his head, full behind and wide above his close-set ears. Lee waited in some curiosity to see if his face was as handsome as his body was well-made. It doesn't often happen.

Judy kept looking over her shoulder toward the entrance to the room. Her face lighted up and she started in that direction. The slick-haired Boris Fanton was coming in. Lee's heart sank when he saw their meeting. So that affair was still on. They left the room arm in arm.

The blond young man turned to look at another picture and Lee saw his face for the first time. He was astonished, as one always is, at the discovery of something absolutely right. It was one of the handsomest young men Lee had ever seen. His features were cast in a mold of classic harmony, but there was plenty of individuality there too. What pleased Lee most in him was that he lacked the cynical assurance that handsome young men so soon acquire in the city. This one was not spoiled yet. People were staring at him, and it made him sore. Lee, searching in his mind for a phrase to describe his fierce expression, thought: Blond Lucifer.

At this moment Rafe found Lee, and led him away to do his duty by the receiving line. At intervals during the afternoon and evening Lee kept remembering with pleasure the proud, resolute face.

On the following morning Lee found another anonymous letter in his mail. Each of these letters had been mailed from a different part of the city. This one was dropped in a Greenwich village postbox.

Lee Mappin:

Everything is all set now. I am only waiting for the train I have laid to produce the particular combination of circumstances that I require. I have left nothing to chance, and within the next three or four days my opportunity will present itself just as certainly as effect must follow cause. The knife is sharp, the hand steady and the grave chosen. If you expect to do anything to prevent this murder, you'll have to look sharp. Yesterday you were in the presence of the destined victim.

X.

Since Lee had been in the presence of hundreds on the previous afternoon the last sentence of the letter did not furnish him with anything of a clue. Many of the persons with whom he was closely associated had been at the Art gallery; Tyrrell and Mary Blair, Rafe Deshon and Peggy, Fanny Parran, Tom Cottar, Judy Bowles and Boris Fanton, besides scores of others that he knew less well.

CHAPTER FOUR

PUTTING THE ANONYMOUS LETTER out of sight, Lee called Judy into his office. Fanny and Judy knew of course that a new letter from X had come, and Lee didn't want Judy to connect the question he was going to ask her directly with the letter. It was painful to have to suspect one who was near to him. He had always boasted that though their business was crime, they, themselves, so far had never been smeared by it.

"Close the door," he said to Judy. "And sit down."

The girl was pale and heavy-eyed; it was evident that the course of her affair with Fanton was not a happy one. Lee thought: So much the better, because it shows that he has not yet obtained a complete ascendancy over her. Judy was alarmed by the request to close the door. In that office they had few secrets from each other.

"You were at the Whitney Galleries yesterday afternoon," said Lee.

"Yes," said Judy, and her sullen glance added: What of it?

He hated to see the secrecy come into her face. "When I saw you, you were standing beside a tall, blond, young man. Is he a friend of yours?"

"No," she said. "I met no young men there that I knew."

"Except Boris," put in Lee.

"He's not blond."

"Well, even if you don't know this other one, did you take notice of him?"

"No."

"He was an exceptionally good-looking young man."

"I didn't notice anybody in particular," said Judy.

"Think back," urged Lee. "You may be able to help me very much. This young man was so good-looking that I don't see how a woman could have failed to notice him. Many people were staring at him."

Judy suddenly began to cry.

"For God's sake!" cried Lee in exasperation, "if the incident means nothing to you, what are you crying about?"

"Because you suspect me of something—I don't know what!" she wailed.

"I don't suspect you of anything. I'm merely asking for information."

"You . . . you think I'm lying to you. I can't bear it!"

"*Are* you lying to me?"

"No!" she wept. "I don't know what it's all about."

"What *what* is all about?"

"Whatever is in your mind?"

"God preserve me from weeping women!" cried Lee throwing up his hands. "Go back to your desk!"

When Judy returned to the front room, Fanny Parran's indignant glance through the doorway at her employer did not help to soothe Lee's feelings. "Sure, I'm a heartless brute!" he muttered to himself. "That's understood." He was exactly where he had stood before Judy came in. He knew enough about women to know that a man cannot hope to follow their erratic emotional courses. Her tears proved nothing one way or the other; perhaps she had guilty knowledge; perhaps when she came in she was on the verge of tears owing to something else, and they had merely overflowed.

He took the letter and jamming his hat on, went out without telling them where he was going. Obsessed with the notion that he was watched, he took a taxi to the main door of the Vanderbilt Hotel and made his way through to the bar entrance in Thirty-third Street. He was positive that nobody followed him through the building. In Thirty-third Street he picked up another taxi and had himself driven down to Police Headquarters. Not that I expect to get much help here, he thought bitterly as he went up the steps.

Lee and Inspector Loasby, chief of the detective division, were old friends and old associates in the investigation of crime. They made a good team because their methods were entirely opposed; Loasby supplied the professional technique, Lee, imagination. Loasby was a handsome man in his late forties who looked his best in the blue and gold of a high police officer and was well aware of it. It was a matter of regret with him that the occasions for appearing in uniform were becoming rarer.

Lee, without comment, laid before Loasby the letter he had received that morning.

"Another?" said Loasby. After casting his eyes over it, he added, "Not much in this one."

Lee jumping from his chair like a grain of corn in a popper, started pacing the room. "It's damnable, Loasby, damnable! It keeps me awake nights. I can't think of anything else. He's got me in a box. There's nothing I can *do!* It's horrible not to have anything for my wits to work on!"

"Easy! Easy!" urged Loasby. "You certainly can't do yourself justice by getting so excited."

"That's all very well, but how can I stand by and wait for a murder to be committed without doing anything about it?"

"Our situations are reversed," said Loasby dryly. "How many times in the past have you told me to keep my shirt on?"

"These letters come from somebody who knows me."

"Sure, that's pretty obvious. Keeping a close watch on everything you do. Somebody who knows you well enough to choose the best way, the only way, of getting your goat. And he has got it. That is what convinces me that there's no more in it but that. It is just somebody who is trying to get at you, Lee, and you are certainly giving him a run for his money."

"I feel that you are wrong there," said Lee. "The psychology running through the whole series of letters convinces me that he means what he says."

"I find it hard to believe that. Murder is a serious business, Lee, and so is the electric chair. I never heard of a man planning murder who advertised it in advance."

"There have been such cases. It's vanity. He said in one of the letters he can't stand the thought that nobody should ever know how clever he was. I don't need to tell you what a large part vanity plays in the makeup of a criminal."

"Well, suppose you're right. Suppose he is going to commit murder. You and I are doing every damned thing that can be done to stop him. The dice are loaded against us because he has given us no workable clues. If the murder is committed, it won't be your fault; you'll have no call to blame yourself."

"But if it is somebody I know; somebody I am fond of. I could never forgive myself."

"You are tormenting yourself with imaginary horrors. In a couple of days he'll write you that the murder is done. It will never come to light because there is no murder. Are you going to worry about it all the rest of your life? That *would* give him a laugh."

"You are wrong," muttered Lee. "Murder will be done."

"Well," said Loasby soothingly, let's see if there are not some additional measures we can take . . . I suppose you've looked into the watermarked paper."

"I did that in the beginning. It's cheap paper manufactured in enormous quantities and sold principally through the dime stores. The envelopes also. I don't see the slightest chance of tracing paper or envelopes. I have looked into the type, too. That sort of type is used by three of the largest makes of writing-machines in the country. No hope there either."

"Would it help to have this latest letter printed in the newspaper?" suggested Loasby.

"I can't see that it would. Newspaper publicity flatters the writer. As for myself, I can work more effectively without newspaper publicity."

"I agree." Loasby read the letter again. "Does what he says about being in the presence of the victim suggest anything to you?"

"No. There were hundreds in the art gallery . . . I have sort of a hunch, but you can't prove a hunch." Lee described the handsome young man who had attracted his attention.

"What reason have you to suppose that he is the intended victim?"

"None whatever, except that when I saw him he was standing beside my girl Judy Bowles, and Judy is linked up with Boris Fanton. Fanton affects me like a sleek snake."

"Any evidence against him?"

"Not a bit except that he has a bad eye. He takes too great an interest in my affairs. He is clever enough to have written the letters."

"Well, we'll keep him in mind as a possible suspect. Anybody else?"

"I can only tell you of the men who are near me whom I distrust. There is Tyrrell Blair."

"Good God!" cried Loasby. "One of the most prominent men in town! What have you got against him?"

"Nothing. But occasionally I have felt that there was something sinister behind his big, bluff, hearty front. I don't like him. His protestations of friendship toward me somehow ring false."

"We would have to watch our step in that direction. Anybody else?"

"Rafe Deshon, Blair's director of promotion and publicity. During the past few weeks he has constituted himself my manager. I have a little more to go on here, because I have heard Deshon threaten to kill his wife."

"Luckily such threats are not always carried out," said Loasby dryly, "or the police *would* be kept busy."

"The Deshons, both husband and wife lead feverish lives," Lee went on; "the man, in particular, never allows himself an honest thought or a natural feeling. Such men are apt to go berserk suddenly."

"Sure," said Loasby, "but you would hardly call this series of letters sudden."

"Right. On the other hand Deshon has made himself very familiar with my affairs."

"We'll keep it in mind. Anybody else?"

"No. The greater probability is, that it is somebody who would never occur to either of us. . . . Look, Loasby, I don't think you ought to take any action against the three men I have named. We have not a scintilla of evidence against any of them and it doesn't seem right to spend the public money on such slender prospects."

"You're so high-minded!" said Loasby, smiling.

"Any clumsy move by the police would only put a clever man on his guard."

Loasby's heavy eyebrows ran up. "Where do you get that clumsy stuff?"

"I propose to hire Stan Oberry to trail them."

"Oh, yeah? Is he any better than me?"

"For this particular purpose, yes. You know it. Your men are handicapped at the start because they look like sleuths, whereas Stan picks up his operatives everywhere according to the special purpose for which they may be wanted."

"Have it your own way," grumbled Loasby. "Saves me trouble."

"What you can do for me," continued Lee, "is to send out a general alarm for the letter-writer. Let every policeman on the force be advised to look out for a man posting a letter to me. The post-office also. Let every carrier and clerk who handles mail be informed."

"I'll do that."

"I'd like to offer a reward," said Lee, "if I could keep it out of the newspapers. To advertise it in the press would only put the letter-writer on his guard. If it scared him he would stop writing letters."

"It worries you to get his letters," said Loasby dryly, "but it would worry you worse not to get them."

"Precisely."

"Well, I'll take care of it. How much do you want to offer?"

"A thousand."

"That's quite a piece of money. Who's going to put it up?"

"I will. It would be worth it to me to regain my peace of mind."

Before returning to his own office, Lee proceeded to Stan Oberry's place on Forty-second Street. He had on previous occasions employed Stan in such delicate matters, sometimes with conspicuous success. Stan's office was no more than a hole in the wall of one of the largest commercial buildings. No one was ever to be found in it except Stan or his secretary, who happened also to be his wife. The operatives had a room elsewhere, frequently changed and connected by private wire. Stan himself was a big clumsy fellow whose principal advantage was that he looked like a moron and wasn't. After hearing Lee out, he said:

"How about the girl, Judy Bowles?"

"Let her alone. If she has any connection with this case it can only be through Fanton."

"Okay. This is a tough assignment; three prominent and busy men, protected by all kinds of employees and servants, and all moving in the smartest society; but I'll do my darnedest."

"I know you will, Stan. In respect to Boris Fanton, remember I want you to take two lines. Dig me up whatever you can about his past life, and also let me know how he occupies himself at present."

"Okay, Mr. Mappin."

"Send the reports to my house in a plain envelope. The men you are watching must not be named in them. Refer to Blair as A, Deshon as B, and Fanton as C."

"Right."

Back in his own office, smoking and brooding on his problem, Lee thought of another measure that he might take. If he broadcasted again, the letter-writer would certainly be listening. It would be a way to reach the man, to influence his acts perhaps. He immediately asked one of the girls to get Rafe Deshon on the wire.

"Hello, Rafe. I've decided to accept the radio offer. I need the money."

"Fine work, Lee!" (Rafe is getting a rakeoff of some sort, thought Lee.) "I'll telephone them at once, and call you back."

In twenty minutes he was again on the wire. "Already?" said Lee.

"Oh, it doesn't take long to cinch it in the case of something they want as bad as they want you, Lee . . . Look, they have fifteen minutes open to-morrow night, and they have asked me if I can persuade you to take it on such short notice."

"All right. That suits me very well. I'll write my stuff this afternoon and it can be edited to-morrow. But look, Rafe, I want you to make this clear. I can't stop them from cutting my stuff according to their peculiar notions of censorship, but I'll be damned if I let them put one word into my mouth. If I had stood firm on that before, look at the trouble it would have saved me."

"Sure, sure," said Rafe soothingly. "Now that you've made a hit on the radio, you can lay down what conditions you like, Lee."

"One more thing," said Lee, "I want you to see that it is well advertised in the papers both morning and evening to-morrow, that I am to speak on the radio to-morrow night."

"I will see to it, Lee."

On the following night Lee duly delivered his spiel to the air. This was not in the form of an interview but was a straight talk, consequently Rafe did not accompany him to the studio. As on the previous occasion, Boris Fanton acted as his announcer, and while he listened to the resonant tones of Boris' introductory words, Lee thought: It would be a queer note if he was my man.

In the course of his talk to the mike, Lee said: "One of the queerest cases I have met with is that of the harmless nut who has been writing me a series of anonymous letters announcing that he was about to commit a murder. Some of you may have read his first letter which was printed in the New York newspapers. Since then the press has dropped him, since neither nuts nor anonymous letter-writers are news, but as a matter of fact he has continued to write to me nearly every day since."

While he was getting this off, Lee, without appearing to, watched Boris' face. The announcer's expression of bored smugness never altered. He appeared to be exclusively interested in the condition of his fingernails; in flecks of dust that had settled on his vest and pants; he watched the progress of the minute hand around the clock. He's overdoing it, thought Lee. It's not possible that he doesn't hear what I'm saying. Lee continued to the mike;

"Of course none of us believe that there is anything in this man's maunderings. Certainly I haven't got time to investigate every crackpot who writes me an anonymous letter. However, I have turned the letters over to the police. They didn't think there was anything in it either, but they considered that it was their duty to investigate. For obvious reasons I can't tell you the methods they used, but they have discovered who is writing the letters. Unknown to him, every move he makes is watched, and if he has any murderous intentions, which I doubt, the moment he attempts to carry them into effect he will be nabbed."

Lee's talk then passed on to something else. While Fanton was making his concluding remarks to the mike Lee was free to watch him. In the depths of those sleepy bored eyes lurked a cold and deadly spark. The startled Lee had seen that look in another pair of eyes; Beau Gramercy when he was brought to bay. Fanton had the eyes of a killer.

The next day was Sunday. Lee had no expectation of going to his office, and there were of course no mail deliveries. Yet at eight o'clock in the morning before he had the least notion of getting up, his man Jermyn came into his bedroom with one of the damnable typewritten envelopes on his little tray. This one bore a special delivery stamp. Jermyn said deprecatingly:

"I thought it might be important, sir."

Lee silently cursed him.

> Lee Mappin:
> It wasn't good enough, Pop. Your talk tonight was too smooth, too obviously calculated to make me mad with its references to nuts, crackpots and so forth. I am wise to you now. You lied to your millions of listeners. If the police knew who I was, you wouldn't have to go on the air to send me a message. You could send it direct. I know that as far as I am concerned you are completely up a tree. I follow all your movements. The police in spite of their general alarms and so on merely make me laugh. Your "warning" on the air will not influence my actions in the slightest. When I'm ready, I'll strike. Since I

wrote you last, the situation has developed. The
pretty fly is caught in the web. It won't be long now.

X.

Lee gritted his teeth. What made him sorest in this effusion
was the word "Pop." He liked to hear it from Fanny and Judy when
no one else was around, and even from Tom Cottar, but nobody
else in the world was privileged so to address him.

The words "pretty fly" suggested that the intended victim might
be a woman.

CHAPTER FIVE

To go back a little, when Lee got home late Saturday night he had found a note on the hall table of his apartment in Jermyn's painstakingly formed characters: "Call TR 7-7616 whenever you get home. This party called twice." Lee knew it to be Stan Oberry's home number, and Stan promptly answered the call.

"Did I wake you up?" said Lee.

"I expected it," said Stan. "The phone is right beside my bed, and my business goes on for twenty-four hours a day. . . . Look, Mr. Mappin, one of my men has contacted C in a big way."

"Quick work!"

"They're together now. It's the beginning of a beautiful friendship. C has offered my man a half share in an act he's putting on, for five hundred dollars. My man says the act looks bonafide, but C does not. This is a man I can rely on. He says if he goes into partnership with C he can find out all there is to know about him, past and present, if it's worth that much to you. Maybe you'll get your five hundred back too, but he doesn't guarantee that."

Lee considered. "C" was Boris Fanton. When Lee thought of Judy's pale, unhappy face, his mind was made up. "Okay, Stan, I'll put up for it."

"Right, Mr. Mappin. My man has already learned a good bit about this bird, but I won't repeat it over the phone. Reports Monday. Good-night."

"Good-night, Stan."

Nothing happened on Sunday. On Monday morning Lee stayed home to receive Stan's reports. They were delivered by messenger about ten. With them came a covering letter from Stan, written on plain paper and signed with a cipher. Each of Stan's operatives was given a number. Lee smiled at the elaborateness of these precautions, but admitted it was a part of the thoroughness which Stan applied to every detail of his business. Stan wrote:

> Having learned that A and B's firm, [Blair and Middlebrook] were doing a very large business, and were short of office help, I succeeded in getting one of my young men employed there on Saturday as a filing clerk. I have not yet been able to contact any of the servants in A's home but have my lines out. Number 38 has scraped acquaintance with a maid in B's house, and something ought to come of that. 38 is a very attractive young fellow. In the case of C, [Boris Fanton] we have been more successful than we could have expected in so short a time. Reports enclosed.

On top was a voluminous communication from the filing clerk in Blair and Middlebrook's office, signed Number 34. The whole of the firm's correspondence was open to this operative, and he could also keep tab on Blair's and on Rafe Deshon's business engagements by consulting their desk calendars when they were out of their offices. Lee learned everything they had done on Saturday morning, but it threw no light on their private lives or secret thoughts. Blair had lunched with business associates at the Biltmore. He was picked up when he left the hotel, but his trailer lost him in the traffic. Rafe Deshon had been driven direct from the office to Wanamaker's store. It was significant that he only walked through the store and hailed another taxi in Fourth Avenue. Evidently he knew he was being trailed or suspected that he might be. Stan's man had been unable to get a taxi in time to follow him further. In respect to Deshon's home, Number 38's report was as follows:

I outfitted myself with a small stock of notions as
suggested, and watched the house on Sutton Court
Saturday morning until I saw B leave and afterwards
Mrs. B. The servants of course always feel freer when
the Mr. and Mrs. are out of the house. There are only
women servants here. I went to the service door, and
by good luck the bell was answered by a maid who
was neither a good-looker nor downright ugly. A
pretty girl wouldn't have any truck with a pedlar, and
an ugly woman always gets suspicious when a man
makes up to her. This one was just right; wasn't accustomed to attention from men, and fell for me in
short order. Her name is Stella and she's the parlor-
maid. When I saw I had her going, I gave her the full
charge; told her I'd been watching her go in and out
for weeks past, and had only bought the pedlar's
outfit for an excuse to make her acquaintance; and I
had a good job as truckman for the A. & P. and Saturday was my day off. She swallowed it whole. I kept
her going until the cook called her back into the
house, and then I made a date to come back in the
afternoon, and I talked to her again, and then I found
she had two hours off Saturday night between 7 and
9 and I persuaded her to take in a movie with me.
Well, we went to a theatre in Fifty-ninth Street, and
I delivered her safe home on the stroke of 9. On this
first date I was careful not to ask her a single question; however, like all house servants, her principal
topic of conversation was the Madam and the Master and I got an earful.

Two pages of servants' gossip followed, which Lee skimmed
over rapidly. There was little in it for him since he was already
acquainted with the situation in the Deshon household. Notwithstanding the popularity of Mr. and Mrs. and all the adulation lav-
ished on them in the press, the servants had a low opinion of their

employers. Obviously Rafe and Peggy had one face for the world and quite another for those who worked for them. Hateful quarrels were described. Yet the servants liked their jobs because it gave them prestige to be working for such well-known people. It did not surprise Lee to learn that both master and mistress were dependent on drugs to obtain sleep. Once Mrs. Deshon got an overdose and a doctor was called in to revive her. She despised her husband, etc., etc. There was one significant piece of information that Lee made a note of:

> On two occasions lately a man about forty years old, trim-looking and a flashy dresser, was seen loitering in the quiet dead end on which the house faces. To the servants he had the appearance of an East Side gangster. B knew him. Once when B came out of the house the man followed him. They didn't recognize each other openly, but they were seen to get into a taxi together at the corner.

Number 38 concluded his report by saying:

> On Sunday Stella wasn't allowed out because the Madam was entertaining. She has Thursday afternoon and evening off, and I have a date with her. Sometimes when the family is dining out, she gets a couple of hours off extra in the evening, and if that happens before Thursday she promised to give me a call.

Lee wrote a memorandum to Stan Oberry to instruct 38 to find out if the maids were ever allowed to have callers in the house. He was to use every endeavor to get inside the house without arousing suspicion, and he was told to make up to the other servants particularly to the cook, who appeared to be the boss. He was to find out if Rafe had a typewriter in the house, and if he was ever seen going out at night to post a letter.

The remaining report, signed by Number 17, presented another picture of the seamy side of life in the upper brackets.

> I presented the letter of introduction that was furnished me to a certain party, and as a result I was put up as a guest in the Heterodyne Club. This is good for two weeks. It is C's regular hangout in his off hours. While I was waiting for him to turn up I talked with various members. I was posing as the son of a wealthy man in Omaha, Neb., who wanted to get into the radio game. I spent freely in the club house. Boris Fanton's name came up and I soon learned that he wasn't popular there. One said that Fanton was hell to women, but I couldn't get anything specific out of this member. Nobody knew anything about Fanton's antecedents before he joined the club last fall. He is considered to have the perfect male voice for radio and owing to that has gone ahead fast.
>
> He came in after his last broadcast. There was some general conversation, and after Fanton got me placed, he separated me from the others. "Money" was the magic word, but he was smart enough not to show his hand right away. I posed as a dissolute kind of fellow as regards women, and this recommended me to Fanton. He likes to be regarded as the modern Casanova who regards all women as fair game, and I encouraged him. He said I was a man after his own heart.
>
> We talked about radio. Fanton told me of an act he was putting on. It's a serial play taken from a popular novel. He said he had his cast engaged and had secured a sponsor; all he needed was five hundred dollars to square the publisher of the novel. Said he had put every cent that he has into it. He said he could get the money in an hour, but only by

parting with a half share of the act, which he didn't want to do. He didn't ask me outright for the money, but he gave me the opportunity to say that I would come in. He's slick all right. He said he wouldn't take a cent from me until he had shown me the contracts, and let me hear the script rehearsed. As soon as I got home I called up the boss, and after a couple of hours word came back from him to go ahead with it.

I met Fanton at the Roosevelt at noon on Sunday and we had breakfast. Afterwards we went to the studios and he showed me the whole works. I acted like a man from Omaha of course, to whom it was all new. After I had watched and listened to a couple of programs, Fanton got his little company together in an unused room, and they read me the script. It sounded all right to me and the contracts looked okay. I believe that this act will go on whatever may happen to Fanton. He's got too good a job with the studios to try to pull anything raw just now. So I agreed to go in with him and we shook hands on it.

By evening Fanton and I were like lifetime buddies. Every now and then in an innocent way, I would try to find out something about his past, but he always blocked it. He must have come of a fine family and had a first-rate education in order to speak so well. I gather that his family chucked him out long ago. He said he had been right up against it before he landed in radio. He has undoubtedly gone under many aliases; he said with a laugh that he had never given his real name to a woman but once in his life, and he had regretted that ever since. I asked him in a simple way what was his real name, and he answered Boris Fanton; that he had had it changed by act of legislature. I don't believe this.

We took a couple of blondes to dinner Sunday night. I was hoping to get Fanton drunk, but he's too cagey. We were supposed to go home with the girls, but I managed to get out of this without exciting suspicion, and as for Fanton, he wasn't going to let me out of his sight. So him and I went to his place to drink and chin. This is a little furnished, walk-up flat; parlor, bedroom and bath in an old building at — West Forty-seventh Street. Fanton referred to it as a crummy place, but said he preferred to live there because there were no doormen or elevator boys to keep tab on him. I noticed that he did not have his name under any bell in the vestibule. It's the third floor rear.

While we were sitting talking, there was a knock, and Fanton went to answer it. The flat has a little hall and I could not see the entrance door from where I was sitting. The moment Fanton got to the door, a woman opened up on him like a cork blowing out of a bottle: "Liar! Cheat! Thief!" and so on. Fanton pulled her inside quick, and shut the door to keep her from arousing the other tenants. He clapped a hand over her mouth; I heard him hissing at her: "Be quiet, for God's sake! I've got a man here!"

She wrenched herself free of him. "It's a woman!" she cried. "And I'm going to have a look at her!" She came to the parlor door. When she saw that it was a man, her face changed and she had nothing to say. The door to the bedroom was just behind her. Fanton hustled her in there and closed it. But I had time to give her the once over. She was a blonde in her early thirties, already a little faded and pinched. Of course no woman is at her best when she's in a rage; her hair was sticking out straight. She wore a navy blue silk suit with a little jacket piped with red. Over her arm she carried a light tweed coat, grey herringbone pattern. Little blue straw hat tipped over in front with a bunch of white flowers on top. I had a glimpse of Fanton's face over her shoulder and it was murderous.

There was another door between bedroom and parlor and I tip-toed over to it, and laid my ear against the crack. I could hear pretty good; that is, I could hear everything she said because she was excited; Fanton was more cagey and I had to guess at what he was telling her. I couldn't repeat exactly what I heard; it was all too broken and confused, but here is the story I pieced together from it.

Fanton married this woman some years ago, and they had a child. This was in South Carolina; the town was not named. Fanton called her Nell or Nellie and she addressed him as Charlie. She had money, and Fanton ran through it. When it was gone he left her. When she pleaded with him to come back for the child's sake, he laughed in her face and told her they were not legally married; that he had a previous wife living. She believed him at the time and took her child and went away to hide their shame as she thought. She changed her name. She went to Baltimore because there was something the matter with the child and she thought she could get the best treatment there. The child died in Baltimore. She accused Fanton of being responsible for the kid's death. Afterwards the girl got a job in a big department store in Baltimore, and she still works there, at the neck-wear counter. The name of the store is Hutzler's.

Just lately she had exchanged a couple of letters with Fanton. I couldn't get this part exactly. Apparently he told her he wanted a reconciliation, and she was all for it. But somehow she had discovered that he was lying to her again and so she had come to New York hotfoot to face him with it. The girl has something on Fanton, something big, but when she threatened him with exposure he shut her up so quick I didn't get the particulars.

That was the situation. The girl was still crazy about Fanton even while she cursed him, and he set out to smooth her down. I couldn't hear much what he said, but I could tell from his silky tone that he was swearing to her she was the only woman he had ever loved, and the poor fool believed it and stopped crying. Anybody but a lovesick woman would have known his voice was false as hell. He succeeded in explaining everything away. She wanted to spend the night with him, but he told her he had to take the midnight to Boston. I heard this. He persuaded her to return to Baltimore. She is to get her things together and return to New York next week. He promised to write her Tuesday with full instructions. He kept telling her they must keep their plans secret. Finally he got her out.

Naturally when he came back he was anxious as to how I had taken all this. I laughed like a fool and clapped him on the back and made out that I had once been through a similar experience with a woman. I took the attitude that any trick was justifiable in getting ahead of a woman. He pumped me to find out how much I had overheard. I made out it was only the opening words. He was satisfied that I was a nitwit and not dangerous to him. He made light of the whole business of course, but his hand shook and his eyes were murderous. He couldn't get a grip on himself. Among other things he said: "*She turned up a few days too soon.*" Then feeling he had given too much away, he added with a laugh: "Damn it all,

I'll have to move to a hotel where she can't get by the desk."

I have another date with Fanton for twelve o'clock, Monday.

17.

CHAPTER SIX

LEE DREW A LONG BREATH of satisfaction upon finishing number 17's report. After his exasperated and baffled days here at last was what appeared to be a hot clue. There was time to run it down, too. The woman's surprise visit to New York must have disrupted Fanton's plans. He would certainly require another day or two to complete new ones.

Lee glanced at his watch. The time lacked a few minutes of eleven. He called up Stan Oberry to ask if it would be possible to arrange a meeting with operative 17 in a hurry.

"Sure," said Stan. "17 thought maybe you would have some instructions for him. I can put my hand on him in one minute."

Stan suggested the sidewalk of Vanderbilt Avenue as a good meeting-place. This street while close at hand was out of the main stream of traffic, yet sufficiently well-traveled in mid-morning so that a meeting would not be too conspicuous. Lee was to walk down from Forty-sixth Street on the right-hand side, and Stan's operative to walk from Forty-second until they met.

"What does he look like?" asked Lee.

"You don't have to worry about that. He knows you and will greet you."

Ten minutes later the meeting took place. Lee was saluted by a good-looking young fellow, well-dressed, but not quite bearing the metropolitan stamp. The only thing that betrayed his occupation was his dead pan; however, a twinkle appeared in his blue eyes at the sight of Lee.

"Where shall we go to talk?" he asked.

"Just walk through Forty-third Street," said Lee. "It won't take long for what I have to say . . . I suppose you can't go down to Baltimore for me?"

"If I don't meet C at noon he might smell a rat. I'm to give him the money then. Maybe I can get away from him soon."

"No. Unless you got the one o'clock plane for Baltimore the store would probably be closed, and you'd have your trip for nothing. You keep C in play and I'll go to Baltimore. Give me a more detailed description of the woman."

"She sells at the women's neckwear counter in Hutzler's department store. C called her Nell or Nellie, but she may pass by a different name in Baltimore."

"After having been parted for so long, how did they get into correspondence again?"

"I took it she had written to him first."

"Co on with her description."

"Between thirty-three and thirty-five years old; average height; a little scrawny; weight about 115; has been pretty in a cheap way; natural blonde hair but has lately applied a wash which makes it look brassy. Last night she was both sore and sour, but if C has persuaded her that everything is going to be right, she'll be looking younger and happier when you find her."

"Well observed," said Lee. "Can you give me one particular feature that would make identification sure?"

The young man shook his head. "She looked like just what she is; salesgirl in a department store. Her rouge was badly applied. Hair hung to her neck and was curled at the ends."

"Four out of five women are wearing it that way."

"Here is something, sir. She has a way of jerking her head a little, like this. A nervous trick."

"That will be sufficient. . . . When you were in our friend's place last night did you notice if he had a typewriter in his parlor or his bedroom?"

"None in the parlor, sir. I didn't get a look in the bedroom."

"If he takes you there again, try to find out without showing your hand. That's all."

They reached the Madison Avenue corner. Lee offered his hand. "Good luck! You've done a neat piece of work and I want to congratulate you on it."

The dead pan broke up. "Thank you, sir," said Number 17, grinning like any young fellow. "That means something, coming from you."

They separated. Lee was only a few short blocks from his office, and the traffic being what it was, he figured he could make it as quickly on foot. While he was still a block away he was surprised and annoyed to see the tall, elegantly-dressed figure of Boris Fanton come running down the steps of his building. Boris turned south and whisked around the corner without having seen Lee.

Entering the front room of his suite a minute or two later, Lee was aware of a tenseness in the air. Fanny's lips were pressed tightly together and Judy was on the verge of tears. He waited for them to say something about Fanton's visit, but they did not. Lee suspected that a crisis was at hand in Judy's affair and he was torn with anxiety.

"Anybody been in?" he asked with a careless air.

"No," said Fanny.

Lee kept his mouth shut. It was impossible to foresee how an infatuated woman might act. If he let fall a single word of what he had learned concerning the radio announcer, it might be carried direct to Fanton, and everything would be spoiled. He wished grimly that he had the power to lock Judy up and keep her incommunicado for a couple of days. He went on into his own room and sat down, thinking hard. He had no time to lose if he wished to make his plane. He called Judy in.

"At last we've got a lead in the anonymous letter-writer case," he announced with a cheerful air.

"That's good," said Judy perfunctorily. Her thoughts were elsewhere.

"The general alarm scared him," Lee went on. "And he's skipped town. Inspector Loasby has a tip that he's in Chicago, but according to my information he dropped off the train in Philadelphia and is watching us from there. Are you free to run out to Chicago for a couple of days?"

Judy looked at him quickly, was on the point of refusing, thought better of it, and lowered her head again. The girls were always so keen to get these out-of-town assignments, she knew it would be a dead give-away if she refused it. "All right," she said.

Lee made believe not to observe the sullenness. "You don't need to fly," he said briskly, "because I can't get your instructions to you until to-morrow morning. Take one of the good afternoon trains; treat yourself to a stateroom, and a comfortable room at the Blackstone when you arrive. Register under your own name. You'll hear from me at the Blackstone in the morning."

When Fanny heard this, she was surprised, a little sore because she had not been chosen, yet relieved on the whole because Judy was being sent out of harm's way. Lee marked all this in her face with inward amusement. Fanny said: "Does it really look promising, Pop?"

"It really does, my girl," he said with honest satisfaction. "I believe we have him stopped!"

"Well! I'm darn glad of that. For the last ten days you've looked like little Boy Blue."

Lee laughed. "I'm flying to Philadelphia. I can't be reached by telephone this afternoon, but I'll call you if I am able. Don't tell anybody where I have gone. Home some time to-night."

Fanny was the office cashier. He drew the money he needed, and running downstairs, hailed a cab and had himself driven to the airport.

He was in Baltimore by mid-afternoon. It took him almost as long to drive in to the city from the airport as it had to fly there. Hutzler's, he discovered, was one of Baltimore's best-known institutions. The women's neckwear counter was near one of the entrances. He walked slowly past it, looking over the salesgirls with a seemingly careless eye. There were two or three that answered in a general way to the description he had. He walked to the far side of the store, and came back, looking for one who jerked her head sideways. None did. Probably only does it when excited, he thought.

There was one salesgirl that answered to all the specifications; slightly scrawny, long bob, goldined and curled at the ends; rouge badly applied. Lee decided to take a chance on this one. There was a lift of anticipation in her face that made her look almost pretty. He was depressed by the thought of the blow he had to deal her. Choosing a moment when she was standing a little apart from the other girls, he approached the counter.

"What can I do for you, sir?"

"Is your name Nellie?" he asked.

She gave him a look of pure terror. "No, sir," she stammered. "My name is Madge, Madge Parker." Her head jerked sideways nervously, and he knew he had made no mistake.

"What time will you be through work?" he asked.

"What's that to you? What do you want of me? I don't know you."

"Easy!" murmured Lee. "The other girls are looking this way. Show me some scarves."

She automatically took down a tray of neckwear and put it on the counter before him.

"My name is Mappin," said Lee, turning over the scarves, "but I don't suppose that means anything to you. We must have a little talk."

She attempted to face him out. "What about? I've got nothing to say to you. I'll call the floorman if you don't stop bothering me."

"Don't do that," said Lee, smiling. "It's about your husband."

Again the look of terror, the jerk of the head. "I have no husband. You've got the wrong person. I never was married."

"I know all about that said Lee. "You went to New York yesterday to see your husband. He calls himself Boris Fanton nowadays."

She looked at him in speechless terror.

"You're giving too much away," warned Lee. "The girls are curious. . . . We can't talk here. When you're through work let's go to some place—a public place. A drugstore, say, where there are tables."

"I've got nothing to tell you," she said sullenly.

"I didn't come to Baltimore to question you," said Lee, "but to tell you something—for your own good."

"Well, tell me and I'll be the judge of that."

"Not before these inquisitive girls. I couldn't."

She gave in. "All right. I'll meet you at Read's drugstore, Lexington and Howard, at five fifteen."

"Thank you," said Lee. He held up a scarf at random. "I'll take this one."

The purchase was completed and he left the store.

Lee moseyed around the outside of the building until he found the employees' entrance. He took up a post across the street where he could watch it in case she tried to give him the slip. He had a long wait. After five o'clock had struck, the girls began to issue out, first in twos and threes, then in a solid stream. Fearful of missing her, he crossed the street.

She saw him the instant she came through the door, but gave no sign of recognition. She was now wearing the grey tweed coat and the blue hat described by number 17. She set off down the street and Lee followed discreetly. They crossed a main street, followed it for a block, crossed another street and entered a busy drugstore. Turning to wait for Lee, she said with a bitter smile:

"Thought I was going to run out on you, didn't you?"

"Well, this is more serious than you know," said Lee. "I couldn't afford to take a chance on it."

They went downstairs and sat at a little table. "What have you got to tell me?" she demanded impatiently.

Lee hesitated. "I'd like to win your confidence first; to convince you that I mean you well."

"You can best do that by telling me what's on your mind."

"You are planning to go to New York to join your husband . . ."

She interrupted him breathlessly. "Did he tell you that?"

"He did not," Lee said meaningly. "He's not telling anybody."

"Then how . . . ? Oh, I see. The man there was a spy. He listened."

A waitress came to the table. They ordered chocolate sundaes. When she had left, the girl said defiantly:

"Well, so what? You haven't told me anything."

"Your husband will never make a woman happy."

She was silent.

"Will he?" Lee asked.

No answer.

"I understand your position," he went on, "and I'm sorry for you."

"You can keep it," she muttered.

"You know he's got a bad heart, but you're still in love with him, and you won't admit it even to yourself."

Her hard face began to break up; she lowered her head.

"This place is as public as a goldfish bowl," said Lee. "I've got quite a lot to say to you. Couldn't we go to a hotel . . ."

She was scandalized. "A hotel!"

Lee smiled. Women of this class always supposed that their virtue was threatened. "I don't mean a hotel room. A restaurant, say, it would be deserted at this hour and we could find a quiet corner . . ."

She rose abruptly. "All right. Let's go."

Lee left money on the table for the sticky messes they had ordered, and they got out of the place.

A few minutes later they were seated in the furthest corner of a dim and empty restaurant. Lee's companion demanded:

"Who are you anyhow? How did you get into this? Are you a detective?"

"Do I look it?"

"No, but . . ."

"I am not a police officer," said Lee. "I'll tell you what my interest is. This fellow who calls himself Boris Fanton is after a girl that I love very much. And I want to show him up to her; to save her from him."

The woman's face was a study in conflicting emotions. "Your daughter?"

Lee did not answer and she took it for an affirmation.

"How do you mean he's after her?" she asked.

"He's trying to persuade her to marry him."

"He can't do that! He's married to me!"

"Would that stop him? Remember, nobody in New York knows of this marriage to you."

"Your daughter is safe from him," she said. "Because him and I are reconciled. I'm going to New York this week to join him."

"And what then?" Lee asked softly.

"What then? We're going to live together, that's what."

"Are you sure, Nell?"

She breathed faster. "What are you getting at, Mister? He proposed it. He always wanted me, he said, but he was broke. Now he's making good money and everything's jake."

"Are you satisfied that he still loves you?"

"Sure, I am! He told me so! He swore it!"

"You have heard him swear many things in the past."

She became more excited. "What's in your mind?" she demanded, softly pounding the table. "For God's sake, Mister, tell me! Tell me!"

"I'd rather have you figure it for yourself," said Lee gravely. "Hasn't he impressed it on you that you mustn't say a word about going to join him in New York, that you must never breathe the name he goes under now?"

The woman sat staring at him in speechless horror. "If he was on the square with you, why the necessity for all this secrecy?"

"You mean . .." she gasped, "you mean . . . he is plotting to kill me?"

"You know him," said Lee. "You know what his past life has been, which I do not. Is he capable of it?"

Spreading her arms on the table, she dropped her head upon them and wept tempestuously. Luckily there was no one within hearing. Lee let her cry it out. She finally raised her head saying stormily:

"I don't believe it! I will never believe such a thing!"

"The suggestion was your own," Lee pointed out.

"You put the thought into my head! That's what you came for!"

"That's right! I came to Baltimore to warn you. The rest is up to you."

"You're only trying to come between us! I won't let nobody come between us!"

"My dear girl," said Lee, "think! Why should I want to separate you? What have I got to gain from it?"

"I don't know. You're up to some game."

"My game is a very simple one. If anything *should* happen to you, I don't want to have it on my conscience."

She wept afresh. "I don't care! If he says he wants me, no power on earth can keep me from going to him!"

"I don't want to keep you from him. I might be mistaken about him."

She stared. "What do you want, then?"

"I want you to let me know every move he makes, and every move you make, so that if any danger *should* threaten you, I can take steps to protect you."

She thought this over. "Suppose he tells me to come Wednesday?"

"Go to him—but let me know in advance!"

As they sat on, Lee's transparent honesty and kindness began to win her. People came into the restaurant and he suggested that they dine where they sat. She had probably never eaten in so fine a place. Suddenly becoming conscious of her besmeared face, she hastened away to a dressing-room. She returned with additional rouge on which scarcely improved her appearance, but she thought it did. Lee gave her a better dinner than she had ever before eaten. The food and wine inspired her with more courage. Bit by bit her pitiful story came out.

The name of the place where she had lived was Bixby, a small town in South Carolina, supported by several big cotton mills. Orphaned as a young woman, she had been left with some money, but not as much as people supposed. She had met Fanton, whom she knew as Charles Lessing, while on a visit to Charleston. He was supposed to be traveling for a big New York concern. His good looks, his ready tongue and his man of the world air made an instant conquest. He followed her back to Bixby and they were married.

She had expected to live in New York, but he told her that all his traveling was in the South and they could be together more if they set up a little house in Bixby. He was away a great deal. He was vague about the exact nature of his employment, but she was too wildly in love to suspect that he was deceiving her. He got large

sums of money out of her on the pretext that he was making in-
vestments that would enable them to live in luxury for the rest of
their days. Their first rift occurred with the coming of the baby
which was apparently a shock to him. When Nell's money gave out
he did not leave her immediately. For some months they lived on
as before, and then one day with cool brutality he told her he was
leaving for good. They were not legally married, he said, because
he had given a false name.

At this point Nell's voice dropped to a whisper. "He said . . . he
said: 'Your brat's got no name at all!' And laughed at me."

"Good God!" murmured Lee. "And after that could you think of
trusting yourself to him again?"

She was silent.

"After he had left you for so long a time how did you find him
again?" asked Lee.

"One day I heard his voice over the radio," she murmured. "It
drove me crazy." Her head went lower still. "It's terrible to love
anybody like that. It makes you sick with longing. But I told myself it couldn't be him and for awhile I didn't do anything. But I
bought all the radio magazines and at last I found a picture of Boris
Fanton and then I knew it was him, though his appearance was so
changed nobody but me would have recognized him. So I wrote to
him. He didn't answer the letter and after awhile I wrote again,
and he answered that one saying that he loved me still and wanted
to make up for what was past . . ."

"Mm!" said Lee thoughtfully. "Why didn't he answer the first
letter?"

"He said he never got it."

"The old story! Letters don't go astray. What did you say in the
second letter that you didn't say in the first?"

"I couldn't tell you," she said evasively.

"Did you threaten him in the second letter?"

Nell said nothing, but her glance of terror was answer enough.

"What have you got on Fanton?" Lee asked bluntly.

No answer.

"Look, my girl," he went on in a kinder voice, "if you don't trust me you've told me too much. If you do trust me you must tell me everything."

Nell began to weep. "I don't know nothing," she whimpered. "It's only a suspicion."

"What do you suspect?"

"Well . . . about the time my money gave out one of the big mills in Bixby was robbed and . . . and the cashier was shot dead. It was late at night and the cashier was making up the payroll because he wanted to get off next day. The money was taken and they never found out who did it. No suspicion fell on Charlie because he was away on one of his trips; he was never known to possess a gun and besides the cashier, a young man, was his best friend in Bixby. Charlie got home for the funeral and he . . . he helped carry the coffin."

"But you suspected him!"

"Not then. Such a thought never came into my head until after he had left me. Then when I was getting ready to sell everything I found in the pocket of a suit he left behind—he wouldn't wear it any more because he'd burned a hole in the coat; I found . . . I found a ticket from a Richmond pawnbroker for a pistol. It was pawned the day after the murder."

"And you want to live with this man again?"

"Maybe he didn't do it! Maybe he didn't!"

"You *know* he did it," said Lee sternly, "or your threat wouldn't have frightened him."

"Well, suppose he did do it, a man isn't bad all his life because he did one wrong thing. Maybe he's sorry for it now and wants to live it down. And anyhow I feel as if I just couldn't live without Charlie."

"That's up to you," said Lee. "Do you happen to have on you the letter he wrote?"

She nodded and drew two much thumbed letters from her handbag.

The false endearments they contained made Lee feel a little sick. Fanton told her he had lately made a hit in radio, but owing to an old contract his salary was still very small and he was still paying off old debts, but he was due for a raise and very soon he would be sending for her and so on and so on. The second letter had obviously been written just to string her along a little further.

"After I got those letters," said Nell tearfully, "I read in a radio magazine that Boris Fanton's new contract called for a fifty per cent raise and he was now among the five highest paid announcers on the air. That made me mad and I went up to New York to face him with it. You know what happened there."

"You let him talk you around again," said Lee.

She hung her head.

CHAPTER SEVEN

LEE TOOK A LATE TRAIN back to New York. He had instructed Nell to communicate with him at his home. In the lounge car he wrote out a long night letter of mysterious instructions that would serve to keep Judy occupied in Chicago next day. Lee was feeling pretty good. He allowed himself to gloat a little over the coming discomfiture of the anonymous letter-writer. In New York he drove direct to his apartment. There were no messages waiting for him. That night he enjoyed a sounder sleep than he had known for a week past.

He was up betimes, and after a hasty breakfast, drove down to his office much earlier than was his custom. He was keen to find out if "X" had written to him the night before. In the light of his present knowledge, Lee expected to get considerable amusement out of his letters and hoped he would write often.

Lee's tread on the office stairs was a light one. He was astonished upon rounding the top, to find that the door of his front office was standing open. It was too early for Fanny to be there. Entering the office noiselessly, he saw a man bending over Fanny's desk, examining the morning's mail. He looked at each letter front and back, held it up to the light. It was the shabby genteel Costin, the janitor.

Spying for Fanton, Lee supposed. It would explain a good deal.

"Good morning," said Lee pleasantly.

The man jumped as if he had been stuck with a knife. A pile of letters slid to the floor. "Good morning! Good morning, Mr.

Mappin," he said fulsomely. He stooped to pick up the letters. "I was looking over the mail to see if there was any foreign stamps, so I could ask for them. My young 'un collects stamps."

Lee affected to believe him. "Sorry," he said, "I don't have much foreign correspondence."

"You are famous all over the world, Mr. Mappin," Costin said fawningly. In order to account for his presence in the room, he started pushing a mop over the linoleum.

"Where's Mrs. Costin this morning?" asked Lee mildly.

"She's feeling poorly, Mr. Mappin. And so I'm trying to help out. Though I might say housework is scarcely in my line."

"I'm sorry she's not well," said Lee. "Give her my best wishes."

"I will, Mr. Mappin."

"How is the book coming on, Costin?"

Costin's smile revealed broken and blackened teeth. This last question assured him that Lee's suspicions had not been aroused, and he said confidently: "Slowly, Mr. Mappin. You can understand that books like mine are not written in a day. The labor is Gargantuan." Costin liked the sound of this word and repeated it: "Gargantuan!"

"What is the nature of your book, Costin?"

"It embodies a new system of economics, Mr. Mappin, in which the capitalist will be limited to a return of five per cent. A tremendous amount of reading for it is required. That is what is so hard on a poor man."

"You should try to find part time employment to help out."

"I am always trying."

"I might have something for you in the way of private investigation."

"If you only would, Mr. Mappin!"

"Ever done anything of that sort?"

"As it happens, I have, Mr. Mappin. I am well fitted for that sort of thing, since I am at my ease in any grade of society."

"Just what have you done?"

"Well, it was confidential work, Mr. Mappin, and therefore I can't say anything about it."

"I see. I'll keep you in mind, Costin."

A slimy creature! Lee thought, as the man went out, carrying his mop. A residue of anxiety remained in Lee's mind. Costin would not be likely to get much from examining sealed envelopes but, on the other hand, after office hours Lee's entire correspondence was available to him, except the few items that were kept in the safe. Lee resolved on the moment to buy a set of new steel filing cabinets that should be locked at night. Fanny had already proposed it.

There was another thing that contributed to his uneasiness. Back of their offices was a room which was hard to rent because it lacked outside light and ventilation. It had been empty for a long time. The dividing partition was a light affair of wood panels and frosted glass, and it occurred to Lee that a person hidden in the empty room might be able to hear a good deal of what passed in his private office, especially telephone conversations. He resolved to be more careful in talking on the telephone.

It was a disappointment to Lee to find that there was no communication from X in the morning's mail.

He telephoned Stan Oberry to send his reports if any to the Madison Avenue office and instructed him in addition to put a man on Costin's trail.

Fanny came in at her usual time, rejoicing Lee's eyes with her flowerlike freshness. The month of May had nothing sweeter to show.

Lee said: "Fanny, has it ever struck you that our friend Costin in the basement was displaying an undue interest in our affairs?"

"Why, yes," she said, "now that you speak of it. I have caught him watching and listening, but I thought nothing of it. I supposed that it was just the nature of the beast."

"If he has been hired by somebody to spy on us, we are rather at his mercy here. . . . I suggest that you order the new filing cases you spoke of."

"Okay, Pop. . . . Did you have a good day yesterday?"

"Excellent!" said Lee.

"Good work!" Fanny was longing to hear more, but she knew he would not tell her. "Anything from Judy this morning?"

"No. There's no occasion yet to hear from her."

They exchanged a smile. The clever Fanny had divined that Judy had been sent west on a wild goose chase.

"What do you think of Judy's situation?" Lee asked.

Fanny's lips tightened. "Bad!"

"What's the man after?"

"Marriage."

"Judy has no money."

"It's her beauty. He plans to make her famous. He figures it would be a greater asset to him than money."

"There's an ugly four-letter word for that kind of man," said Lee.

"I'm acquainted with the word," said Fanny, ". . . But what can you do with an infatuated woman? Judy ought to be committed."

"My idea exactly," said Lee. "But we must find another way of saving her."

"We'll have to act quickly, Pop. It's touch and go with Judy."

A sheaf of reports arrived from Stan Oberry's office by messenger. Today they contained nothing of first rate importance. The doings in the office of Blair and Middlebrook on Monday were faithfully retailed; Tyrrell Blair had lunched with one of his numerous lady friends; Rafe Deshon had again shaken off his trailer. This operative was positive that Rafe could not have seen him. Apparently Rafe made a practice of darting through buildings with two entrances, and running down and up subway stairs just to be on the safe side.

Number 38 had not seen the maid Stella again, but had had a loving misspelled letter from her. He had answered it asking if he would be allowed to call. Number 17 had spent the greater part of Monday in the company of Boris Fanton, but reported nothing suspicious in his actions. Their intimacy had ripened considerably. 17 had satisfied himself that Boris had no typewriting machine in his rooms. There were however many typewriters available in the broadcasting offices, and since Boris had often to copy or revise scripts, he might have been typing at any hour without causing comment. Boris' expressed intention of giving up his rooms was only a stall. He intended staying where he was.

In the middle of the morning Boris Fanton himself came saun-
tering into the outer office beautifully dressed, manicured and
pomaded. Lee, watching him through the open door of the inner
room, felt the back of his neck prickle, just as he had seen a dog's
hair rise at the approach of an enemy. Boris sang out:

"Hi, Fan! You look too beautiful this morning. It's indecent!"

Though it was offered as a compliment, there was a hateful edge
to his voice. He knew that Fanny disliked him. Fanny said with a
rising inflection:

"Oh yes? What shall I do about it?"

"Wear a basket over your head. You hurt my eyes!"

He came into Lee's office. "Hi, Pop."

"Good morning," said Lee. "Sit down."

Fanny was so annoyed by his insolence, that she snatched up a
letter at random and brought it in to Lee's desk. "This is what you
asked for, Mr. Mappin."

Boris didn't get it—or didn't choose to get it. "Pop, I dropped
in to talk to you about your next broadcast."

This was a palpable lie because the next broadcast was still four
days away. Lee wondered what he had come for. It gave Lee a queer
start to be sitting face to face with a prospective murderer. It had
never happened before so far as he knew. He had been in the presence of discovered murderers and confessed murderers, but never
with a man who nursed murder in his heart. As far as he could see,
it wasn't worrying Boris any.

"They made a list at the office of all the telephone calls that
came in after your last broadcast. This will show you what they
liked and what they didn't like." He handed over a typewritten list.

"This will be valuable to me," said Lee dryly.

Boris did not hear the irony. "You and I ought to work together
closely, Pop. Of course you're a great writer, and I would never
think of interfering with your books. But speaking your thoughts
is something else again. I can show you how to speak."

"Certainly is kind of you, Boris."

"It's a pleasure, Pop."

Lee thought grimly: The next time I broadcast you will not be the announcer, my friend!

"When will Judy be back?" Boris asked carelessly.

"Depends on what she succeeds in turning up out there. Say, Thursday morning."

"Is she on the anonymous-letter-writer case?"

"Yes."

"If this fellow is what he says he is, isn't that pretty dangerous work for a young girl?"

Lee thought: He thinks he's having a bit of fun with me, but it's the other way 'round. He said: "Not the part that Judy has to play."

"Have you made a rough draft of what you want to say next Saturday night?" asked Boris.

"Not yet," said Lee. "It won't take me all that time."

"Well, I thought I had better mention it as I'll be out of town all day tomorrow."

"Where are you going?"

"To Poughkeepsie. They're having an anniversary dinner at Vassar and I am to conduct the broadcast. I'll stay all night."

Lee thought: He's preparing an alibi. That's what he came in for.

"If I knew what train Judy was coming back on, maybe I could board it Thursday morning at Poughkeepsie," said Boris.

Lee thought: With blood on your hands! He said: "Well, keep in touch with Judy. She's at the Blackstone."

When Boris had left, Lee, consulting the newspaper, learned that there was in truth to be an anniversary banquet at Vassar the following night, and that the speeches were to be on the air from eight until nine P.M. Lee reminded himself that you can get back from Poughkeepsie in an hour and a half or so.

He wrote another telegram to Judy with instructions that would keep her occupied until the following afternoon. She was then to take the Century for New York.

Later Rafe Deshon called up to say that Tyrrell Blair was giving a dinner at his home that night in honor of a visiting British publisher with whom he had business relations. It was essential for Lee to attend, Rafe said, because an English contract for his books was hanging in the balance. Unfortunately Rafe himself could not be present. He warned Lee not to accept any offer that might be made him until they could talk it over. "These Englishmen are the most charming fellows in the world," said Rafe, "and the slickest."

This was the day that Lee had a date to take Mary Blair to tea. She called up after lunch to say she couldn't go. She said she was sorry but Lee heard a lift in her voice unusual in the self-contained Mary.

"Will you set another day?" he asked.

"I'll have to let you know, Lee."

At seven Lee presented himself at the Blair penthouse. The sun was still shining and the view of the towers of Manhattan gilded in its horizontal rays was fantastic and gorgeous to a degree.

Cocktails were served in the open air. It was to be a stag dinner for ten. Lee inquired of a footman for Mary, and was told that Madam was dining out. He was disappointed. He enjoyed stag affairs well enough if the guests had wit, but this lot did not look promising. Excepting the Englishman they were all a little in awe of their big host.

The dinner was perfection. Blair, who had an idea that the English considered themselves more civilized than Americans, was on his mettle to show what New York could do. Lee doubted if this particular Englishman, rather a dry specimen, appreciated it, but Lee himself did. It was nothing to the lordly Blair if his guests lacked conversation. Booming from the head of the table, overriding them all, he supplied what was necessary. In more ways than one he reminded Lee of King Henry VIII. Bluff King Blair! Watching him, Lee wondered if he always succeeded in seizing what he wanted and what would happen if it were refused him.

Blair wearied of his guests at last and let them depart early. Lee was preparing to leave with the others, when the big man laid a hand on his arm.

"Stop a little while, Lee. It's too late to go anywhere, and too early to go to bed."

They sank into easy chairs in Blair's luxurious library. This room, which was furnished in massive carved oak suitable to the build of its owner, had a whole row of casement windows looking east over the river. A wasted moon was rising above the factory chimneys of Newtown. Blair unbuttoned his capacious waistcoat.

"Now we can talk about women," he said.

"You can," said Lee smiling. "I have nothing to contribute to the discussion."

"Come off! Come off!" chuckled Blair. "You're one of these sly fellows. You can't fool me!"

"I am only interested in the psychology of the pretty dears."

"Well, that's as good an approach as any!" Blair said with a great laugh.

He launched forth on his favorite subject. Lee, listening and studying him, speculated on what it could be that constituted his attraction for women, elderly and gross as he had become. It must be the sheer force of the man that bowled them over, he decided. They liked to be bowled over. After a particularly spicy anecdote, Blair boomed:

"Would you blame me? Would you blame me?"

"Not in the least," said Lee coolly. "I suppose you are just fulfilling your nature as we all do, each in his own way.

"Sure! I was made for women and women were made for me!"

"The only thing I don't understand is, why did you marry?"

"Because I wanted a wife. I wanted everything that belongs to a man. A fine wife adds to a man's prestige. I had to have the finest; the handsomest, the best bred and the rarest; the kind of woman that all men desire. I'm no worse than other men, Lee, but only honester. When her beauty begins to wear, I pay her off and stick a fresher flower in my buttonhole. Do you blame me?"

"Not if you can get away with it," said Lee dryly. "How about the wives?"

"Look what I can give them; money, position. Each enjoys her day in the sun. What more could a woman desire?

"What about her emotional life?"

Blair laughed. "Hell, that's her lookout. Sleeping with your own wife is like a slice of cold veal."

"In that case I'm glad I never married," said Lee dryly.

Blair glanced at Lee with a spice of resentment. It annoyed him that such a little man should be so independent.

EARLY NEXT MORNING Lee was awakened by Jermyn with a telegram from Baltimore.

He read:

> Mailing special delivery your address. When you get
> it call Madison 3120M.
>
> Parker.

Lee did a little mental figuring. A letter mailed before nine o'clock in Baltimore ought to be delivered in New York between one and two. He instructed Jermyn to bring it to him at the office as soon as it arrived, and not to let it out of his hands.

CHAPTER EIGHT

THE ENVELOPE THAT JERMYN BROUGHT to the office for Lee contained two enclosures; a brief, scrawled note on sleazy paper, blistered with tears, and a longer letter in a man's hand on the note paper of the St. James Hotel, New York. The first read:

> Dear Mr. Mappin:
> The enclosed just came. Oh, I want so to believe that it's true! I want to believe it so bad! Maybe he means what he says. I can't believe he's as bad as you say. Call me up and tell me what I should do. I'll be waiting near the phone all day. I have the money he sent me.
>
> Your friend, Nell.

Lee's face hardened as he read the second letter.

> My darling little wife:
> Everything is all set now for the start of our new life together. I can hardly wait till I see you! I long to make you forget all the bad past. I have rented a little apartment but I have not furnished it because I thought it would be fun to go around together and buy the stuff. We can afford the best now. Take the 6:43 P.M. train Wednesday for New York on the Pennsylvania. It arrives about ten o'clock. I can't be

there to meet you because I have a broadcast, but I won't be long. Check your trunk to New York from Baltimore and when you get there, let it stay in the station. If you have any valises check them in the parcel office in New York and bring me all the checks. Only bring an overnight bag with you to the hotel. It will be easier to send all your stuff next day direct to our apartment. Take a taxi from the station to the Governor Van Buren Hotel. That's a swanky place, but the best is none too good for us, darling. Register at the hotel under your own true name which I never told you before. It is Mrs. Herbert Deaves. Hereafter we'll always sail under true colors. Engage a nice room with bath and the heck with expense. Remember this is going to be our second honeymoon, darling. Get a room on the 12th floor because that has the best view. I'll be at the hotel shortly after you get there. I can't wait until I clasp you in my arms. I enclose $50 but I wouldn't advise you to buy any clothes. You can do better in New York.

Yours devotedly, Herbert.

P.S.—Don't tell a soul in Baltimore where you're going or what for. We want to make a clean break with the past. This is going to be a brand new fresh start.

Lee grunted. A loving woman will believe anything, he thought. The letter puzzled him because he could hardly imagine a more unsuitable scene for a murder than a busy, modern hotel in the heart of the city. Perhaps Fanton meant to take her on to some other place, but if so, why all the bunk about checking her bags at the station, getting a room on the twelfth floor and so on. Time would tell.

Lee had saved his Pennsylvania time table. Spreading it on his desk, he called the Baltimore number. The telephone on Lee's desk was an extension from the front office. The door was open and since he had his eye on the other instrument, he could be sure nobody was listening in on his talk. When he heard Nell's faltering voice on the wire, he answered close to the transmitter so that his voice could not possibly carry beyond his own room.

"That you, Nell?"

"Oh, Mr. Mappin! You got the letter? What am I to do? What am I to do?"

"Easy, my dear! You must keep your wits about you today for all our sakes."

"Can't I come to New York like he wants me?"

"Certainly you are coming to New York. You are going to do exactly what he tells you. With this exception; you are to take the 5:46 from Baltimore instead of the 6:43. Get that?"

"Yes, sir. 5:46 from Baltimore."

"That will bring you here an hour earlier. That's to give me a chance to talk to you."

"But shan't I see Charlie, Mr. Mappin? I've got to see Charlie."

"You shall see him. I might be mistaken about him. In any case we must act as if he was on the square, until he proves that he isn't."

"Oh, thank you for that, sir. I wouldn't be satisfied if I didn't see Charlie."

"Are you sure you can remember everything he told you to do; check your trunk in Baltimore; check your bags in the New York station; take a taxi to the Governor Van Buren; get a room and bath on the 12th floor?"

"I've got it all written down, Mr. Mappin."

"Very good. You ought to be in your room at the hotel shortly after nine o'clock. You'll hear from me there."

"You won't let him see you?"

"I will give him every chance first to prove himself."

"Thank you, sir."

Lee dropped the telephone in its cradle and wiped his face. This situation was too exciting for his comfort. The risk to the woman was terrible—but how could he act otherwise?

He drove down to Headquarters and laid the whole case before Loasby. The Inspector, when he recovered from his astonishment, agreed that the measures Lee proposed were the best that could be taken.

"Man!" he exclaimed enviously, "if you take him in the act so to speak, what a coup that will be for you, Lee!"

"You can have all the credit for it," said Lee. "God knows I've had too much publicity already."

Lee didn't want a detective to accompany him to the girl's room. It might arouse somebody's curiosity. He agreed though, that Loasby's men should be secretly planted in the hotel within call. Loasby gave him a police whistle.

"Who will you take with you?" asked the Inspector.

"Tom Cottar," said Lee. "I can depend on him like a son. . . . Fanton's a tall fellow," he went on, "but weedy. He's got no guts. If Tom gets the jump on him he'll give no trouble."

"What a story for to-morrow's papers!" said Loasby.

Lee, who knew of old what a fatal attraction newspaper publicity had for the handsome Inspector, said dryly: "Well, don't give them any hint of it to-day!"

Lee spent a restless afternoon. He was a student and a writer; he was not happy with the raw material of crime. He asked Tom Cottar to dine with him. Lee could eat but little, but young Tom was under no such disability. Tom was all lighted up with anticipation. "What a scoop! What a scoop!" he kept saying.

Lee asked anxiously: "Are you sure you can handle Fanton by yourself?"

Tom flexed his biceps. "Don't make me laugh, Pop!"

"I'll be there to help you, of course."

"If there's any rough stuff you'd better stay out of it."

It suddenly occurred to Lee that the train might be delayed, and his heart sank. Why hadn't he timed the girl's arrival for earlier in the evening? However, upon telephoning to the terminal, he learned that number 154 was on time. At nine fifteen he called the Governor Van Buren. Too early. Five minutes later he was successful in getting "Mrs. Herbert Deaves" on the wire. So far everything had gone off according to schedule.

"I only want the number of your room," Lee said to her, "so I can come there without sending up my name from the desk."

She could hardly speak.

"1224," she whispered. "Oh, Mr. Mappin, I'm so nervous I'm like to jump out of my skin!"

"Keep cool," said Lee with more confidence than he felt. "Everything is going to be all right."

Lee called up Loasby to let him know that everything was set. He and Tom then taxied around to the Governor Van Buren and ascended to the twelfth floor. Tom had a gun in his pocket, Lee a pair of handcuffs. Lee knocked on the door of 1224, and a frightened voice spoke from inside:

"Who is it?"

"Mappin."

Nell let them in. Seeing Tom she asked suspiciously: "Who is he?"

"My friend, Mr. Cottar," said Lee. "I brought him along just in case . . ." He left his sentence in the air.

She closed the door. The unfortunate woman was in a bad state of nerves. Her face was pale and sweaty with a patch of rouge on either cheek standing out like a red seal. Her brassy curled hair had fallen into damp strings. She was wearing a new silk dress of the worst possible shade of red for her; it hung awkwardly on her thin frame. Not a very appetizing sight for a bridegroom, Lee thought. Out of the tail of his eye he saw Tom's face fall. It would not be nearly so much fun saving the life of a homely girl.

"If he doesn't come soon I'll go crazy!" she said wildly.

"Now, my girl," said Lee soothingly. "There's no occasion for you to fly off the handle. Maybe everything's going to be all right. You want to look your best for him, don't you?"

She flew to the mirror, applied fresh lipstick, powdered her face, attempted in vain to fluff up her damp hair. "Oh, I look terrible!" she wailed.

Lee and Tom were taking stock of the room. There wasn't much to see. With its neat wallpaper, inoffensive pictures, striped satin coverlets on the beds, it resembled a hundred thousand other such rooms throughout the country. Lee wondered how they contrived to make hotel bedrooms all look so exactly alike. As you entered, the twin beds were on your left; in the right wall toward the front of the room was the door into the bathroom; in the same wall, nearer the entrance from the corridor, another door. When Lee threw it open, a capacious clothes closet was revealed. The bureau stood against the left hand wall near the windows, and there were two arm chairs at that end of the room; also a desk between the two windows.

"Please to sit down, gentlemen," said Nell. "You must excuse me. I can't sit still. . . . Oh, it's awful, just waiting like this, not knowing what's going to happen!"

"Tell yourself that everything's going to be all right," said Lee.

She suddenly turned on him. "Everything would have been all right maybe, if you hadn't stuck your nose into it. It was you put the bad thoughts into my head. I would be happy now, I wouldn't be worrying if it wasn't for you! Oh, I wish I'd never laid eyes on you! I wish . . ."

Lee stood up. "We can still go."

The threat quieted her. "No," she said sullenly. "As long as you're here you might as well stay."

Lee sat down again.

"Are you aiming to stay until Charlie comes?" she demanded.

"That's the idea."

"He mustn't find you here," she said excitedly. "What could I say to him? He knows I don't know nobody in New York."

"He won't find us here."

"Where'll you be then?"

Lee pointed to the clothes closet.

"No!" she said. "I'm not going to have you listening to everything we say. He's my husband and this is our private room! You'll have to get another room to wait in."

"There might not be time for us to get back here," Lee said grimly.

Nell started to cry. "Oh, I don't know what to do," she wailed. "You've got me all mixed up. I don't know what to do!"

"You had better go in the bathroom and wash your face," said Lee mildly. "Charlie would wonder to find you crying."

She obeyed him. When she came out of the bathroom she made up her face again before the mirror. Turning around, she said sullenly:

"You keep telling me maybe everything's going to be all right; maybe Charlie is on the square. If so what will I do with you two hiding there in the closet? Do you think I'm going to let you stay there?"

Lee looked at her compassionately. The notion that the elegant Boris Fanton would acknowledge this poor creature as his wife was grotesque. However, Lee wasn't going to tell her that. All he wanted was to stave off hysterics until after the man got there. He said:

"If you are satisfied that Charlie is on the square with you, tell him you're hungry; tell him you didn't have any dinner, and make him take you downstairs to a restaurant. Then my friend and I can slip out."

This seemed to satisfy her.

There was nothing to do then but wait. Nearly an hour must pass before they could expect Fanton. It stretched before them to infinitude. Lee found himself calculating; sixty minutes, three thousand six hundred seconds. Good God! how would they get through it. He and Tom sat like a pair of waxworks in the easy chairs. They could not even smoke because the fumes would have betrayed them. Conversation was impossible. Nell paced the floor, biting her lip and twisting her hands together. Every few minutes she stopped in front of the bureau to tinker with her makeup.

The level-headed Tom Cottar had come prepared for just such an emergency. He pulled a newspaper out of his side pocket and unfolded it. "Sit down on the bed, Miss Nell," he said in his pleasant, virile voice, and I'll read you the news."

She dropped on the bed with a sigh. "Maybe the woman's page will be more interesting to you," Tom went on. "I know the girl that edits it. She's smart all right. Did you ever think of newspaper work, Miss Nell? It would pay you better than standing behind a counter."

He began to read about a parade of summer clothes in a Fifth Avenue store, and Nell in spite of herself listened. The time passed.

When the telephone rang all three of them started violently. Nell without moving, stared at the instrument with wide eyes of horror. The bell shrilled again. Lee signed to her to answer it.

"I can't! I can't!" she whispered. "I'm shaking so!"

"If you don't answer it he won't come," said Lee.

That fetched her to the telephone. "Hello," she faltered. ". . . Yes, this is Nell. Hello, Charlie. Yes, I'm scared. I'm scared being alone here in the hotel . . ."

Not so scared, Lee thought grimly, but you can lie handily.

She continued: "The number of my room is 1224 . . . Yes, I left my bags and my trunk at the station. I registered as Mrs. Herbert Deaves . . . No, I ain't told a soul, Charlie . . . All right, I'll be looking for you."

When she hung up she swayed on her feet. Lee caught her and Tom ran into the bathroom for a glass of water.

"Let me put some whisky in it," urged Lee.

She shook her head. "He would smell it on me." She recovered herself and went to the mirror. "Oh, I look terrible!" she mourned.

"Where is he?" asked Lee.

"He phoned from Thirty-fourth Street. He just wanted to get my room number, so he wouldn't have to ask at the desk downstairs."

"Just like us!" said Lee.

"Said he'd be here in five minutes."

Lee looked around the room to make sure they had left nothing to betray their presence. He and Tom took their hats and retired into the clothes closet. Lee pulled the door to after them, but did not allow it to latch. Thus, while they could not see what took place in the room outside, they could hear everything.

Lee and Tom stood side by side in the dark, breathing fast. After what seemed like an endless wait, there was a knock on the door. Nell went to open it, and, judging from the sounds, Fanton strode in, slamming the door behind him. He dropped a heavy valise on the floor, and gathered the girl in his arms. A pitiful cry of relief and joy escaped her.

"My Charlie!"

"Darling!" he cried emotionally. "My blessed little wife! How I have longed for this moment!"

A little breath of disgust was forced from Tom Cottar. Lee laid a warning hand on his arm.

Fanton continued to fondle the girl and murmur endearments. "My own girl! There is nobody in this whole world for me but you! What makes you tremble so? You're not afraid of your own boy, are you?"

"Not now," she whispered. "Oh, Charlie, it's all right, isn't it? Tell me it's all right!"

"You bet it's all right! We're never going to be parted again!"

He left her and they heard the sound of the windows being pulled down. "All the windows in the hotel are open," he explained. "We don't want them to hear us." He returned to her.

After a moment Nell said in a small voice: "I'm hungry, Charlie."

"Didn't you get your dinner on the train?"

"I couldn't eat then. I was too excited. Let's go down and get something now."

"After awhile. I can't let you out of my arms yet."

"No, please, Charlie, wait!"

"What's the matter? Don't you love me any more?"

"I'm hungry!" she wailed.

He laughed. "I never knew a girl to be hungry at such a time. . . . I can't order anything sent up because I'm not registered, see? They'd put us both out."

"Not here, Charlie. Let's go downstairs and eat."

An ugly note of suspicion came into his voice.

"What do you want to leave the room for? Is it a trap?"

"No, Charlie, no!"

"After awhile we'll go and eat. Now . . ."

"I'm hungry!" she wailed.

He couldn't keep up the pretence any longer. His voice turned hateful. "Do you think I'm going to show myself in public with a cheap floozey like you? Oh, my God!"

"Charlie . . . !" she gasped.

"You're horrible to me!" he snarled. "Horrible! You're never going to leave this room, see?"

She started to scream. The sound was choked off at the beginning. Lee and Tom ran out of the closet. Fanton had forced the girl down on the bed on her back. One of his knees was planted on her breast and both his hands were around her throat. Nell's hands were clawing feebly at his wrists; her eyes starting from her head.

Tom, catching the man by the shoulders tore him off the girl, and flung him to the floor. Fanton was up again like a cat, only to be met by a crashing blow in the face from Tom's fist which stretched him flat again. Tom flung himself on his body. They threshed wildly on the floor. Fanton contrived to pull a gun. Lee, watching for that, kicked his wrist and the gun flew harmlessly across the room. Tom roused to a terrible rage by what he had heard and seen, banged Fanton's head on the floor until he became groggy. They handcuffed him then and stood up.

Fanton recovered almost instantly, and handcuffed as he was, scrambled to his feet and started toward the window. Tom pulled him back. Lee fetched a towel from the bathroom and they bound his ankles together. He was then helpless. No sound escaped him. He rolled from side to side on the floor with an inhuman expression of rage. Lee took a double pinch of snuff.

Meanwhile the girl was lying motionless half on, half off the bed. She was not seriously injured, and they brought her to without difficulty. It seemed cruel to do so, for when consciousness returned she only moaned piteously and reproachfully:

"Charlie! . . . Charlie! . . . Charlie!"

"We'd better have in the police," said Lee.

He knew they were waiting near by, but the affair had been so brief and had made so little noise, they were not drawn to the room.

There was no hurry now, and instead of alarming the guests by using the whistle, Lee called up Headquarters and obtained the number of the room they had engaged. He then called them in, four husky plainclothes men.

"There's your prisoner," he said.

"What's the charge, Mr. Mappin?"

"Attempted murder."

"No! No!" wailed Nell. "He didn't mean to hurt me!"

"She's his wife," explained Lee. "We've got evidence enough to convict without hers."

The valise that Fanton had brought still rested by the door. It was of the "Pullman" type as big as a trunk. One of the detectives tried it; found it locked. The key was in Fanton's pocket; when the lid was thrown back the contents were significant; several iron sash weights wired together; a hatchet, ground to a keen edge; a knife with a pointed blade ten inches long; a cheap cotton comforter.

Lee, studying these articles, said: "One begins to see what his plan was. You will find that he registered in this hotel early today. He had his valise with him. Tonight he had only to return to his room and fetch the valise here." Lee tried the edge of the knife. "One can understand why he instructed his wife to engage a room with a bath."

"Oh God!" murmured Tom in horror.

"She would have left the room in the valise in pieces," Lee continued. "It is big enough. All he had to do was to pay his bill at the desk and carry the valise away with him. How he planned to dispose of it, I don't know. Drop it from the after deck of a ferryboat no doubt; the sash weights would sink it. He would have secured the checks for her baggage, and disposed of that at his leisure. Also the letters he had written her, the only evidence against him."

Lee offered his snuff box to the headquarters men who hastily declined. "A very cleverly-planned crime," he went on. "The girl brought only an overnight bag to the hotel. That could have been shoved into the big valise with the rest. When the hotel management discovered the room to be empty they would naturally have supposed that the lady had slipped out without the formality of paying her bill, which sometimes happens. They would not have reported a disappearance. No inquiry would have been made from Baltimore. The murder would never have come to light."

The towel was removed from Fanton's ankles and he was stood upon his feet none too gently.

"Well, my ingenious letter-writer," said Lee, "what now?"

"I don't know what you're talking about," muttered Fanton.

A car was summoned from Headquarters and the prisoner taken down in a service elevator and out through the hotel basement without alarming any of the guests. They all accompanied him downtown.

At Headquarters Nell was incapable of giving testimony even had she been willing to do so, and she was handed over to the care of a matron. Lee and Tom Cottar told their tales and Fanton was committed to the Tombs. He had only one merit; he never whined nor sought to excuse himself.

Lee said to Loasby: "Have him well watched. He has suicidal tendencies. That would be too good for him."

While they were at Headquarters Tom Cottar was fretting to get away to the newspaper office with his sensational story, but Loasby would not let him go until all the preliminaries were settled. When Tom was finally released, Lee said to him,

"Don't reveal the fact in your story that you were acting as my assistant tonight. If you do, I'll never be able to employ you in such a capacity again. It would get me in wrong with all the other boys of the press. Another thing: I want the police to have the credit for this capture. You can start your story by saying: 'Acting on a tip from Amos Lee Mappin, Inspector Loasby planted his men in the Governor Van Buren Hotel,' and so on, and so on."

This was not the way that Tom had visualized his story, and his face fell. "Okay, Pop, if it must be so," he said.

IT WAS VERY LATE before Lee got home and turned in. He had scarcely fallen asleep, it seemed to him, when he was awakened by Jermyn. It was morning. The servant had a special delivery letter on his salver. Lee's eyes almost popped out of his head when he saw the cheap plain envelope, the typewritten address. A feeling like fear crept into his breast. This smacked of the superhuman. The letter contained but a single line:

> Wrong man, Pop. I'm still on the job.
>
> X.

"Mr. Mappin, sir, what's the matter?" cried Jermyn in alarm.

Lee put his legs out of the bed. "Jermyn, you have murdered sleep!" he said. "Bring me a stiff whiskey and soda."

CHAPTER NINE

LEE WAS FORCED TO TODDLE DOWN to Police Headquarters with his tail between his legs so to speak, and show his latest letter to Inspector Loasby. After the way Loasby had congratulated him the night before upon nailing the letter-writer, and after Lee had accepted the congratulations as no more than his due, it was bitter to have to confess error. The stories in the newspapers too: ANONYMOUS LETTER-WRITER FOUND! IDENTIFIED AS BORIS FANTON, WELL-KNOWN BROADCASTER!—made Lee feel a little ill. He took no steps to put the newspapers right. Let them discover the mistake for themselves.

Loasby was sympathetic. "Mr. Mappin," he said, "this may be some comedian who reads the newspapers, and has got the notion of taking up the joke where Fanton left off."

Lee shook his head. "Same envelope, same paper, same kind of typing."

"All that has been described in the newspapers."

Lee pointed out that the letter had been dropped in a box in midtown New York at ten o'clock the previous night. "That was before Fanton had even entered the hotel, and of course hours before the story broke in the newspapers."

"Somebody close to you," suggested Loasby. "Somebody with advance information."

"There's nobody close enough to me for that," said Lee. "Except you," he added dryly.

Loasby puffed out his cheeks. "Lee, I swear I never mentioned this case to a living soul except the four men I sent to the hotel. And they didn't know what they were sent for. . . . Couldn't Fanton himself have posted the letter as a blind?"

"Fanton didn't know what was going to happen in the hotel, or he wouldn't have gone there . . . It's no good, Inspector. I can't explain it, and neither can you. The letter-writer *knew beforehand* what was going to happen. There's something uncanny about it."

"Well, we'll tighten our lines all over town," said Loasby soothingly. "I think I can promise you results within twenty-four hours."

Lee got small comfort out of it. "I seem to have heard that before," he said.

LEE FOUND HIS OWN OFFICES EMPTY. Fanny, he knew, had gone to Grand Central Station to meet the Twentieth Century, bringing Judy from Chicago. Presently Fanny came in alone.

"Where's Judy?" he asked anxiously.

"Gone home to bathe and dress after her journey," said Fanny. "She'll be here soon."

"What did you say to her?"

"I didn't say anything. She had read the newspaper. What could I have said? She was carrying the newspaper in order to show me she had read it, and that it wasn't necessary for me to say anything. So I just gave her a sisterly kiss."

"Is she all right, do you think?"

"As far as I can tell, she is. She couldn't have loved the man, Pop. It was an infatuation. If I am right, in her heart she is relieved at being saved from him, though of course she isn't going to admit it to anybody."

Lee pinched Fanny's ear. "Who would ever believe there was so much sense in that curly head!"

"Some day you'll appreciate me at my true worth," said Fanny.

Soon afterwards Judy arrived, very smartly dressed and entirely mistress of herself. Her beautiful face was like a mask. Lee listened gravely while she reported on her activities in Chicago. By this time she probably knew that she had been sent on a fake errand and was aware that Lee knew she knew it. However, for each other's sake they kept up the comedy. Lee said:

"If you've read the papers you know what we've been doing while you were away."

"I know," said Judy briefly.

That was all. Lee observed with relief that she attacked her office work with more attention than she had shown in many a day. The new files had been delivered and both Fanny and Judy were engaged in transferring the correspondence from the old boxes to the new.

A bundle of reports was sent down from Stan Oberry's office. It included the first account of the activities of Jim Costin who in alphabetical progression had naturally become "D."

I was unable to contact D. until he came home to supper at six-thirty on Tuesday. About an hour later he left the house and I tailed him to a little tavern on Third Avenue near Thirty-sixth, called Hymie's. D. appeared to be well known there. He lined up at the bar with some of his cronies, talking loud. I listened, but it's not worth putting down. Just bar-room boasting. Later he sat at a table with a man. I couldn't hear so good now, but I got enough to tell there wasn't anything private or secret in it. Just empty talk to pass the time. He went home shortly after one. By that time he was pretty drunk.

He came out at 9:48 Wednesday morning and proceeded to the main reading room of the New York Public Library. He got out a big bound volume of the *New York Graphic* for 1877 and sat at a table thumbing over the pages and looking at the pictures. He kept glancing at the clock and at 5 to 12 he got up and left and went down to the terrace in front of the Fifth Avenue side and stood there by the balustrade waiting for somebody. At 12:09 he was joined by a tall, thin, dark-complected man about 35 years of age. Dressed very careless, but clothes of good material. Close-set eyes, pasty skin, like a night worker. They had a little low-voiced talk, then D. gave this fellow a fat sealed envelope which the fellow put in his pocket, and he gave D. something which I took to be a bill or a couple of bills folded small, and they parted.

I followed D. to Hymie's Tavern where he ordered a ham sandwich and proceeded to drink up the money he had earned. I heard him telephoning home that he was kept out on important business. He stayed there all afternoon. If he's going to stay in Hymie's all the time I can't sit around without their getting on to me.

43.

Lee, with a spurt of anger, seized a pen and wrote a few lines to Stan Oberry.

Your Number 43 is a washout. From his report it appears that he had what was possibly the key to the whole case right in his hand yesterday and muffed it. He knew he could pick up D. at any time. Why the devil didn't he go after the man who gave D. money? Now that C. is lodged in jail, number 17 is free. I suggest you fire 43 and give the job to 17 who has a head on him.

Upon thinking the situation over, another and a better means of keeping tab on Costin occurred to Lee. He sent downstairs to ask Mrs. Costin to send her husband up to his office as soon as he had eaten his dinner.

Among the other reports there was a lengthy communication from number 38. There wasn't much in this one for Lee, but all of 38's reports made amusing reading. He was evidently a devil among

the women and didn't mind confessing it. In this report he described how he had taken supper at the servant's table in the
Deshon house on Wednesday night by special invitation of the cook.
In addition to the cook and his girl, Stella, there were two other
maids and 38 had laid himself out to charm them all. Evidently
there had been a gay time in the servants' hall. Mr. and Mrs. Deshon
were dining out.

After supper the two maids went out to meet their dates, while
38 sat on in the servants' hall, holding Stella's hand, while the cook
sat on a sofa nearby, playing propriety with her knitting. Soon the
cook fell asleep and 38 had little difficulty in persuading Stella to
take him on a tour of the rooms upstairs. He took the precaution
of putting the front door on the chain so he couldn't be surprised
by the return of the family. But they never came home in the middle
of the evening, Stella said. A description of the house followed,
which Lee skimmed over as he already knew it. The part that interested him came at the end of the report.

> There is no typewriter visible in any of the rooms,
> and Stella says she has never seen or heard her mas-
> ter using one. He has a suite of three rooms on the
> third floor of the house; study, bedroom and
> dressingroom. There is a desk in the study; all the
> drawers are locked. On the pretext that I wanted to
> see what a gentleman's clothes were like, I got Stella
> to open the wardrobes in his dressingroom. I noticed
> behind his regular clothes was hanging a complete
> sailor's suit and also a shabby, worn outfit which
> suggests that C. occasionally has a fancy for disguis-
> ing himself.

Lee, making a note of Rafe Deshon's "disguises" put the reports
in his safe.

Costin appeared after lunch; shabby, frayed, revealing his broken teeth in an insinuating grin and filling the front office with
the fumes of swallowed whiskey. Lee, watching him through the

open door, saw him rap the new filing cases with his knuckles in passing. He said:

"Steel, eh? That's a good precaution to take against fire."

"They're thief-proof, too," said Fanny. "Locked up at night."

Costin's smile faded.

He came on into Lee's room. "I hope you've got a job for me like you said, Mr. Mappin."

"Well, I have," said Lee.

"That's fine! As it happens, I just finished a little job yesterday, so I'm at liberty to take it."

"What kind of job?"

Costin held up a grimy hand impressively. "My lips are sealed, Mr. Mappin."

"Good!" said Lee. "I hope you'll be as secret about my affairs."

"You can depend upon me, Mr. Mappin."

"Shut the door and sit down," said Lee.

Costin seated himself with all the manner of a prominent executive, crossing his legs, pressing his fingertips together.

"Are you acquainted with my servant, Jermyn?" asked Lee. "He's been to the office occasionally."

"I have exchanged a few words in passing with Mr. Jermyn."

"Very good. That will make it easier. . . . Costin, someone close to me is betraying the secrets of this office."

Costin, without changing a hair, shook his head and made sounds of disapprobation.

"I hate to think that it may be Jermyn," Lee continued, "but I must neglect no precaution. Your job is to make friends with Jermyn, to gain his confidence, to find out what he is up to."

"You came to just the right party, Mr. Mappin," said Costin earnestly. "Making friends is right in my line. . . . What about the remuneration?"

Lee satisfied him on that point.

"Well, give me some message or something to carry up to your house and I'll start in right now," said Costin.

Lee shook his head. He wanted time to warn Jermyn first. He said: "It would look more natural if I sent Jermyn down here after

dinner tonight to fetch something for me. You will hear him and
come up to see who it is, and then you can get into talk."

"Very good, Mr. Mappin. Maybe he will accept an invitation to
come down to my place for a drink. But, unfortunately I haven't
got anything in the house." He paused suggestively.

Lee gave him a couple of dollars on account.

LATE THAT AFTERNOON Lee was greatly surprised to see Mary Blair
entering the front office. She had never looked handsomer. Tall
and slim with her remote and exquisite air, she was like a legend-
ary woman, a demi goddess; like the beauty that a man remem-
bers when he is old. Lee always had a feeling of gratitude towards
Mary because she embodied a dream. He could not describe what
she was wearing; it was of no importance beside the invisible
mantle of grace that clothed her. In the outer office she was her
usual reticent self, but as soon as she turned her back on the girls
and came in to Lee, the mask dropped from her smiling face.

"So this is where you concoct your plots!" she said. "It is not
what I expected."

"What did you expect?" asked Lee, hastening to meet her.

"I don't know. But not this. It is all so matter-of-fact."

"Camouflage, my dear. Terrible secrets are concealed here."

He made to close the door, but she stopped him with a gesture.
"They would think it strange," she murmured.

She sat down with her back to the open door.

"Did you come to tell me you were going to tea with me?" asked
Lee.

"No. I'm sorry. I have an engagement at five."

Wondering then why she *had* come, Lee offered her cigarettes;
she shook her head. She started to talk like one whose tongue suddenly finds release—but she did not tell him why she was there.

"As I came out of the back door of Altman's I remembered that
your office was close by, and I thought how nice it would be to
drop in on you. So I sent the car home and here I am. I suppose I
ought to apologize for interrupting a man at his work. I am bringing you no business.

"I'd rather see you than any amount of business," said Lee.

She smiled delightfully. "You say such nice things! And the best of it is, you look as if you meant them!"

"I wish I had an opportunity to prove that I mean such things about you," he said to give her an opening.

She sheered away from it. "A woman always feels a little in awe of a busy man. My life is filled with such trifles."

"Some women only need to exist," said Lee.

She laughed. "Oh, that's going too far. That's sentimental. A woman has got to be useful just as well as a man. That's always been my trouble in the past; I felt like such a useless creature."

"And you're going to change now?"

"I am!"

"What are your plans?"

"Oh, no plans," she said quickly. "Just a resolve."

"Please don't ever change," said Lee.

"There's room for improvement," she answered almost gaily.

After a minute or two she got up saying: "Well, I must run along."

He could not induce her to stay longer. She did a strange thing; she retreated to the front corner of the little office where she was out of the range of vision through the open door, and beckoned to Lee. He went to her wonderingly. She was a little taller than he. Her dark blue eyes were big with feeling.

"Lee, dear," she murmured; "I wanted to tell you . . . I wanted you to know that I am grateful for your kindness, your understanding. It is so rare in this world. You're a fine person, Lee. I count myself lucky to have known you."

The demi-goddess took his face between her hands and kissed his lips. She went out quickly leaving Lee the most astonished man in New York at that moment—anxious too, because the kiss had the nature of a farewell. He heard her bidding the girls good-bye with that mixture of sweetness and shyness that was characteristic of her. The outer door closed.

THAT NIGHT LEE DINED QUIETLY at home. Jermyn broiled a chop the way he liked it, and put the makings of a salad on the table. This with cheese and a half bottle of Chateauneuf du Pape satisfied his every desire. When it was before him, he said:

"You needn't wait, Jermyn. Get your own supper. Are you free this evening?"

"Always free, sir, if you have need of me."

"Yes," said Lee. "You will smile when you hear what it is. Have you ever taken notice of Jim Costin, the husband of the caretaker at my office?"

"Yes, sir, I have spoken to him."

"What do you think of him?"

"Rather an unpleasant specimen, sir."

"Quite. I have reason to believe he is selling information about my affairs. The personal investigator that I put on the job has bungled it badly, and I have a mind to try you." He looked up with a smile at the tall, thin figure; plain, decent and correct. "Nobody would ever suspect you of doing detective work, Jermyn."

"No, sir. I expect not, sir."

"In order to lull the fellow's suspicions," Lee went on, "I have engaged him to investigate you, understand?"

"Sir!" exclaimed the astonished Jermyn.

Lee chuckled. "He is instructed to worm himself into your confidence and you are to allow him to do so. Confide anything you like in him. Invent crimes for yourself. While you are doing so, find out what he is up to. He's an educated man and shrewd in his boozy way. He's not the principal; somebody has hired him to spy on me. That's the man I want to find."

"Yes, sir. I understand. It has always been my desire to help you in your work, sir. I'll do my best."

"I know you will. Here are the keys to the office. The little one is for the middle drawer in my desk. Bring me the letter that lies on top of the pile. I've forgotten what it is. Any letter. Costin will hear you and come upstairs. He'll ask you to have a drink with him. The rest is up to you."

"Yes, sir. I want to thank you, sir, for this proof of your confidence."

"Shucks, Jermyn! We've been together for—how long is it? twelve years! It would be a nice thing if we didn't have confidence in each other. . . . Run along now. You can clear away when you get back. People like the Costins have their supper early, and Jim will be listening for you."

Half an hour later Lee heard Jermyn leave the apartment and smiled. He would have liked to borrow an invisible mantle in order to overhear the scene that would presently take place in his office. There would be rich comedy in it.

CHAPTER TEN

ON FRIDAY MORNING at the office Lee, with a sinking heart opened another plain envelope with a typewritten address. The enclosed communication was not a long one.

> Tonight's the night! The trap is baited and set; the victims are fatally attracted. I am using a more irresistible bait than cheese, Pop; the most potent bait in the world; physical desire! At ten or thereabouts the blow will fall. We will neither bury the body in earth, nor sink it under water. So find it if you can! When the clock strikes ten, think of me as enjoying the greatest thrill a human being can experience; the thrill of gratified revenge; the thrill of murder! I'll sleep sounder tonight than you will, old top!
>
> X.

Lee carried it down to Loasby. The latter said: "I still can't feel that there is anything in this, Mr. Mappin. It sounds too melodramatic."

Lee shrugged. "People have a way of sounding melodramatic when they cut loose."

Loasby said: "Notice that he refers here for the first time to victims in the plural."

"That's one of the things which makes me feel that it's bona-fide," said Lee. "If it was an imaginary situation he would always refer to it in the same terms. This suggests that there is a wealth of real circumstances and conditions surrounding the situation."

"Then you actually believe that more than one murder is to be committed tonight?"

"No. Only one murder. I take it that the victims he refers to are those who will suffer by reason of the murder. Notice that there is only one blow to be struck and one body to be disposed of."

Loasby was impressed by his acumen.

"There is another significant plural," said Lee. He read from the letter: "'We will neither bury the body in earth nor sink it under water.' He speaks of an accomplice."

"Maybe he just stuck that in to confuse us."

"Why should it confuse us? More likely it slipped out unconsciously. The whole letter suggests supreme confidence. He doesn't care whether we know it or not."

"That is, if it's not all a hoax," Loasby stubbornly insisted.

"If he has an accomplice, it gives us something to go on. . . . Though the time is terribly short!"

"How?"

"Murder can be committed singlehanded," Lee went on, "but it generally requires two to dispose of a body—though Boris Fanton had doped out a way to do it alone. All the letters have suggested that this murder is being carried out to satisfy a private vengeance. If that is so, the accomplice has no interest in it except his pay. He has been hired. There are plenty of murderers for hire in this fair town of ours. You have a list of those known to be killers and suspected of it. Round them up without the loss of an hour. Use every resource of your department. Round them up and question them. If you don't succeed in learning anything, detain them over night. If we can deprive the murderer of his accomplice his plan must fail."

Loasby began to take fire from Lee's earnestness. "Okay, Mr. Mappin, I'll do that." He reached for the telephone.

Lee got up. "Keep in touch with me, Inspector. You can always reach me through my office."

Lee passed a bad morning. He was unable to apply his mind to anything. The sense of helplessness was maddening. Rafe Deshon

came into the office and Lee looked at him with a grim, specula-
tive eye. He had heard this man threaten to kill. Was he the letter-
writer? Rafe's facetious style was not unlike the manner of the letters.

"Hi-ya, Lee, my bucko! Do you know we're going to sell near
two thousand copies of your lousy book this week? That'll put it
way up among the bestsellers. I hope you appreciate what we're
doing for you. A book like yours might lie absolutely unnoticed in
the ruck if it *wasn't* pushed. We've got the booksellers eating out
of our hands. We'll go to their convention next week and you can
charm them . . ."

Lee could make nothing of him. The real man was completely
hidden behind this parade of hearty good fellowship. He had come
in to tell Lee that the biggest bookseller in Chicago was to be in his
office that afternoon, and if Lee would drop in, they could make
him double his order for "Murder and Fantasy."

"Sorry," said Lee firmly, "it's impossible. I'll be occupied all day."

"Well, if you can't, you can't," said Rafe.

"What about tonight?" Lee asked curiously.

"I've nothing on for you tonight."

"Couldn't you and I spend the evening together?"

"Sorry, I'm tied up, Lee." He made no offer to explain.

He lingered in the outer office to chaff the girls gaily. Rafe
labored to make everybody feel that he was their friend. It was a
funny thing about him, everybody praised him publicly—such a
good fellow!—but nobody liked him privately.

When he had gone, the uneasy Lee called up Peggy Deshon.
After he had submitted to listening to her brittle chatter for awhile,
he said:

"What are you doing tonight, Peg?"

"Let me see. . . . Dining with the Warringtons at the Plaza."

"Is Rafe going with you?"

"No."

"What's he doing?"

"God knows! . . . If you're free, Lee, drop in at the Plaza after
dinner. The Warringtons would be tickled pink to be noticed by
such a celebrity."

"I'll let you know, Peggy."

Lee's mind endlessly revolved in its problem like a squirrel in a cage. Surely Peggy would be safe enough dining with a party in a public restaurant. At this point thinking of X's letter, it occurred to him that "Vengeance" was perhaps not the word that a man would use in connection with a woman. Maybe after all, the intended victim was a man. Lee thought of the redheaded Tom Cottar. He did not believe that Tom had ever injured Rafe Deshon, but Rafe might believe that he had. According to Peggy's story, the mere existence of the man she loved was an offense to Rafe.

Lee called up Tom at his office. "What are you doing tonight?" he asked.

"Sorry, I'm tied up, Lee."

"Sure! But how?"

"Well, to tell you the truth, a fellow is taking me to a cock-fight somewhere in Jersey. Keep it under your hat."

"Who are you going with?"

"Nobody you know."

"Don't go," said Lee. "Tell your friend the paper has given you an important assignment. Tell him anything you like but *don't* go!"

"Okay, Lee," said Tom in a wondering voice. "But . . ."

"I can't explain over the phone."

Lee, after he had hung up, reflected that it was not going to be any too easy to explain further without betraying Peggy's confidence. Tom, who had his full share of human curiosity, was not long in coming round for more information. Lee threw himself on his mercy.

"Tom, I can't tell you what is in my mind. I have a certain reason to suspect that somebody has it in for you. Maybe I'll be able to explain the whole business later. In the meantime, for tonight take Fanny out, and stay with her all evening."

"That wouldn't be too difficult," said Tom, grinning.

At intervals during the day, Lee talked with Loasby. The Inspector described the operation of his dragnet and how the suspects were being brought into Headquarters one by one. In addition to Loasby himself, the most skillful and ruthless cross-examiners in the department were assigned to the questioning of these men, but up to the time Lee left his office, nothing had been elicited which even remotely suggested a connection with the anonymous letter-writer. All the suspects were able to give a clear account of their recent movements and present intentions. They all had criminal records, and Loasby was prepared to stretch the law a little and detain them in custody during the night.

He had not been able to lay his hands on the man he most wanted to see. This was one Loney Frasca. Frasca had been heard to boast during the past few days that he would soon be in the money. Throughout the underworld Frasca enjoyed the reputation of being a silent and solitary killer. The police had never been able to pin a homicide on him. He was a mysterious fellow who always worked alone; hence his moniker of "Loney." He belonged to a "Pleasure Club" in Stanton Street, but had never taken any of the other members into his confidence. He was a good-looking young fellow and presumably he had a girl—such men are often tracked through their girls; but Loney was as secretive about this as everything else, and none of his men associates knew who the girl was. Loney had a respectable father and mother, brothers and sisters, but he rarely troubled them. Nobody knew where he slept.

Later in the day the police received a tip that Loney was preparing to take an ocean voyage. A detective making the rounds of the steamship offices with Loney's photograph learned that he had engaged passage for Bermuda on the *Monarch* to sail Saturday. The name given was C. Wilson and wife, Hotel Vandermeer. No such persons were registered at the Vandermeer.

Loasby assured Lee that every man of the force who would be on the streets that night had been warned to keep a special lookout for trouble. "I also warned the Jersey police to watch for suspicious characters from Manhattan. I want you to be satisfied that I am doing everything possible. Have you anything further to suggest?"

"No," said Lee heavily. "We're working in the dark."

He made a trip to Stan Oberry's office to make sure that a special watch was put on Rafe Deshon that night. "Use as many men as you need," Lee urged; "your best men. I expect them to give me an exact account of where Rafe was and what doing up to and at ten o'clock. . . . Stan," he said, "this may be the means of preventing a terrible crime."

Afterwards it occurred to Lee that Peggy Deshon might be lured away from the dinner party by some trick, and he called her up to say that he would join her at the Plaza at eight-thirty.

"Grand!" said Peggy. "I told Ruth Warrington there was a chance of your coming, and she was delighted."

With the passing of each hour that brought him closer to the end of the day, the tightness in Lee's breast increased. After the girls had gone home at five, he could no longer bear sitting around the office. He walked the crowded sidewalks for a couple of hours wondering if any among the faces that passed was that of the murderer or his victim. Hunger drove him into a humble restaurant for a hasty dinner. At eight o'clock he went home to dress. Jermyn recounted his séance with Jim Costin the previous night, but Lee was in no mood to appreciate the humor of it.

Before setting out for the Plaza he called up Loasby again. The Inspector had remained at Headquarters to receive the reports of his men. There was nothing new, he reported. Loney Frasca had not been rounded up. Loney had not been seen in any of his usual haunts during the day. Lee told Loasby where he could be found during the next few hours.

The dinner party was already in an advanced state of hilarity when Lee joined it. Lee had the reputation of possessing a neat wit, but tonight he was a disappointment to his hostess. He rarely spoke, and at the sallies of others his smile was strained, his laughter forced.

"What's the matter?" whispered Peggy.

"A touch of lumbago," said Lee.

To the wall above their table was fixed a little brass clock. It announced the hour of nine with a single silvery stroke. Lee watched the progress of the minute hand thereafter with a horrible fascination. It traveled so fast! Like the hand of doom. At quarter to ten he excused himself and went to call up Loasby for the last time. Nothing new!

Returning to his seat, he continued to watch the relentless minute hand drawing closer and closer to the top of the clock. Up to the final moment he hoped to hear from Loasby. His nerves were stretched to the snapping point. Would it never strike? When the little silvery sound was at last heard it seemed to reverberate through the room and Lee wondered that everybody did not start and look that way. Well, it was done now. A sensation of fatalism took possession of him and the tension was a little eased. At any rate Peggy Deshon was still safe beside him. Lee took a stiff drink.

After awhile somebody suggested that they go on to another place. Lee whispered to Peggy

"Will you let me take you home now?"

Peggy's eyebrows ran up. "At eleven o'clock! Why?"

"I couldn't stand a nightclub," said Lee; "yet I don't want to leave you. I dreamed last night that you were in danger."

Peggy laughed. "You dreamed about me? How exciting! What sort of danger?"

"I don't know. You know what dreams are, a terrible danger hanging over your head. I wouldn't sleep a wink tonight unless I saw you safe at home first."

Like most women, Peggy was not proof against superstition. Her laugh was a little shaky. "All right, Lee. I'll let you take me home."

When Lee himself got home there was no message waiting for him. Finding it impossible to sleep, he sat up in bed reading. In the morning he was up before Jermyn and was out of the house by half-past seven. He knew that the first mail was delivered at his office about eight.

Upon entering the front room Lee received a shock. There sat Jim Costin at Fanny's desk slowly tapping the keys of her typewriter. Lee's jaw dropped. Was it possible that the anonymous letters had actually been written here in his own office? Costin was startled also. He jumped up, snatching the paper from the machine. He was tearing it across when Lee, leaping across the room, jerked it from his hands. Costin stared.

The paper was a disappointment. It contained only the well-known legend about the quick fox and the lazy dog written over and over. Lee was sorry then for the excitement he had betrayed.

"I was just practicing," explained Costin. "I would like to make out my reports on the typewriter like the other operatives."

"It is no matter," said Lee recovering himself. "You may go downstairs now. I'll talk to you after I have read the mail."

Lee noted that Costin had betrayed knowledge of the other operatives and their reports.

The postman was already on the landing. Lee's hands trembled as he took the morning's allotment of letters. Inwardly he was trying to reassure himself. It was not certain that anything had happened the night before. Loasby might be right after all. Or, the various measures they had taken yesterday might have prevented the murder. In that case the murderer would not confess that he had been balked. He would still make believe that the deed was done.

The plain envelope with the typewritten address fell out of the pile of its own weight. Today it contained something bulkier than note paper, a curiously uneven lump. Stooping to pick it up, the feel of this lump through the paper caused Lee's blood to run cold. He slit the envelope, the enclosed paper partly unfolded and a human ear fell on Fanny's desk. It was a fresh human ear. Judging from its size, it might be that of a small man or a large woman.

Lee fell back from the desk. He was no weakling; in his mind he could face out anything without flinching, but the piece of human flesh took him unawares. He was glad to drop on a chair and wipe his face while the beating of his heart quieted down. Some moments passed before he felt able to read the letter. It was brief.

> Lee Mappin:
> Everything passed off tonight like clockwork. My enemy is dead and safely put away, and my breast is easy. You will never find the body. In order that you and your friend Loasby may not kid yourselves into

believing that it is all a stall, I am enclosing a little
memento of the deceased. This may be my last letter, but you can be sure I will always be watching
you and laughing to myself at your clumsy attempts
to find what belongs to the ear.

X.

CHAPTER ELEVEN

NONE OF THE LINES that Lee and Loasby had put out produced any results. The *Monarch* was watched but Loney never turned up and the ship sailed without him. Every policeman in New York and in the nearby towns was looking for the gangster, but he eluded them. When Lee went down to Headquarters, the Inspector showed him a photograph of the triggerman. Lee saw a smooth-faced youth with a comely oval face and the suggestion of a derisive smile. He had a noticeable look of resolution which of course a crook may possess as well as an honest man. Decidedly an uncommon criminal. A small man but very trimly made.

Lee grew hot upon learning that in spite of his special orders, Rafe Deshon had succeeded in shaking off the men who had been assigned to watch him during the previous night. Rafe had come out of his house in Sutton Court at half-past seven, carrying a suitcase, and had taxied to the Pennsylvania Terminal. In the basement of the terminal he had engaged a dime-in-the-slot dressing room, and after half an hour had issued from it wearing an old shabby outfit, with a longshoreman's cap pulled over his eyes, and still carrying the suitcase. He had deposited the suitcase in a lock box in the station. He then led his two trailers a dance up and down stairs in the subway, and succeeded in shaking them off in the press of the theater-going crowd in the Times Square station. One operative returned to watch the lock-box in the station, while the other took up his stand across the street from the house in Sutton Court. It was all they could do. Shortly after two Rafe had retrieved his suitcase, dressed in his usual clothes and returned home. Stan Oberry was as angry as Lee at the failure, but there was nothing to be gained by abusing the unlucky operatives. The mischief was done.

Number 17, who had been detailed to watch Jim Costin, reported that his man had entered a large apartment house in the Bronx at 8 o'clock Friday, and had not come out until past midnight. Jim appeared to be sober which was unusual for him at that hour. The apartment house had two entrances and since Number 17 was alone, he could not watch them both. It was therefore not certain that Costin had remained in the building the entire time.

The operative (Number 9) assigned to watch Tyrrell Blair, reported that the publisher upon leaving his office, had drunk several cocktails with a woman friend at the Hotel Biltmore, and had then driven to his own home where he arrived at 7:30. Number 9, who had remained watching the apartment house until 2:30 a.m. (both the main and the service entrances were visible to him) asserted that Blair had not left the house again.

Lee checked his various friends with feelings of relief. Fanny turned up at the office at the usual time; likewise Judy. Lee called up the *Herald-Tribune* office and was relieved to hear the nonchalant voice of Tom Cottar on the wire. Peggy Deshon he had delivered safe at home the night before; he talked to her during the morning. Recalling Mary Blair's curious farewell with some anxiety, he called the Blair apartment. Madam had gone to spend the weekend in the country he was told. Lee then called up the Blair place at Old Westbury and was rewarded by hearing Mary's own voice. It sounded listless, but it was certainly herself. She said she was all right.

Rafe Deshon came into the office and Lee, without appearing to, studied him keenly and weighed every word he uttered. If this man had been through a great emotional experience during the past twenty-four hours, no sign of it showed; there was no secret glint in his eye, no tremor in his voice. But what could you tell about a man who displayed an artificial personality at all times. To the outward appearance Rafe, blond, good-looking, perfectly groomed, was the successful young New Yorker, par excellence. Hoping to surprise him, Lee asked casually:

"What did you do last night?"

Rafe answered with perfect readiness: "I went slumming."

Lee affected a friendly curiosity. "Slumming? Where?"

"Oh, you can read about it some day in my memoirs.

The day passed and the following day. Inspector Loasby, in his endeavor to satisfy his friend, put himself and his whole department at Lee's disposal. He carried out all Lee's suggestions. It was Loasby who decided that the story should not be given to the newspapers for the present. "No use starting a murder sensation until we have better evidence that there is a murder," he said.

No crime of violence was reported to the police and no unexplained disturbances. Several persons were reported to be missing, but during the next two days all these were checked and accounted for. The various automobiles reported stolen on Friday were subsequently recovered without showing any evidence that they had been used for murder. It was little wonder that Loasby held more firmly than ever to his belief that the whole thing was a hoax. The letter writer could have obtained the ear from a medical student, he said.

Lee could not comfort himself so easily. "Less than twelve hours before I received it that ear was on a living head, Inspector."

"Well," said Loasby, "you've prevented one foul crime. I should think you'd be satisfied."

Murder or no murder, Lee was determined to discover who had written the letters. His professional pride was at stake. If I can't solve a mystery which touches myself so closely, he thought, I might as well give up all claim to be a criminologist. He gave his whole time to the case, surveying what he had to go on from every possible angle—it was not much.

The report of Stan Oberry's number 9 did not eliminate Tyrrell Blair from his consideration. But Lee had never had anything positive against Blair. Rafe Deshon's unexplained actions provided more matter; his threats, his disguises, his acquaintance with sinister characters. True, Rafe's suggested victims had both escaped, but there might be another person in Peggy's life or in Rafe's. Peggy might have put forward Tom Cottar as a blind. She was clever enough. Next there was Jim Costin. Costin seemed too foolish a character to have engineered so ingenious a crime, but Lee had it in mind that if he was clever enough to have conceived the crime, he was clever enough to have assumed the foolishness. Finally there was the unknown quantity. The supreme confidence expressed in the anonymous letters suggested to Lee that his suspicions had not yet fallen on the real criminal.

In respect to Jim Costin, the police questioned every tenant in the Bronx apartment house into which Costin had disappeared on Friday night. This building, which was on the corner of the Grand Concourse and Swithin Street, contained nearly a hundred suites. Every tenant denied knowing a man answering to Costin's description and denied having been visited by such a person. Lee had arranged with Stan Oberry that while Jermyn was with Costin all other watch on Costin should be withdrawn.

On Monday morning while Jermyn was shaving his master and giving him a facial massage, he made a report.

"On Thursday night, sir, as I told you, Costin invited me down to his rooms in the basement to have a drink. He is fixed very comfortable there. His wife was out. He said he had given her and his boy the money to go to the movies. 'She works hard,' he said; 'she's entitled to it.' This hardly coincides with other things I have heard about his treatment of her. I expect he wanted to get her out of the way while I was there.

"I couldn't stay very long with him because I was supposed to be fetching something up to you that you had sent for. Costin spent the time in feeling me out, so to speak. He's a good deal smarter than he lets on. His line was the wrongs of the poor, you understand, sir, and how the masters oppressed them that was under them. I played up to it, but not so quick as to arouse his suspicions. I kept my own counsel at first and only little by little let him see that I was with him. He was flattering me all the time, and I appeared to swallow it. We parted the best of friends. Friday night I did not see him. He said he had a particular engagement."

"Didn't give you any inkling as to the nature of it, I suppose," put in Lee.

"No, sir. Very mysterious. Is always letting on that he is not what he seems; that he is engaged in big affairs."

"Go on."

"Thursday night he had asked me if I could get off after supper Saturday night. I said I could go out any night unless the master was entertaining. He said: 'Huh! I shouldn't think an able fellow like you would be satisfied to have a master.' I said: 'What is a poor man to do?' He said: 'Oh, of course, if you're content to be a servant, it's all right.' I said: 'I didn't say I was content.' He said: 'We only live once, Jermyn. Might as well live in a big way,' and let it go at that. We made a date to meet at Hymie's saloon on Third Avenue on Saturday night at eight. 'Don't come to my house any more,' Costin said; 'my old woman, she's too nosy.' So we met on Saturday."

"Did you notice any alteration in the man on Saturday; in his appearance, in his manner of speaking, in his spirits?"

Jermyn thought this over before answering. "No, sir. Can't say I did. But I wouldn't expect to, because he's always putting on with me; he's never natural."

"Well observed," said Lee. "Go on."

"Nothing particular happened Saturday night, sir. He was still testing me out. He put in many a sly question with the object of finding out if I had ever robbed you or played you false in any way. I denied that I had, but let on that I would not be averse to it if I thought I could get away with it. We drank a good deal. Luckily I have a strong head, sir. I made out to be more affected by liquor than I was. That night I fell for everything. 'Jermyn,' he said, 'every man is entitled to a place in the sun. There's not enough of the good things to go 'round, and a strong man must seize what he wants and the hell with the weaklings!' I said: 'That's true, Jim! I've been a fool to submit so long!' We shook hands on it. Evidently he was satisfied with my performance, for he said on Sunday night he would take me up to see a friend of his, a big shot, who was in a position to do something for me if I made good with him.

"On Sunday night we went at the Fifty-first Street subway station and went to the Bronx. Got off at the 177th Street Station and walked to a big apartment house on the Grand Concourse, the Wellwood, it was called. Costin said: 'We just walk through this building for a stall, see? I don't think anybody's trailing us, but my friend that we're going to see, he don't want his private address known. He don't want to be bothered with curiosity seekers. If you ever come to see him by yourself, always make certain you're not being tailed, see? Or you'll get into bad trouble.'

"There was a side door to the apartment house opening on a one-way street called Swithin Street. We came out that way. There was a private automobile standing in front, a new Dodge sedan I noticed, black in color, but I couldn't get around behind to see the license number, for Costin had me by the arm. We got in it. I couldn't get a good look at the chauffeur. Nothing was said. We started off and drove around so many corners I lost my sense of direction. We traveled too fast for me to read the street signs."

"Could you retrace the route?" asked Lee.

"No, sir. I'm afraid not, sir. But I'm to go there again, and next time I'll be prepared for them. I have a map of the Bronx. Next time I'll count the blocks and note every corner we turn."

"Good."

"We came to a stop in an out-of-the-way street of little, old-time, single-family houses. The street was paved with cobblestones; so little traffic there was grass between the stones. The house we stopped in front of was a wooden house, very old. It had a porch with fancy trimmings, painted white. I would know the house again if I found the street. The chauffeur preceded us up the walk, and telling us to wait on the porch, let himself in with a latch-key. Opened the door presently, saying it was all right. In the lighted hall I got my first good look at him; tall, lean, dark man about 35 years old, dressed careless . . ."

"But clothes of good material," put in Lee smiling. "Close-set eyes, pasty skin like a night-worker . . ."

"Why, yes, sir," said the surprised Jermyn, "you know him then?"

"I wish I did," said Lee. "It fits with another part of the puzzle, that's all . . . Go on."

"He opened a door into the sitting-room on the right. There was a man sitting there . . . one of the strangest men I ever saw, sir." Jermyn hesitated.

"Go on," said Lee.

"I am trying to find the right words to describe him, sir . . . A horrible sight! Made my skin prickle like I had the goose flesh. A little old man wasted away to skin and bones. Was something the matter with his legs. Sat in a wheel chair with a shawl across his lap. His head was bald and egg-shaped, with just a fringe of white hair around the base; wicked, grey eyes—terrible eyes, big nose, and a mouth like a hawk's beak—I mean the upper lip folded over the lower like a beak. I never saw a creature that looked so wicked.

"Well, we sat down and his eyes bored into me. The tall fellow was in and out of the room. He never spoke, but I could feel his eyes on me. The two of them were sizing me up. Other men also come in to look me over. Liquor was served and under the guise of friendly conversation the old man plied me with sharp questions. There was nothing the matter with his wits. He had a powerful voice that surprised you, coming from that wasted creature. Some of his questions made me sweat, but I don't think it was noticed, because the windows being closed, the room was hot, and Costin was sweating worse than me. I expect I looked somewhat confused too, but that would be natural; that old man must have been accustomed to it from strangers. Many of his questions was about you, sir. If I may say so, he had a special feeling against you."

"I suppose I have enemies I do not suspect," said Lee. "It would be natural in my line." He repeated Jermyn's description to himself: "Bald, egg-shaped skull, big nose, mouth like a beak, powerful voice . . . I can't connect it with anything out of the past, Jermyn."

"Very likely his appearance is much changed by age and disease, sir. His fingers were bent like a bird's claws from arthritis. . . ."

"Well, go on."

"He asked me if it wasn't true that you kept your most valuable papers in your home, sir. I said I didn't know, and anyway your papers wouldn't be valuable to anybody but yourself. 'All right,' he said with a horrible grin, 'if they were lost, Mappin would pay well for their return.' I said if they disappeared, I would certainly be suspected because you had no other servant. 'What harm to be suspected if they couldn't prove anything?' he said. 'Only the boobs get themselves caught, Jermyn. If you were properly instructed beforehand you would never be caught. You wouldn't have to snitch the papers yourself, but only to receive a friend some night when Mappin was out. If you lost your job, I could put you in the way of a better one. You are wasted, working for a . . . for a single man . . .'"

"What were his exact words, Jermyn?" Lee asked smiling.

"Begging your pardon, Mr. Mappin, lousy old bachelor was what he said."

Lee laughed. "I expect he asked you many a question about my personal habits and so on."

"Yes, sir, he did. I hope I may be excused from repeating his words. I answered all such questions truthfully. Nothing could be more to your advantage than the truth, sir."

"You're a good fellow, Jermyn. Go on."

"He said that with my front I ought to be employed in one of the richest houses in the country, sir, a house where the women wore ropes of pearls and collars of diamonds. I wouldn't have to do any of the dirty work, he said. He would arrange it so that I would never even be suspected, but would go on to better positions until I wished to retire and live at my ease. Such was the style of his talk. No actual proposal was put up to me last night but I am to go up there again. Costin will let me know the night. The tall man drove us back to a point near the subway station. I thought it safer not to turn around and look at the license number, sir; Costin was watching me so close."

"That's all right," said Lee. "We can be certain that the car wasn't registered as from that address."

"I'm pretty sure I made good with those people, Mr. Mappin," Jermyn said simply. "If I had not, I doubt if I would ever have been allowed to leave the house."

"Have you the courage to go there again?" asked Lee.

"Yes, sir. I am afraid, naturally, but that recommends me to the old man. He likes men to be afraid of him. And if you'll excuse the liberty, sir, it's very exciting. It takes me out of myself. I have always wanted to do something important in this line. My place with you is most pleasant, sir, but it's too easy. I want . . . I want to do something bigger."

"If you no longer served me here, I should miss you very much, Jermyn."

"Why couldn't I carry on both together, sir? My place here would afford good protective coloring, so to speak, to a criminal investigator."

"We'll try it," said Lee. "What we've got to do is to establish the connection if any, between this old man and his gang and the anonymous letter-writer. The next time you see him tell him that I have begun to suspect that my papers at the office have been tampered with, and that I have brought all my notes and papers in connection with the anonymous letter-writer to my home. I'll prepare a set of dummies to leave in my desk here, and then we'll see what happens."

"Very good, sir."

SHORTLY AFTER Lee had arrived at the office, Jim Costin came to the door of his room to ask if he might speak to him. "Or perhaps you would prefer that I communicate with you by writing?" he added.

"That's not necessary," said Lee.

Costin carefully closed the door and sat down by Lee's desk with the air of one gentleman calling on another. Lee half expected to be addressed by his first name. Since Lee had hired him Costin had visited the barber and had bought himself a suit of clothes and some badly needed haberdashery. Curiously enough, the new clothes had the effect of making his grinning face look more disreputable than before.

He slapped the new gloves against his leg. "I have made friends with a certain party," he said, "according to your instructions. We have spent a couple of evenings together—perhaps he has mentioned it to you," he put in slyly.

"No," said Lee, "I am hardly on such terms of intimacy with this party."

"So far as I can see thus far," Costin continued, "your suspicions of him have no foundation, Mr. Mappin. He appears to be a simple fellow, and the very soul of honesty. He is absolutely devoted to your interests. The suggestion that it might be to his advantage to act otherwise, was rejected with indignation."

"I am delighted to hear it," said Lee.

"I may say that even under the influence of liquor this party showed no weakness. To put it bluntly I got him a little drunk on Friday night, but he still appeared to be the same honest, simple fellow."

"Servants have to learn to conceal their real feelings," Lee suggested with a grave air. "He may be pulling the wool over your eyes."

"Possibly, possibly. But I flatter myself I'm a pretty fair judge of human nature, Mr. Mappin. However, I will continue to watch him and to draw him out."

"Do so," said Lee. He reached for his wallet. "You will need something for expenses."

Costin's eyes glistened at the sight of the bills. "Filthy stuff," he said airily, "but indispensable."

He swaggered out with all the assurance of an old actor. A comic figure, Lee thought, but, remembering Jermyn's story, nonetheless dangerous.

CHAPTER TWELVE

MONDAY MORNING provided Lee with a series of disappointments. The reports of Stan Oberry's operatives gave him absolutely nothing new to go on. Since Friday night all Rafe Deshon's actions both inside his house and out, had been open and aboveboard; no disguises, no attempt to shake off his trailers. If he is the guilty man of course he would be careful now, Lee thought bitterly. Tyrrell Blair was reported to have spent the weekend at his country place.

Inspector Loasby's report of progress was equally discouraging. After the *Monarch* sailed from New York the captain acting on instructions from the police had made a check-up of the passengers and had searched the ship. Loney was certainly not aboard. The only new clue that turned up was obtained from a salesman in a fashionable clothing store who had sold Loney two new suits a week before.

In the middle of Monday afternoon Judy came to the door of Lee's office to tell him he was wanted on the telephone. Her face was one great round O of astonishment.

"Who is it?" asked Lee.

"He says . . . he says," she stammered, "it's Loney Frasca."

Lee shrugged. "Some comedian, I expect. However, switch him on. You listen in, and take down what he says. Send Fanny out pronto, to another phone. She is to try to have the call traced, while I am keeping the man in talk."

He picked up the instrument. "Hello?"

A male voice answered—a good-humored voice: "Is this Mr. Mappin?"

"Yes."

"I'm Loney Frasca—do you know me?" The voice had the rough intonation of New York's East Side; it was a tenor voice fresh and young in timbre.

"I have heard of such a person," said Lee dryly.

He heard a chuckle. "Just so. And been looking for me, eh?"

"Where are you now?"

Another chuckle. "All in good time, Mister. You and me got to come to an understanding."

"What's your proposition?"

A suspicious note came into the young man's voice. "First-off, Mister, I believe there is somebody tapping this wire. The connection is weakened."

"That's right," said Lee. "My secretary's listening in. I told her to."

The man laughed outright. "Pretty cute, ain't you?"

"I shall be perfectly honest with you," said Lee; "and you can do what you like about it."

"Suits me, Mister."

"First," Lee said, "tell me something by which I may know that you are the real Loney Frasca, and not some fresh guy having a little fun at my expense."

"Fair enough. Listen, Mister, there was a certain person put away on Friday night, and I was present when it happened. Are you interested?"

"I might be," said Lee. "I'd have to know more particulars."

"All right. But I got to protect myself, Boss. I didn't finish this person, see? I didn't know there was going to be a killing. But I was present."

"Who did it?" asked Lee.

"Wa . . . ait a minute," drawled the humorous voice. "It'll cost you money to learn that, Mister Listen! A certain guy hired me, see? I ain't saying what for. Well, I'm known. I never sang to the police about any guy that hired me and paid on the nail. But I didn't like this guy, see? This was a dirty murder. This guy wasn't satisfied with killing; he had to mutilate the body and I didn't like it. I would have called you up before, but I didn't know who the guy was."

"How could you make a deal with him, without knowing who he was?"

"This guy is smart. He got my name from some friends of mine. He wrote to me at my club asking if I was open for a proposition, and if I was, to put an ad in the 'Business Opportunities' column of the paper. So I did, and he wrote again making a date to meet in a hotel in Hoboken. So we met there, and fixed up this deal. But I didn't know who he was."

"Describe him."

The young man laughed. "Not until I see the color of your money, Mister! . . . Well, first-off I was going for a little trip with my girl on Saturday, but I got to thinking it over and decided I would see that he got his first. I did a little detective work and now I know him."

"What's your price?" asked Lee.

"Is it worth two grand, two thousand dollars to you, to learn who did this murder and where the body is hidden?"

Lee considered for a minute. "Yes," he said, "I would pay that for the information if correct. But there's a difficulty in the way."

"What's that?"

"I take it you would expect me to protect you from the police?"

"Sure!"

"If I did that, it would make me an accessory after the fact."

"Well, that's up to you," said the voice indifferently.

"It's a hard choice," said Lee. "Up to now I've always played along with the police. They trust me."

"I only ask for an hour's start of them, Mister. They have my mug down at Headquarters, my finger prints and all. It ought to be a cinch for them to catch up with me. I only ask for an hour."

"All right," said Lee. "Give me the information. As soon as I can prove its correctness, I pledge myself to send or leave the money any place you specify."

A derisive laugh came over the wire. "I believe you're a good guy, Mister. You have the reputation of being on the square. But I wouldn't trust no man on earth as far as that. I got to have the money in my hand before I tell."

"And I've got to know what I'm buying before I pay."

"I'll have the proof to show you. I got the guy's two letters to me."

"Well, what do you want to do?"

"We got to have a meeting."

"Where?"

"Somewhere in the suburbs. It's got to be after dark because every sidewalk-slapper and every auto-bull in the city's got his eye peeled for me right now. Bronx or Westchester; over in Jersey if you want. Not Long Island; it's too easy for them to put a watch on the bridges."

"And you expect me to come to such a spot alone at night?" said Lee. "It's out of the question."

"Well, that's up to you," said the voice with pretended indifference. "You want the information."

"You want the money," retorted Lee.

There was a silence. The young voice weakened first.

"Well, what have you got to propose?"

"Come to my office at nine o'clock tonight," said Lee. "I'll have the money here. At that hour lower Madison Avenue as you may know, is quiet and deserted. There will be nobody in this building except myself, and perhaps the caretaker in the basement. The outer door of the building is locked when the tenants go home. I will leave it unlocked for you. My offices are one flight up in front. You will see a light there."

"Oh yeah?" drawled the voice. "And walk right into a trap!"

"I give you my word that I will not notify the police until one hour after you have left me."

"And how about the girl who's listening in? How about her, eh?"

"She would not be working for me unless she could keep her mouth shut. I will answer for her, too, just the same as for myself."

"It's not good enough, Mister!"

At this moment Fanny came into Lee's office holding up a piece of paper on which she had written: "It's a city dial call. Cannot be traced." Lee nodded.

"I'm sorry," he said into the phone. "We can't do business unless you are willing to trust me. It wouldn't matter how lonely or out-of-the-way the spot that you might choose, if I wanted to it would be just as easy for me to set a trap for you there as it would be here."

"Well, that's true, too . . . Will you swear that no word of this shall reach the police until ten o'clock tonight?"

"I swear it!"

"Okay, I'll take a chance on it." A hard edge came into the voice. "You understand that if you play me false, I'll have time to get you, however quick they are!"

"I understand that."

"Okay, I'll see you nine o'clock tonight."

The connection was broken.

Lee sat back in his chair and took a pinch of snuff. This was pretty exciting. Judy came running into his room wringing her hands.

"Pop, you sha'n't do this! You sha'n't do it!" she cried excitedly. "It's too dangerous!"

"Calm yourself, my girl," said Lee. "I shall be armed. I shall deal fairly with the young man and no danger will threaten me."

"I can't bear it!" wailed Judy.

"I'll call you up as soon as he leaves me. Just to relieve your mind."

Fanny added her protests. "Pop, you have no proof that it was Loney Frasca that you talked to. It may have been the murderer himself . . ."

"I have a hunch that I would recognize his voice," said Lee. "Otherwise he would have called me before. A man of his peculiar humor would have had more fun in taunting me over the phone."

"Perhaps he was getting another to speak for him."

"Why should he want to come see me?"

"To kill you! He's afraid of you!"

"Unfortunately I have not come close enough to the murderer to give him the slightest uneasiness as yet."

"He may think you have."

"He seems to know everything I do."

"Well, suppose it *was* Loney Frasca," said Fanny. "How utterly foolhardy to receive such a man alone! If he was hired for one murder, he could be hired for another. Murder's his business!"

"I shall be armed," said Lee. "And on my guard."

"At least have somebody here with you. I don't mean the police, but just a friend."

"Meaning a certain redheaded fellow of our acquaintance," suggested Lee, slyly.

Fanny couldn't see any humor in the situation. "You couldn't have anybody better than Tom," she said stormily.

"You are right," cried Lee. "But I can't have him tonight. This place will be watched before the meeting takes place. It may be under surveillance now."

The girls glanced nervously towards the windows.

"If I was to bring anybody else into the situation, my friend Loney would not come."

"But Pop . . ."

"It is useless, my dears. Don't force me to speak with the voice of authority. Come on, let's get a little work done before closing time."

Fanny and Judy went back to their filing with heavy faces. Lee departed for the bank to supply himself with the cash he required.

At five-thirty he sent the girls home.

An hour later Fanny called him up. "Pop," she said bluntly, "will you have dinner with Tom and me at the Gamecock?"

"I'd be delighted," said Lee, "on one condition."

"What's that?"

"That you do not look like a mourner at my funeral. It would spoil my appetite."

"All right. I promise."

They dined in one of the little alcoves along the wall of the restaurant. Fanny was game. At least she gave a good imitation of her usual smiling self. As for Tom, he was always smiling when in Fanny's company. Lee liked to listen to these two abusing each other while quite other feelings shone in their eyes.

"Darn glad you could join us, Pop," said Tom. "I'm outmatched here. I need male support."

"As big as you are!" said Fanny scornfully.

"It's not a question of size, but of explosive power."

"You really do annoy me," said Fanny, "when you talk as if I were a small child having a tantrum."

"You see," said Tom, turning to Lee, "whatever I say is wrong. See what you can do with her, Pop."

"Pop's got more sense than you," said Fanny; "he never tries to 'handle' a woman; he treats her like a human being."

"Go ahead, Pop," said Tom; "treat her like a human being and see what happens. Maybe I'll learn something."

"Impossible," said Fanny. "You're too conceited."

"That's the fault of the girls," said Tom. "Once I was a modest boy. The girls have turned my head."

Fanny turned a scornful shoulder to him. "For goodness sakes, Pop, let's have a little sensible conversation."

Throughout the meal, no reference was made to what was coming later. They lingered over their coffee. Lee was grateful to the young pair for providing him with a distraction in that difficult hour.

When they got up to leave, Tom said hurriedly: "Lee, I could be waiting in that hotel on the corner of 38th street for the next hour or so. It could do no harm."

"It couldn't do any good, either," returned Lee calmly.

"It would ease Fanny's mind a lot, not to speak of my own. She won't show it, but she's near crazy with anxiety. Look, Lee, if I got a table by the window in the café, I could command a view of your windows down the street. You will have the shades pulled down. If you wanted me, you could snap up one of the shades, and I'd be there in three shakes. Look, I'll approach the hotel from the East, so that if a watch is being kept in Madison Avenue, nobody will see me."

Lee was a little touched by the young man's concern. "All right,"
he said good-naturedly. "But don't come to my aid unless you're
sent for."

They parted at the door of the restaurant. Since there was still
plenty of time, Lee walked down Madison Avenue smoking a cigar.
Well aware that he would be watched, he was determined to show
a confident front. Below 42nd street the avenue was quiet; a few
taxis sped noiselessly up and down; an occasional pedestrian
strolled on the sidewalk. The converted dwelling where Lee had
his offices, showed a dark front to the street. Mounting the steps,
he let himself in with his key, and caught the latch of the door so
that his visitor could follow him.

There was a single bulb burning in the lower hall, and another
on the first landing. Lee climbed the long stairway with its heavily
carved balustrade. The silence in the old house was oppressive;
Lee felt more comfortable when he got into his own front office
with the lights turned on full. He caught the latch on his office
door and drew down the front shades. He fetched his pistol from a
drawer of his desk and laid it on Fanny's desk. He paced the wide
room, analyzing his own feelings humorously. He was not enjoying the situation; he reveled in mental excitement, but the physical kind was not his dish. The accelerated beating of his heart annoyed him, and the moisture that crept out on his palms. He was
afraid, not a doubt of it, but that, he told himself, was because he
had to wait; in the actual presence of danger he would be too busy
to feel fear.

Somewhere outside he heard a clock striking nine. He sat down
in the chair at Fanny's desk, facing the door. The automatic was
close to his hand. He was listening for the sound of the downstairs
door. But whoever came in there opened and closed it noiselessly.
The first sound he heard was on the landing outside his office door.
It was just a little sound; the soft scuff of a foot on the floor. His
heart slowly rose in his throat; he swallowed hard, and touched
the gun beside him for reassurance.

He heard more slight sounds outside the door; certainly somebody was moving there. He waited for a knock, but moments passed

and it did not come. The suspense was unbearable. He would not open the door because that would have been to expose himself. Finally there was a modest knock on the glass.

"Come in," said Lee. He picked up the gun.

The door did not open. Perfect silence outside. "Come in!" Lee repeated sharply. Only silence. Unable, finally, to bear it any longer, he approached the door from one side to keep out of range of a possible shot.

Holding the gun ready in his right hand, he turned the door handle with his left. There was a pressure against the door on the outside. It swung in swiftly and the body of a man pitched to the floor. Lee saw the handle of a knife protruding between the shoulder blades.

Lee's instant thought was, *this* one had not knocked. Gun in hand, he ran out on the landing. The light had been switched off, but enough light streamed out of his office for him to see by. There was nobody visible. He ran to the head of the stairs. The light was still burning below; the hall was empty. The assassin had had time to get out. Lee ran back into his front office, snapped up one of the shades and leaned out the window. The pavement below was empty; it was only fifty feet to the corner; the man had disappeared.

If he had left the building! Lee tried the other doors on the landing. The middle door was unlocked; there was nobody in that room. The door to the rear suite was locked. Lee ran down the stairs and on down to the basement. Mrs. Costin heard him, and showed a frightened face at the door of her kitchen.

"Is Jim home?" demanded Lee.

"No sir, no sir," she stammered. "He went out right after supper."

Lee believed this woman to be honest. "There's been an accident upstairs," he said. "You'd better not come. I'll send for the police."

The front door of the house banged open, and when Lee got to the head of the basement stairs he came face to face with Tom Cottar.

"Thank God!" gasped Tom.

"Bad work here," said Lee. "Come upstairs."

The body lay where it had fallen. It was the trim figure of a young man a little under the average height. His head was turned to one side, and Lee distinguished the smooth oval face that he had studied in the photographs at Police Headquarters. A wet crimson stain had spread around the knife handle, but the blood was not welling out. His heart had ceased to beat.

"Loney Frasca?" asked Tom.

Lee nodded. "Must have been followed here. Killed by the man who hired him . . . You were watching my windows. A minute or so before I snapped up the blind, did you see anybody run out of this house?"

Tom said, "I couldn't have seen it, Pop. Too dark."

"Well," said Lee, "get Loasby on the wire. Tell him there's been a murder here. Tell him to bring the Medical Examiner and so on, but not to make any noise about it until we find out where we stand."

While Tom was telephoning, Lee made a closer examination of the body. There was something very saddening in the sight of the wrecked youth. He appeared no more than nineteen or twenty, a comely sophomore on the threshold of manhood—but this boy had already served a dark apprenticeship to life. He was wearing one of the new suits he had bought the week before for a honeymoon in Bermuda. No more love and laughter for him. In his pockets Lee found a handkerchief, cigarettes, matches, a neat and effective "silencer" and a handful of change—no gun. He had undoubtedly carried a wallet, but it had been taken. There was no scrap of paper on him, nor anything else for Lee to work on; the murderer's secret was safe.

Lee examined the walls and the floor of the landing under a magnifying glass. There was sufficient dust on the floor to reveal that Loney had been struck as he rounded the top of the stairs. The murderer had been waiting hidden at the corner. He had been marvelously deft and silent. Must have flung one arm around the boy's head while he stabbed him with the other. Had held the body from dropping to the floor; had carried it to the door of Lee's office and propped it there.

Several police cars arrived in the street below, without, Lee thankfully noted, any braying of sirens. He felt as if he could not stand the uproar of a public sensation just then. Loasby entered with his various assistants and experts; photographers, fingerprint men, Medical Examiner and so on, and the usual investigation was set on foot.

CHAPTER THIRTEEN

THE STORY OF LONEY FRASCA'S MURDER as related in the press next day was somewhat incomplete. It was represented as an accident that Loney happened to be killed in the building where Lee Mappin's offices were. No connection was established between the dead man and the celebrated criminologist and author. It was explained that as Mr. Mappin was working late in his office, the outer door of the building had been left unlocked, and Frasca, supposedly, being pursued by one of his underworld enemies, had sought safety there. Just another gangster murder! The public was not much interested. The feeling was, that the more such fellows got killed, the better it was for decent people. The case of the radio announcer who had planned to murder his wife still occupied more space on the front pages than this new murder.

On Tuesday morning the inevitable anonymous letter came in the mail. The sight of the envelope affected Lee with a kind of sickness of disgust. The cold-blooded writer was becoming a nightmare figure. He wrote:

> You have forced me to commit another murder and to write another letter. This is a bore. Not that I feel the slightest remorse on account of liquidating Loney Frasca; the kid was a public enemy and the world is better off without him. For him to rat on me after he had taken my money was a dirty trick and I

felt I was performing an act of justice in rubbing him out, and in getting back at least part of my money. The business is finished now, and I don't want to be troubled with it further. My revenge is complete; I have other fish to fry. The second murder was a lot more exciting than the first, because there was real danger in it. If anything had gone wrong, I was prepared to finish you, too. Be careful you don't give me too great a taste for this sport, or I'll have to go after you just for the fun of it. I admit it was a mistake to hire a man like Loney to help me, but I didn't see how I could dispose of the body without him. Anyhow, Loney's gone now, and there's nothing left in the world to connect me with the murder, or to lead you to the spot where the body is hidden. So you had better save yourself—and me, trouble by dropping the case. If you ever begin really to annoy me, you won't last twenty-four hours.

Lee smiled dryly at the writer's notion of "justice." He showed the letter to Inspector Loasby and locked it up with the others. Loasby could no longer pretend that it was all a hoax. He was working faithfully with Lee to solve the mystery, but they found themselves faced with an almost blank wall. There were no fingerprints on the handle of the knife. The knife itself was a cheap utensil which there was no possibility of tracing. The murderer had neither dropped anything, nor made any mistake, nor left the slightest clue to his identity.

How had he got into the building? When Lee went out to dinner the outer door was already locked. Mrs. Costin testified that she had locked it at six o'clock. She always locked it at that hour unless one of the tenants advised her that late customers were expected. When Lee returned a couple of hours later the door was still locked. True, for the next twenty minutes or so it stood unlocked, but Lee could not believe that Loney would venture into the house without having kept a watch on it beforehand.

The murderer then, must have got in before six o'clock unless he had a key. Or unless Jim Costin or Mrs. Costin had let him in. Once inside the building, there was no lack of hiding places. In addition to the middle room on the second floor, there were other unoccupied suites above. The building though small, was a busy one. There was an agency for photographers' models on the ground floor, and a school for accountants on the third. Consequently up to six o'clock numbers of people were always passing in and out; people of every class and condition.

Was Jim Costin himself the murderer? Lee doubted it. But he might have guilty knowledge of the crime. Costin had left the house about 7:30 and had proceeded to Hymie's on Third Avenue. The tavern was crowded, and the man who trailed him there, could not swear that Costin had remained in the place during the next hour and a half continuously. When the body was discovered, Costin's boy was sent in search of his father and found him at Hymie's. Costin when he arrived, had expressed the utmost astonishment and horror at what had happened. Lee had not been much impressed by it, knowing what a good actor he was. Today Costin hung around Lee's offices on the pretext of helping the police. To get him out of the way, Lee invented an errand to take him over to Brooklyn.

How had the murderer learned of the intended meeting between Lee and Loney Frasca? In talking to Loney on the phone, Lee had been careful to keep his voice down. It could not have carried beyond his own small room. Besides himself, only the two girls and Tom Cottar knew about the conversation, and Lee was very sure they had not told. Neither could be believe that Loney, knowing it was as much as his life was worth, had told anybody. Yet the murderer had learned of it in time to make his plans. Once again Lee was faced with that suggestion of the uncanny which shakes the strongest breast.

The only rational explanation that occurred to him was that his telephone wires had been tapped. He phoned to an official of the telephone company who was a friend, and asked him to start an investigation without making any noise about it. Soon afterwards a discreet expert arrived at Lee's office and was able almost immediately to point out the spot where a tap had been made. There were no conduits in this ancient building; all wires were exposed. They found that the extra wires were led out through a hole in the partition at the back of Lee's little room.

Lee and the telephone man hastened into the vacant office. The wires passed around the base board, and disappeared under a desk. The drawers of the desk were locked.

"Whose desk is this?" asked the telephone man.

"It belongs to the landlord," said Lee. "Left here by the last tenant in payment of rent."

"Better send for the janitor to open it."

Lee was thankful that Costin was out of the way. "No," said he. "If there's anything funny about this desk, the janitor may be implicated."

"Will you take the responsibility of breaking into it?"

"Sure! Co ahead."

A chisel did the trick. They found the desk empty until they pulled out the oversize bottom drawer on the righthand side. In this drawer lay a beautiful little electrical machine, the like of which Lee had never seen. There was an oaken box which evidently contained a motor. To the top of the box was affixed an arrangement of two metal spools with a fine steel wire passing from one to the other. Midway on the wire was a pair of tiny electro-magnets. The telephone wires entered the bottom of the drawer and were connected to posts on the box, with sufficient slack in the wire so that the connection was not broken when the drawer was pulled out.

The telephone expert studied this gadget with keen professional interest. "Wait a minute," he said. "I have seen one of these before somewhere." After a little further study, he said: "Ask somebody in your office to take the telephone off the hook."

When this was done, the little machine in the drawer began silently to move. The fine wire unrolled from one spool and passing between the electromagnets, rolled up on the other.

"Good God, how ingenious!" exclaimed Lee.

"Now I know what it is," said the telephone man. "The company has one in its museum. It is called a telegraphone, and it records telephone conversations. A Dane, Vladimir Poulson, invented it forty years ago. In this country it was made the excuse for a stock-selling scheme which went bust; consequently there is a debt of millions attached to the machine and nothing could ever be done with it. Go into your office and say something over your telephone, then hang up and come back."

When Lee returned, the telephone expert reversed the wire, then ran it forward again. There was a pair of ear phones attached to the machine; Lee placed them in his ears and heard his own voice, low, clear, and without mechanical interference.

"Marvelous!" he said.

They then ran the wire back to the beginning, and listened. All the conversations which had taken place over the telephone in Lee's office that morning, were clearly recorded. The record for the previous day had been removed.

"Not more than three or four of these machines were ever imported," said the expert. "They were used as demonstrators to sell stock in the company. Presumably they were sold at auction when it failed. My company got one for their museum. I can't say what became of the others."

"He would have to buy additional wire," said Lee, "and have those special spools made. Perhaps we can trace him that way."

The expert shook his head. "Not unless he wanted to preserve the records. By reversing the current you de-magnetize the wire and wipe it clean. It can be used over and over. What do you want me to do with this, sir?"

"Nothing," said Lee. "Leave everything as is. You will oblige me very much by saying nothing about it."

"You can depend on me, Mr. Mappin."

After the man had gone, Lee explained the working of the machine to Inspector Loasby, and it was arranged to have a watch kept on it. Among other articles left by the last tenant, was a screen used to mask the washbasin in a corner of the room. Night and day thereafter, there was always a headquarters man sitting in a chair behind the screen.

Through police channels an investigation was started of the affairs of the defunct American Telegraphone Company. As this concern had been out of business for more than thirty years, Lee had not much hope of tracing the machines they had sold. At any rate the discovery of the telegraphone removed the superhuman element from the affair. It was now clear how the murderer had been able to inform himself so well of all Lee's moves.

During the morning Tyrrell Blair and Rafe Deshon came up to Lee's office. On the part of the great publisher this was an unusual condescension; Blair was accustomed to make men come to see him. Rafe explained the visit by saying:

"By God! it's something to have a murder committed just outside the door of a friend's office! We came around to have a look at the spot."

Was it simple curiosity, Lee wondered, or curiosity of a more morbid sort? Lying on his desk at that moment were reports of the movements of these two on the previous evening. Rafe Deshon was said to have been working at his office until ten o'clock. Lee did not feel that he could place much reliance on this statement, because the office building was a very large one with many doors. In addition to the main entrances there was another for the delivery of goods, and it would have excited no remark for a tenant to have used this door. Tyrrell Blair was reported to have been in his own home between the hours of six and nine-thirty.

"Where did the fellow get it?" asked Blair.

"They caught him there at the head of the stairs."

"What on earth brought him into this building?"

"No one will ever know that," said Lee blandly. "I suppose it was just a blind impulse to escape."

"Come off, Lee!" said Rafe teasingly. "You don't have to be so prudent with us. We know you deal with all kinds of queer customers."

Lee passed it off with a smile.

"I've read that those fellows always duck through the nearest doorway when pursued," said Blair. "They're seeking a way to the roof and over the roofs."

"Were you in your office at the time?" asked Rafe.

"Yes."

"Bet you were scared!"

"I had no time to be scared."

"Could you hear anything?"

"No noise at all. Just the sound of a soft blow, a fall, and rapid feet on the stairs."

"Did you see the killer?"

"Not a glimpse. By the time I got to the poor fellow the killer was out of the house, and when I ran back to my office and looked out of the window, the street was empty. He had got around the corner."

The two men stared down at the spot at the head of the stairs as if they could see a body lying there still.

"There's no blood," said Rafe. "Has it been washed up?"

"He was struck clean through the heart," said Lee. "What little blood flowed was soaked up by his clothes."

"It's a nice thing when these gangsters come right up here on Murray Hill to pull off their killings" said Blair indignantly. "Why can't the police confine them to their own districts? That's what I want to know!"

As they were leaving, Rafe said: "Anyhow, it will make a good story to put in your next book, Lee."

Lee shrugged. "I've got better stories than this." Privately he was thinking: It will be the best story I ever wrote in my life—if I am able to finish it!

With people coming and going and the telephone ringing almost continuously, it was impossible for Lee to concentrate at his office on such a day. The girls too, were in a bad state of nerves, and no wonder. Therefore, as soon as the police had concluded their investigations, Lee gave Fanny and Judy a holiday, and locking up the office, went home.

After lunch he paced the long living-room with his hands behind his back, looking at his problem from every angle. He considered Rafe's disguises, his disappearance on Friday night; his unexplained gangster friend. This fellow did not answer to the description of Loney Frasca. There was also the bald paralytic in the Bronx, who, now that disease had laid him by the heels, had become a promoter of crime. That morning Jermyn, taking suitable precautions, had made a secret visit to Headquarters but had been unable to pick out the Bronx Fagin from among the photographs in the police files.

Lee went over the letter he had received that morning. It was not necessary to have it before him because he knew it by heart. The writer boasted that there was now nothing in the world to connect him with the first murder or to lead Lee to the spot where the body was hidden. Lee doubted if this was true. Never in his experience had he been faced with a completely blank wall. There was always a loophole, and the loophole in this one was the girl who had been cheated of her honeymoon in Bermuda. True, the police had been looking for her several days without success, but the police were not infallible. She existed somewhere, and she must know something about the first murder. Lee made up his mind to try looking for her on his own.

CHAPTER FOURTEEN

DURING THE COURSE OF THE DAY the body of Loney Frasca was released to his relatives. Lee read in the afternoon paper that the Stanton Street Pleasure Club to which the dead man had belonged, was going to give him a fine funeral. The bishop of the diocese, mercifully assuming that Loney might have repented in the brief instant between the striking of the knife, and the passing of his soul, had granted him Christian burial. The body would be "lying in state" at the Johnson Funeral Church on Delancey Street on the following morning, and the services would take place at eleven o'clock.

Lee dressed himself plainly and inconspicuously, and was on hand at the undertaking establishment at nine. Already a stream of people was passing in and out. Lee was astonished at the size of the place, and its luxurious appointments. However poor they might be, the East Siders somehow contrived to provide a magnificent exit for their dead. Rather late, Lee thought, to give a man his first taste of luxury then.

The handsome bronze casket rested in a side parlor, almost hidden under masses of exquisite flowers. A line of people moved slowly up to it and out by another door. They appeared to be mere curiosity seekers, drawn by the notice in the newspapers. It was a fine show and it cost nothing. One by one the faces bent over the coffin; worn faces and smug, smooth and wrinkled, clean and dirty, crafty and simple, the eyes widening a little in awful curiosity. Lee saw no tears falling. Around the room stood several of Loney's clubmates, dark and watchful young men, proud of themselves and of the occasion, each wearing a white badge with Committee printed on it.

When it came Lee's turn to look, he was saddened by what he saw. The young face resting against its white satin cushion, smooth and olive-skinned, was purely beautiful. It bore an expression of proud dignity that none of the living faces could match. The dead man appeared to scorn the living. Lee could have wept—not for Loney Frasca, but for the cruel chaos of life in which youth wasted itself and was so soon destroyed.

The room in which the casket rested adjoined the main chapel of the establishment with an arched opening between. After making a turn in the first room, Lee went around and took a rear seat in the chapel. Here, while he was himself partly hidden by curtains hanging in the archway, he could look at every face in the adjoining room as it bent over the body. A decent, ordinary-looking little man, middle-aged, and wearing an ill-fitting suit, nobody looked twice at Lee. Other persons were sitting in the chapel. The endless procession wound into the adjoining room, came to the flowery casket and wound out again. Women were in the great majority, and of these, the most were poorly-dressed, older women, mothers come to look at another woman's son. Many brought small children and held them up to see.

After hundreds had passed in and out, Lee saw what he was looking for, one grief-stricken face. No tears; this grief was too deep for tears. It was a pretty young woman whose smart and colorful attire was out of keeping with her tragic expression. A strong girl, taller than the average of her class and wonderfully graceful. Like Loney, she was of Italian extraction with a creamy skin, immense brown eyes, and curled raven hair. At this moment she was more than pretty; the intensity of her feeling gave her face the immemorial beauty of a Greek mask. It touched Lee to see how, as she passed beyond the casket, her face was turned back to allow her eyes to dwell for the longest possible moment on the face of the dead youth. She was entirely oblivious to everything else in the room.

Lee got up, and leaving the chapel by another door, caught up with the girl in the outer hall of the establishment. He followed her out into the street. In order to keep the line moving, a policeman directed those leaving the building to the east while the new comers approached from the west. The girl circled around the crowd that partly filled the middle of the street and attached herself to the end of the line approaching the building from the other side. Lee was close behind her. Her absorbed glance passed over him unseeingly. They entered the building again and passed into the room with the casket. The girl's rapt eyes clung to the dead man's face so long that the people behind Lee began to murmur complainingly. Recalled to her surroundings with a start, she hastily made her way into the chapel and sat down. Lee seated himself across the aisle from her. She prayed.

The chapel was filling now. Presently the priest in cassock and surplice came to the door and paused to say a prayer. He proceeded to the altar, followed by a boy with a vessel of holy water. More prayers in Latin and English were recited. The casket was then wheeled in, and there were more prayers. Sounds of weeping were heard from the front row, where Loney's black-clad sisters and sisters-in-law were sitting. The girl across the aisle from Lee cast a look of scorn in that direction. Her eyes were dry, but with what a passion of longing they followed the flower-covered casket when it was wheeled out!

Lee had no trouble in following her through the streets. Lost in her thoughts, it never occurred to her to look over her shoulder. The only thing that irked Lee was that she forced him to walk faster than was consistent with his years and plumpness. He admired her trim figure, admirably turned-out from daintily shod feet to smart little hat. Her dress was a simple, springlike affair of blue and white. The humble east-side girl, like most of her sisters, would have been well dressed in any company. It was not the most suitable outfit for a funeral, but perhaps she had no other.

She led Lee to East Broadway, a wide street that was fashionable in the early days of the Republic. Some of the steep-roofed old dwellings of that time remain, now sadly reduced in condition.

The girl went up the steps of such a house and disappeared through the door. Lee was about fifty yards behind her. The door was not latched, and he pushed it open. The house was one of those that are rented out room by room to all comers. There was a sharp contrast between the gaily-dressed girl and her dingy domicile. She had already disappeared up the first flight; he heard her above. Listening with a hand on the rail of the stairs, he heard a door close; third floor front hall room. He went up.

She opened the door promptly; the light was behind her, but he sensed surprise in her attitude. "What do you want?" she asked. Her voice was hard with pain.

"Can I talk to you for a moment?" he asked.

Her glance was devastating in its indifference. "Nobody is stopping you."

"May I come in?"

"No. Let me hear what it's about first."

"It's about Loney Frasca."

She made no start, but Lee could feel caution drawing over her. "I don't know him," she said.

"You have just come from his funeral."

"You're a liar."

She tried to close the door but Lee had his foot in it. "I am your friend," he said.

"The hell with you," she said, kicking at his foot. "I know your kind. You'd better get out of here." She ground her heel into the top of Lee's foot, and he withdrew it with a yelp of pain. The door closed and the key was turned. The girl continued to abuse him through the door.

When Lee could make himself heard, he said: "I know that you and Loney were going to Bermuda last week."

She fell silent. She was frightened and being a courageous person, she unlocked the door and threw it open to face him out. "I think you're crazy," she said. "Who are you anyhow, and what do you want with me?"

"I'm looking for the man who killed Loney and I want your help."

She scowled. "I don't get you, Mister. Police?"

"No. Private investigator. Name of Mappin."

Her eyes widened. "Why . . . why it was outside your office . . ."

"That Loney was killed. Exactly. He was on his way to see me."

"What about?"

"He came to sell me some information that I wanted."

"Don't sound like Loney," she said with a bitterly curling lip. "I think you're lying. How do I know it wasn't you croaked him?"

"Do I look like it?" said Lee. "I'm hardly big enough."

She studied him from under frowning brows.

"If you don't want to let me in your room," suggested Lee, "let's go out and sit in a restaurant where we can talk."

She shook her head somberly. "I don't want to show myself in no restaurant." She opened the door wider. "You can come in. I ain't afraid of you."

Lee entered, and she closed the door. The small room, though cluttered, was clean and tidy. The ceiling sloped down in front, enframing a dormer window. There was a complete housekeeping outfit; gas ring just inside the door, with shelves above for utensils and dishes, bureau, oilcloth-covered table by the window and two chairs. On the other side a narrow bed, and behind the door, more shelves and clothes hanging behind a curtain. Lee sat down. The girl looked at him with a bitter indifference that suggested nothing could touch her now.

"What's your name?" Lee asked.

She shrugged. "What does it matter? Call me Marta."

"Don't you want to see Loney's murderer punished?" asked Lee.

"If I knew you was on the level," she muttered.

"You'll have to make up your mind about that."

She stood, studying him with a scowl.

"The man who killed Loney wrote to me boasting of what he had done," Lee said. "It wasn't signed."

"What did he have against Loney?" she demanded. "Loney wasn't mixed up with no mob. He was Loney; he worked by himself!"

"Loney talked with me on the telephone Monday afternoon. He said this man hired him to help do a job. That was on last Friday night. Do you know anything about that?"

"No. Loney never talked. Not even to me."

"Loney said he didn't know what he was wanted for. Which may or may not have been true. I didn't expect him to tell me everything. Well, as it turned out, there was a murder in it."

"It wasn't in the papers," she put in quickly.

"The body has not been discovered. That's my job. Loney said it was a dirty murder. It made him sore. He wanted to see the man get his before he left town. That's why he wouldn't sail with you on Saturday. He didn't know who the man was, and he had to take the time to find out. He did find out, and I agreed to pay two thousand dollars for the information. Somehow or other the man learned that Loney was coming to my office. He laid for Loney, and struck him down before he could speak."

Marta listened to this without giving any sign. "Did you see the man?" she asked.

"No. He got away."

Standing like a statue, she considered what she had been told.

Lee looked around the little room. "I take it this was where Loney was hidden while we were looking for him."

"Sure," she said defiantly. "I kept him here since Wednesday a week ago. Anything to say against it?"

Lee shook his head. "I guess you're glad now that you had him," he said softly.

The simple words reached her. She suddenly dropped on the bed and covered her face. "No! . . . Yes! . . . How do I know?" she whispered. "To have him such a little time and lose him!" Tears crept under her hands and dropped to the floor.

Lee let her alone. She bowed her head; no sound of distress came from her. She presently took down her hands. Her face was composed, but big tears continued to roll down her velvety cheeks, one after another. One of the rare women who cry beautifully, Lee noted. After awhile she said:

"How could I help you?"

"You must know something about the job he was engaged for."

She shook her head. "All I knew was, he had a job because he said he was going to be in the money. He got an advance payment. Last Wednesday he bought a couple of new suits, and the tickets for the ship and a watch for me." She exhibited the watch on her wrist. "He gave me money besides, for me to buy clothes for the trip These are some of them I got on. After Wednesday he never went out in the daytime. Said it was better to let on that he had already left town."

"Wouldn't he be recognized just the same if he went out at night?"

Marta smiled distantly. "He wore my clothes. At night he could get away with it. He passed for a good-looking girl. I fixed him up. Wednesday and Thursday he was out near all night."

"Have you no idea where he was?"

She shook her head. "He didn't tell me. I never asked Loney questions. I knew better."

"I find it hard to believe that," said Lee. "You were crazy about him. Didn't it make you jealous not knowing what he was doing?"

She smiled again. "No. I knew there wasn't no woman in it. He was mine."

"What about Friday? Did he appear to be excited?"

The smile was scornful now. "Loney never got excited. Friday he was talking about the trip. Neither him nor me had been on a ship. He went out at nine o'clock and come home about three in the morning. He was just the same as usual."

"Did he wear women's dress that night?"

"Sure. But not my clothes. He brought home a green dress, a white evening coat with white fur on it, and a green scarf to go over his head. He said he got the stuff from a costumer's. Maybe he was lying."

"He was used for a decoy, then."

Marta's eyes blazed up in a startling fashion; she clenched her hands. "Don't you go to say anything against Loney, Mister! If he was a decoy, that's his business!"

"Sure!" said Lee. "I am just trying to dope out what happened. ... Afterwards, on Saturday did you notice anything different about him? Was he sore or anything?"

"If he was sore he didn't let me see it. All he said was that the business wasn't finished and we couldn't go on the ship. I felt awful bad and he promised to take me on the next trip. I'll never go now."

"Let's go back a little," said Lee. "How long had you and Loney been keeping company?"

"Since last Fall. We always kept it a secret. Loney said it would get me into trouble some day if it was known that I was his girl, and I said I didn't care if it did, and then he said they might reach to him through me, and I said the police could kill me before I'd tell them anything."

"I believe you," murmured Lee.

"I left home along of Loney," she continued simply. "And took this room where he could come without anybody seeing him. I could afford a better room. Until last week I had a good job in a dress shop on Clinton Street. In this house the door is always open and there's no landlady to watch the halls. Loney used to come through a house in the next street behind this, and climb the back fence."

"Didn't you ever go out together?"

"Sure, we did. But not around here where we would be seen by them who knew us. I would meet Loney somewhere outside this neighborhood and we'd drive uptown or out in the country or any-where we wanted."

"He owned a car then," said Lee eagerly.

"He never owned a car," she said scornfully. "That would be as good as handing your address to the police. He borrowed a car when he wanted it."

"How could he be sure of finding a car at the time he wanted it?"

"It was always the same car; a blue Dodge sedan that was parked every night in Frankfort Street, near Gold. Every night it stood there just as regular, from eight o'clock until four in the morning. Loney watched it and found out it belonged to a linotyper who worked on a morning newspaper. It was an old car, faded-looking, but the fellow kept it up good. Ran like a breeze."

"Did Loney know the owner's name?"

"Mike Slattery. It was on the license card."

"Where does he work?"

"I don't know. Loney found it out, but he never told me."

"Didn't Slattery lock his car?"

"Locked the engine. Loney made up to a mechanic in the Dodge repair shop, and got a key for it. After that he could borrow it whenever he wanted. Always left it where he found it, and the fellow never suffered by it. Many's the gallon of gas Loney put in. Wasn't nothing cheap about Loney."

"Maybe this car was used on Friday night."

"Sure, but what good will that do you? It was taken back. And cars can't speak."

"Just the same, I'll look into it," said Lee.

It was now Marta's turn to ask questions. "Why did you come to me to-day, Mister?"

"You were the only link I had with Loney," said Lee.

"You followed me to the funeral parlor this morning?"

"I didn't follow you there. I found you there."

"What do you mean, found me?"

"I knew Loney had a girl, but I didn't know who she was. I went to the funeral parlor and I watched the faces until I saw the one that truly grieved for Loney. Then I followed you here."

She glanced at him in astonishment.

"I wish I knew if you was lying," she murmured.

"Do you still think I'm lying?"

"There was somebody knew I was Loney's girl before this morning."

"What makes you say that?"

She continued to study him with somber eyes. "I think you're a good guy," she said slowly. "Anyhow what difference does it make? I don't care what happens to me. . . . I got a letter yesterday morning."

Lee leaped from his chair. "A letter! Good God, girl! What kind of letter? Who from?"

She smiled darkly. "You're surprised at that. I guess you're on the level."

She went to the shelves by the door, and lifting the cover of a dish, took out a letter. When she brought it to him, Lee's heart suddenly failed at the sight of the cheap, plain envelope, the type-written address. Snatching it from her, he tore out the contents and read:

> Marta Corioli:
> I killed your boy because he was about to sell me out. I took his wallet and in it I found a letter from you written from the shop where you worked. I called up the shop and they told me you were no longer working there. They gave me your address. Nobody in the world but me knows that you were Loney's girl, and if you keep your mouth shut you'll be all right. But if you ever open your mouth to a living soul about Loney, you will follow him, see? Remember, I know who you are and I'm watching you. You can't escape me.
>
> X.

"God!" cried Lee. "Why didn't you show me this in the beginning?"

"I thought maybe it was you who wrote it," she said dryly. "I thought you was feeling your way along to see how much I knew, and if I showed you I didn't know nothing, you would leave me alone."

"Look out of the window," said Lee. "Can you see anybody watching the house? Is there a car waiting in the street with men in it?"

She obeyed, without betraying any excitement. "I can't see anybody. He wouldn't be showing himself. There's a car parked across the street, but I can't see if there's anybody in it. The engine isn't running."

"You take it coolly," said Lee. "If either you or me go out we are likely to be received with a burst of bullets and if we don't go out they'll come in after us . . . Is there a telephone in the house?"

She shook her head.

"Have you got a friend in the house who would go out and tele-phone for you?"

"There's the girl in the next room. She's my friend. She's not what you'd call a good girl, but she's on the level with me."

"See if she's there."

"She's always there mornings," said Marta. "She's sleeping." Marta went out and knocked at a door outside. There was a brief whispered colloquy. Marta returned, saying: "She'll go as soon as she gets her clothes on."

They waited. Lee, unable to sit still, paced the narrow room. "I would never have come here if I had known I was leading you into such danger!"

Marta sat on the bed with her hands in her lap. "You don't need to trouble about me," she said evenly.

"I'm not even armed," said Lee. "By God! I'll never go out again without a gun."

"Loney had a gun," she said, looking down at her hands, "and it didn't do him no good."

In due course, a feminine voice spoke outside the door: "Marta." Marta opened the door, and her friend entered. She was no longer young; she had dressed in a hurry and she looked pretty ghastly without her war paint. Lee made up his mind on the spot to do something for this woman if he was spared.

"Look," he said to her, "Marta and I are in a jam. Will you go out to the nearest telephone booth and call up Inspector Loasby at Police Headquarters. Tell him that Lee Mappin is in danger at this number East Broadway, and that he requires police protection quickly."

She hastened away.

Marta started for the window to watch her come out below, but Lee put out his hand. "Better not. If somebody sees you looking he might connect her with you."

They waited. There seemed to be nothing to say now.

In ten minutes or so the woman returned. She reported that she had spoken to the Inspector and that he had said he would come himself immediately.

Lee gave the woman a five-dollar bill and wrote down his address for her. "You had better commit that to memory and destroy the paper," he said. "Come and see me at my office after this business blows over. Go back to your own room now. It won't do you any good in this neighborhood to be seen associating with the police."

To Marta he said: "Better pack your clothes. You won't be coming back here for awhile."

She silently drew a smart new suitcase from under the bed, and started laying her clothes in it.

In no time at all they heard the screaming of a siren far away. It quickly swelled louder. "I think we may go downstairs now," said Lee.

The Inspector's long scarlet sedan drew up at the door, followed by an ordinary police car. Half a dozen plainclothesmen swarmed out on the sidewalk. Instantly a crowd filled the street from walk to walk. People seemed to spring out of the very pavement. Loasby and Lee met just inside the house door, and Lee quickly explained the situation.

"I can't be sure that anybody was watching us," he said, "but I didn't want to take a chance on risking the girl's life."

"Not to speak of your own," said Loasby. "You did right. But you ought to inform me in advance of your movements. That funeral was no place for you to show yourself."

Lee made believe to agree with him; privately he was thinking that after all his object in going to the funeral was gained. He said: "Do you want to make a search of the neighborhood before starting back?"

Loasby shook his head. "Useless, now. Whoever was here, he certainly faded when he heard the sirens."

Lee and Marta drove down to Headquarters in the big red car, leaving the gaping crowd excitedly speculating on what had happened. They possessed no clue.

In Loasby's office the story was told in more detail. Marta submitted to a lengthy questioning but nothing was obtained from her beyond what she had already told Lee. She agreed with an indifferent shrug to be detained for the present as a material witness.

"You'll be safest with us," Loasby assured her. "Not like a prisoner but a guest."

When she had left them Loasby said to Lee: "And what am I going to do with you? You can't be allowed to go around loose. You must have a police guard night and day."

Lee shook his head. "Grand fellows, all of them, Inspector, but they look the part too well. To have them along with me would be like a walking advertisement. I'll take a guard, but he must not be a professional. All I'll trouble you for, will be a license for him to tote a gun."

Calling up the *Herald-Tribune* office, he got Tom Cottar on the wire. "Tom," he said, "do you think you can persuade your employers to give you a brief leave of absence? Maybe they'll be more inclined to it if you suggest there is a story in it."

"Not a doubt of it, Pop! Consider it settled. Where do I report?"

"Police Headquarters, Inspector Loasby's office, as soon as convenient."

CHAPTER FIFTEEN

SHORTLY AFTER SEVEN-THIRTY that evening, Lee and Tom Cottar turned up in Frankfort Street and strolled up and down in the neighborhood of Gold Street. They had brought a plainclothesman with them, thinking his badge might be useful; this was Sergeant Rafferty, a detective of the old school, wise and humane. It was not yet dark when they came. Nobody lives in that neighborhood, known to many generations of New Yorkers as "the swamp"; after working hours it is one of the most deserted in town. High over their heads rumbled the traffic on the approach to Brooklyn Bridge.

"This is a forlorn hope," Lee said to Tom, "but we've got to try everything."

At ten minutes to eight a faded blue sedan drew up to the curb and two stolid mechanics stepped out. Approaching them, Lee asked:

"Which one of you is Mike Slattery?"

"That's me," said the bigger of the two truculently. "So what, Mister?"

Lee glanced at Rafferty who quietly showed his badge on the palm of his hand; whereupon Slattery modified his attitude.

"We just want a little information," said Lee mildly. "This is your car. Are you aware that it was borrowed on many occasions and brought back here while you were still at work?"

"Often borrowed?" said Slattery in surprise. "How could that be?"

"The man had a key to the switch."

"To my knowledge it was never borrowed but once," said Slattery, "and that was last Friday night."

Lee pricked up his ears. "How did you find it out, Mr. Slattery?"

"About three o'clock in the morning—I won't swear to the exact time, a guy called me up at the place where I work. He says: 'I'm sorry fellow, but circumstances beyond my control have prevented me from returning your car to the place where I found it!' Fresh guy, see? 'You'll find it,' he says, 'in East Second Street, halfway between First and Second Avenues. Much obliged for the loan,' he says, and hung up on me. I looked in Frankfort Street first and the car was gone, so I walked up to Second Street and there she was, just as he said. I looked her all over and I ran her. She wasn't harmed any. In fact there was more gas in the tank than when I left it."

"Did you happen to notice the speedometer?"

"Yes. Being as I was trying to figure how much gas she used, I looked at the speedometer when I left her that night. When I got her back she had been driven eleven miles only."

"Did those who used her leave anything behind them?"

"Not a thing, Mister."

"Not the slightest bit of evidence that might help to identify them?"

"Nothing at all, Mister. I keep her nice. I brush her out every morning when I get home. If there was anything I would have found it."

"Do you mind if I look?"

"It's all right with me. What do you think you might find?"

"An old bloodstain, perhaps; even a little one would be evidence."

The owner of the car whistled softly between his teeth.

Lee searched with a flashlight and found nothing. He said to Slattery: "If I make it up to you, could you take time enough off from your work to show me the exact spot where you found the car?"

"Sure, Mister." To his fellow-workman he said: "Tell the boss I'll report in an hour, Jack."

Lee said to them both: "If you don't say anything about this for the present I'll make it worth your while."

Slattery slid under the wheel, and Rafferty sat beside him. Tom and Lee got in behind. Lee was greatly elated.

"Tom," he said, low-voiced. "This is the first real clue we have picked up."

"I hope it may be, Pop. If Loney was accustomed to return the car, why the hell didn't he bring it back Friday?"

"I don't know. Maybe it wouldn't start."

"Slattery had no trouble starting it. If Loney didn't bring it back, why in God's name did he telephone Slattery?"

"I can answer that one. It was because he didn't want the police to find the car in Second Street. That's how I know we have a real clue."

East Second Street proved to be a little backwater of the town that the current of progress had left behind. Slattery stopped the car in front of a short row of small eighteenth century houses that had once been the dwellings of the well-to-do as indicated by the remains of their graceful doorways and iron railings. They had come down lower and lower in the world, until at last the Housing Authority had stepped in and condemned them as unfit for human occupancy. They now stood abandoned and forlorn with the front doors and the lower windows boarded up. Across the street there was a similar row in slightly better condition. These housed the businesses of dealers in rags, bottles, old paper and other fag-ends of industry. Already at half-past eight the block was empty and silent.

"A fit place for murder!" murmured Tom.

Lee nodded. To Slattery he said: "If you can remember the exact spot where the car was standing, it will help us a lot."

"This is it, Boss," said Slattery. "I mind when I got in to start her, there was a lamppost about forty feet ahead of me just like now."

Lee glanced up at the house alongside. "Let us try this one first," he said to Tom.

"Why this particular house, Pop?"

"If there was a man to be carried in, living or dead, they would stop as close as possible to the door to lessen the risk of being seen."

"The door is boarded up."

"There's another door under the stoop."

Slattery would have been glad to stop and see the affair through, but Lee settled with him and sent him back with his car.

"Had we better phone for more men?" suggested Rafferty.

Lee shook his head. "We won't find any living persons here."

The house had a low stoop. Beneath it, six steps led down to an iron gate such as is customary at the basement entrance to an old New York house. These gates always have an iron plate surrounding the lock to prevent a hand from slipping through to draw the latch. They noticed at once that the plate on this gate had been broken off. It was thus a simple matter to open it. The wooden door inside was not locked. Lee left Rafferty standing within this door, gun in hand, to prevent anybody from taking them in the rear.

He and Tom went forward with guns and flashlights. The house stank of mildew and old dirt. Evidently the roof had leaked for years and rain had seeped down from story to story; parts of the floors were rotten and patches of plaster lay where they had fallen. On their right was a square room where the decorous eighteenth-century family had eaten its meals; since then the room had witnessed a long progress of squalor and misery. All the fittings had been ripped out, including the mantelpiece.

The kitchen occupied the rear of this floor. Lee's flashlight searched every corner of the pantries and cupboards without finding anything but endless dirt. They paused at the head of the cellar steps. It took a pretty strong stomach to brave that foul place. Tom went first. Lee warned him to test each step before trusting his weight to it. The cellar was empty. In that neighborhood rags, paper, even the smallest piece of wood had its value, and the place had been stripped. The floor was paved with brick which showed no sign anywhere of having been disturbed. Lee was keenly disappointed, for it was here that he had expected to find what he had come for.

From the kitchen one climbed half a dozen steps to the backyard. This was much shorter than was usual in a city lot and was likewise paved with brick. No bush, no flower, not even a weed grew there. The bricks were covered with a sooty greenish coating that had not anywhere been disturbed. Instead of the usual wooden fence, the yard was bounded at the back by an ancient brick wall ten feet high, topped with a line of rusty iron spikes.

"An unusual feature," said Lee. "By daylight we must see what is on the other side of it."

Above the basement were two well-proportioned parlors. The mantelpieces had been ripped out. On the hearth in the rear room lay a little pile of fresh ashes which caused Lee's eyes to brighten. It was the first evidence they had come upon that the house had recently been visited. On the hearth stood a bottle which Lee put to his nose.

"Kerosene," he said. "They had something to destroy which would not burn by itself. Don't disturb the ashes until daylight."

Family bedrooms above and attic rooms above that. The higher they climbed in the house, the lower fell their hopes. "There is no conceivable reason why they should go to the trouble of carrying him up here," said Lee. He was right. The upper floors yielded no body, but Lee noticed that some of the exposed laths under the ceiling of the top floor were loose. Wrenching them down, and sticking his head into the hole he discovered two iron crow bars lying across the floor beams of the attic.

"Yet I could swear that the bricks in the cellar and the yard have not been disturbed," he said.

They returned to Rafferty in the basement. The air from the Street was good in their nostrils.

"Not much luck," said Lee to the plainclothesman. "We'll have to go over everything again by daylight. We may have been seen to enter the house. Will you keep watch on it from the street until morning?"

"Sure, Mr. Mappin. Please telephone for a relief to be sent me at midnight."

After communicating with Headquarters Lee and Tom taxied up to the former's apartment and lay down without undressing. At four o'clock they were back in East Second Street. At the corner they picked up two plainclothesmen, for Rafferty, having had a sleep, was back on the job. His mate was detective McGaha. In the cold light of morning the surroundings were infinitely more sordid. The once comely houses, broken, patched, decayed, like human derelicts had lost all self-respect; the sidewalk was uneven, the roadway full of holes; even the street-cleaners had abandoned this no-man's land; papers, rags and other litter blew where it listed.

They discovered that the house they were interested in bore the ominous number: 13. There was not a living creature moving in the block, not even a cat. With quick glances up and down, the four men ducked through the basement gate and let it close behind them. McGaha was left on guard in the lower hall, while Rafferty accompanied Lee and Tom.

Lee led them direct to the hearth in the back parlor. He had brought a magnifying glass and he went down on his knees to study the ashes. The freshly burned stuff stood up clean and distinct upon the old litter beneath. After studying for a little, Lee said:

"Hemp. One may assume that rope, and quite a lot of it, was burned here. There are a few threads that escaped the flames."

"Maybe they brought rope to tie their man up," suggested Tom.

Lee shrugged. "Why go to that trouble when they could hit him over the head. Loney was never without his pacifier . . . Anyhow, there was a lot more rope than they would need for that purpose. A rope ladder is suggested, and a ladder suggests a wall."

Scrambling to his feet, Lee trotted to one of the windows, only to discover that the brick wall that backed the yard was still higher than his eye level. He made for the hall, Tom and Rafferty following. The stairway went up at the back. Half way up it turned on itself and there was a window on the landing. Lee needed to go no further. An exclamation broke from him. On the other side of the brick wall lay an ancient graveyard with rows of flat grey slabs let into the verdant grass. It was a strange, peaceful oasis, a relic of long ago, surrounded by the backs of dingy tenement houses with clothes flapping on lines from the windows.

"This is the Old Marble Cemetery," said Lee. "I have seen pictures of it, but I didn't know the location. . . . Each one of these stones is the entrance to a burial vault. It is a hundred years since they have been used. Perfect for the purpose of a murderer."

"There must be some passage into the place," suggested Tom.

"Let's not wait to look for it," said Lee. "We want to get in there before the town wakes. . . . Telephone to Headquarters for an emergency truck to be sent here. They carry ladders. We already have crow bars. Tell them to drive through the streets quietly."

Rafferty left the house for this purpose.

A few minutes later the truck arrived without sounding a siren or ringing a bell. Nobody had yet appeared in Second Street. Ladders were carried through the house and planted against the wall in back; Lee, Tom and several policemen went over. Others had been left on guard in front to prevent anybody from entering the house. Lee pointed out how those who preceded them over the wall had hooked their rope ladder over the spikes on top. In the graveyard the men spread out on the springy green turf to examine each stone that covered a vault.

The murderer, never expecting to be followed as far as this, had chosen one of the first vaults at hand. He had taken no special care to obliterate the traces of his work because the graveyard was never visited from one year's end to another except by the man who cut the grass. Lee's searching eyes presently detected some fresh scratches on one of the stone frames in which the slabs rested. Going down on hands and knees he felt through the grass all around the slab, and was rewarded by finding a small key, an automobile key. The other men came to him.

Holding up the key, Lee said: "This is why they had to leave the car standing in the street. Loney dropped the key. They must have gone back over the wall and burned their ladder before he discovered the loss. So they couldn't return to look for it. If it hadn't been for that, we would never have been led to this place. . . . There is always something forgotten or something lost. Perhaps after all the old saying is true; murder will out."

Nearby at the base of the surrounding wall, they found two bricks that had been used as fulcrums. The crowbars were inserted under the edge of the slab and it was lifted a few inches. Hands seized it and turned it over in the grass. A black pit yawned below. Lee cast the light of his flash into the hole, and the men peering over the edge saw that they had come to the end of their search. Eight feet beneath them lay the body of a man, hideously sprawling on his back as he had been thrown there. A young man, judging by his clean limbs and flat belly. When the light fell where his face ought to have been, the watchers exclaimed in horror. It had been cut and slashed beyond all human semblance. One of his ears was missing.

"I agree with Loney Frasca," said Lee. "A dirty murder . . . Rafferty, go to the nearest telephone and rouse up Inspector Loasby."

CHAPTER SIXTEEN

W HEN THE M EDICAL E XAMINER had finished his work, the body of the unknown and unrecognizable young man was carried to the morgue. The ancient vault was sealed again. The only entrance to the graveyard was by a narrow passage between two buildings fronting on Second Avenue. After the story of the strange discovery was published in the afternoon papers, a crowd stood in Second Avenue for hours dumbly staring at the rusty gates that closed the passage. An ancient caretaker turned up who scarcely knew who his employers were, and didn't care so long as his weekly check arrived from the bank. He admitted curiosity seekers at a dollar a head, and made a handsome thing of it until the police stopped it.

When the story was published Lee was well aware that he became a marked man. It was not pleasant to know that somewhere in the city lurked one who would stop at nothing in order to take his life. He could picture the rage of the egomaniac upon learning that he had been worsted in the contest that he himself had provoked with Lee. If he had restrained his itch to write letters, his crime would never have come to light. Not only rage but fear, for half his secret had been disclosed and the remaining half ought to prove less difficult. Tom Cottar stuck close to Lee's side wherever he went; furthermore, Lee now yielded to Inspector Loasby's urging, and allowed himself to be followed by two plainclothes men. Rafferty and McGaha were assigned to that duty.

Lee went to the morgue to study the pitiful, wrecked body. It was that of a superb specimen of young manhood, tall and strongly made; he could not have been more than twenty-four years old.

Lee was teased by something familiar in his aspect. When the attendants turned him over, the well-shaped blonde head seen from
behind, full at the back, broadest over the ears, and the small close-
set ear, gave him a clue. It was the handsome young man that Lee
had marked in the art gallery some days before.

After consultation with Loasby, Lee engaged a well-known plas-
tic surgeon to restore the face as far as might be possible. It was
not a success; too long a time had intervened since death. A portrait artist was then called in to paint him, with the assistance of
Lee's description of the young man as he had appeared in life. But
a verbal description may not be translated exactly into pigment
and the finished painting bore little resemblance to the handsome
youth as Lee remembered him. However, it was the best they had,
and it was published in the press.

Nobody came forward who had known the dead man. It was
one of the most baffling features of the situation that such a man
could disappear and not be missed. A constant succession of people
viewed the body at the morgue but no one could—or would, identify it. The expressions and the actions of the visitors were carefully observed. Nothing came of it.

Each morning at this time Lee went through his mail with ap-
prehensive eagerness. No further letters were received from Mr.
X. Had he been scared off? driven away by the hue and cry raised
in the newspapers? Lee rather thought not. The silence increased
his uneasiness. It would have been some satisfaction to know what
the man was thinking about. Neither he nor any agent of his had
ever returned to listen to the telegraphone, and the watch upon it
was finally dropped.

Lee's full connection with the case was now revealed, and an
enormous amount of publicity accrued to him. The usual amount
of mail was doubled and trebled; all sorts of people stormed the
office, largely crack-pots; the telephone rang all day. All this was
very troublesome to a busy man. On the other hand, the sales of
"Murder and Fantasy" increased by leaps and bounds; Blair and
Rafe Deshon were delighted.

Blair cried with his big laugh: "By God, Lee! you are your own best publicity man! I believe you croaked the guy yourself!"

Rafe, who, in Lee's opinion never could let well enough alone, thought up a dozen schemes to push his author even further into the limelight. He should show himself here, speak there and so on. Lee firmly declined all such opportunities. He had enough to do.

There was one big show that he could not get out of because an invitation had been accepted in advance. This was the annual banquet of the Booksellers' Association. He went hoping to refresh his eyes with a sight of Mary Blair's beautiful face, but her husband came without her. Mary was still lingering in the country he said; couldn't be persuaded to leave her garden. Peggy Deshon was placed beside Lee at the table.

"Lee, darling," she said, "what's the inside dope about the young man without a face?"

Lee conceived a sudden dislike for the brilliant and beautiful Peggy. "There isn't any," he said. "That's just the trouble."

"Do you mean you haven't got a thing to go on?"

"Not a thing!"

"You disappoint me! Why don't you talk over your problems with me? They say sometimes a woman's wit is a help."

"Here?" asked Lee dryly.

"Don't be silly! Let's have lunch together."

"All right. I'll give you a ring." He wondered if Peggy had been put up to this and by whom.

Meanwhile a further examination of the young man's body revealed a blemish on the left forearm which might have been the result of a recent burn. The doctors were of opinion that the injury had been received about ten days before death. Lee had this fact added to the description of the man that was published in every edition of the newspapers. Out of town newspapers copied it.

As the days passed the lines in Lee's hitherto bland face deepened. Had he come so far only to be stopped now? It was not pleasant to picture how the murderer's smile would be correspondingly broader with each passing day.

On an afternoon when the discovery of the body was six days old, Fanny brought a woman into Lee's little office. Tom Cottar, who refused to let Lee out of his sight for a moment, was sitting in the corner. The woman had been a pretty blonde long ago, and was still trying to convey that impression. She had dressed with care for this visit but her agitation had disarranged the effect. She looked like a good-hearted creature, but there were permanently harassed lines in her face. She gave her name as Mrs. Folsom. Lee recognized her type before she described herself; the immemorial landlady.

"It's about the young man who was killed," she said nervously.

"Sit down," said Lee. "Will you smoke?"

She accepted a cigarette, holding it awkwardly like a woman who had learned late in life. She kept glancing uneasily at Tom.

"Mr. Cottar is my friend and assistant," said Lee. "You may speak freely before him. He knows all about the case."

"Perhaps I should have gone to the police," said Mrs. Folsom, "but I couldn't bring myself to face them at Headquarters. I'm a timid woman. I read your name in connection with the case; I thought it would be more private coming here."

"It's all the same thing," said Lee. "I am working with the police. What have you to tell me?"

"When I read of the finding of the body," she went on, "it never occurred to me that such a terrible thing could happen to my young man; such a clean-cut, quiet young fellow. I couldn't imagine him mixed up in anything bad; everybody liked him. And the picture that was in the papers didn't look like him at all, so I thought no more about it. But when I read that he had burned himself on the arm it started me thinking, and I remembered two weeks last Sunday my hot-water heater got out of order and he offered to fix it, and he did, but he burned his arm. I dressed it for him."

Lee let her take her own time. "He lodged with you?" he suggested.

"Yes, sir. My second floor front hall room. Was with me for three months, a southern young gentleman new to New York. One of the nicest who ever come into my house. Everybody was sorry when he left. You see, my house is much too big for a lone woman, so I rent some of my rooms. Mostly for the sake of the company, you understand."

This story was familiar to Lee. "I understand," he said politely. "Where do you live, Mrs. Folsom?"

He had some trouble in obtaining her address. "Oh, if it's published in the newspapers the police will come and the reporters will hound me; the neighbors will start gossiping . . ."

Lee promised to keep it out of the papers if he could. She finally gave him a number on West 89th Street.

"You say he left you," Lee continued. "When was that?"

"A week ago Friday, sir."

Lee's face turned grave. Friday was the day of the first murder. "Mrs. Folsom," he said, "don't you think we'd better drive up and take a look at him. That's the quickest way of settling the matter."

"No, sir! No, sir!" she cried in affright. "The morgue! I couldn't bear it! If it is the same man . . . his handsome face all scarred and spoiled! Indeed I couldn't bear it!"

"Well, let it go for the moment," said Lee soothingly. "You say you dressed his arm when he burned it. Which arm?"

"The left, sir."

Lee rolled up his sleeve. "Put your finger on the exact spot where he was burned."

"The water was boiling. He turned off the gas and in fooling around, he laid his arm against a hot pipe. Just here."

Lee rolled down his sleeve. "It is the same," he said.

Mrs. Folsom hung her head. "Oh, the poor fellow!" she mourned. "The poor young fellow!"

Lee drew a sheet of paper towards him. "What was his name?"

"Walter Ashley."

Lee described him as he had looked in life. "Does that fit, Mrs. Folsom?"

"Yes, sir. That's the man."

"You say he gave up his room, left your house a week ago Friday. Where did he go?"

"He didn't say where. Out of town as I thought. Said he had got a better position in another city. His trunk was taken to Grand Central."

"Didn't he ask to have his mail forwarded?"

"He never received any mail at my house."

"Where did he work?"

"Somewhere down town. I couldn't tell you, sir."

"You said he was from the South. Whereabouts?"

"I don't know, sir. He never mentioned the town."

"But you got the impression that he had lately come to New York?"

"Yes, sir. Everything here was new to him when he came. He was deeply tanned."

"Ah! And this was in February. It's only in Florida that the sun is hot enough to bum the skin in February."

"I suppose so."

"Who sent him to you in the first place, Mrs. Folsom?"

"He answered my ad in the paper, sir."

"Did you ask him for references?"

"No, sir. His appearance and manner were references enough. He liked my house; took the room at a glance. He paid in advance."

"You have drawn me the picture of a very secretive young fellow."

"Not to say secretive, sir. Nothing ugly or suspicious about him. Always the same; pleasant and polite to all, but just silent."

"Didn't it strike you as strange that he never told anything about himself?"

"No. He just wasn't interested in anybody in the house. Lived a life of his own."

"Did he have any visitors?"

"No."

"Telephone calls?"

"No. He was out a lot."

"And never any letters?"

"No, sir. Not all the time he was in my house. Naturally I was curious about him, and I looked over the mail. But that's not strange, because most young men like to get their letters at the office."

"Can you give me any idea of the nature of his business?"

She thought awhile. "He might have been in a steamship of-fice. I say that because he seemed to know all about the ships. Sometimes when I cleaned his room Sunday mornings I would get into talk with him."

"What else did he talk about?"

"Oh, anything that might come up, sir. The news of the day, and so on. Never about himself."

Lee suspected that Mrs. Folsom had done most of the talking on these occasions. "Did he talk to anybody else in the house?"

"No, sir. I'm sure of that. All were curious about him, he being such a handsome young man and nice-mannered. They came to me for information."

"He left suddenly?"

"Yes, sir. On a Tuesday he said he might be leaving town; Thurs-day he said he was going next day. Wanted to pay me an extra week's rent, but I wouldn't take it."

"What were his movements that Friday?"

"He went to his office in the morning but soon came back and packed his trunk . . ."

"Wait a minute. Any marks on his trunk to suggest where he came from?"

"Nothing on his trunk, sir."

"What about the maker's name in his hat?"

"I never thought of looking in his hat."

"Well, go on."

"He telephoned for the transfer company to call for his trunk and they came. In the afternoon he went out, but left his suitcase here. Came back about nine o'clock, took his suitcase, and said good-bye. That was the last I saw of him."

"Was anything left in his room?"

"Not a thing, sir. I looked myself."

Lee went over the whole ground again. He learned all about the young man's wardrobe, a modest one; what books he got out of the library; what he liked for breakfast Sunday mornings—that was the only meal he ate in the house, but nothing to establish where he had come from or with whom he had associated. He had displayed no personal knickknacks or photographs in his room. His trunk was always locked.

"Well, Mrs. Folsom," Lee said, disappointed, "you haven't told me much, have you?"

"I've told you everything I know, sir. If I may say so, Mr. Ashley seemed to be living in a world of his own. Always polite and friendly, but not quite there, if you know what I mean. Busy with his own thoughts. Miss Parker said—she's an unmarried lady lives with me, she said it was her opinion he was in love, and truly that Friday evening when he went away his blue eyes were shining like stars."

"Soon to be put out!" murmured Lee.

Feeling sure that there must be more to be learned—possibly from the unmarried lady, Lee made an appointment to call at Mrs. Folsom's house the following morning.

He had no sooner arrived at the office next day than she called him up. She could scarcely speak she was so agitated. "Mr. Mappin, don't come here! I haven't got anything to tell you. Nobody here can tell you anything; there's no use your coming!" Her voice scaled up hysterically. "Don't come up here! I'm warning you for your own good! It's dangerous! I won't see you. I'm going out of town! Don't come up here!"

When Lee attempted to explain that she would be provided with protection, he found himself speaking to a dead wire. She had hung up.

Naturally, he and Tom Cottar immediately took a taxi for 89th Street. Rafferty and McCaha went along. Mrs. Folsom's house was one of a long row of stone-fronted dwellings of the better class, most of which under modern conditions had become apartments or furnished-room houses. Lee ordered the taxi to wait, and left the plainclothes men sitting in it. Nobody answered the bell, and he and Tom were left standing rather foolishly on the stoop.

"In a house like this there must be somebody home," said Tom.

Lee, glancing down at a basement window, saw an eye applied to the crack between shade and frame. "Let's try the basement," he said.

The basement door was promptly opened by a sturdy Irish maid servant, whose plain face bore a curious expression between fear and determination. "I was told not to open the door, but it don't seem right," she said with a rush. "Come in, gents."

They stood in the basement hall, and she closed the door.

"My name is Mappin," said Lee.

"I know it, sir."

"Is your mistress at home?"

"No, sir, she went away. Pack her bag right after she telephone you and go to stay with her sister in Connecticut. She was scared."

"She got a letter?" Lee suggested dryly.

The woman's eyes widened. "Yes, sir. How did you know? She got a letter and it scared the daylights out of her. I don't know what was in it. She's gone away and I don't know the address neither."

"Never mind that now," said Lee. "What can you tell me about the young man who was killed?"

The maid told a long and voluble story, referring to herself from time to time as Katy. Allowing for the difference in viewpoint, it was the same story as her mistress'. A fine young fellow, but very closemouthed about himself. Katy was all for him. "Not like some I could mention, sir; never forgot to pay me when I did any little extra thing for him."

"What extra things did you do for him?" asked Lee.

"Well, one day he take a silver cup out of his trunk and it was all tarnished, like. And he ask me to polish it for him, and I did, and he give me half a dollar."

Lee's eyeglasses glittered. "Was there any inscription on the cup?" he asked quickly.

"Yes, sir. I read it over and over while I was rubbing it. It say: 'Walter Ashley . . .'"

"That then, is his real name," Lee said to Tom.

"It say," the woman continued; "'For the 100 yard free-style swim.' Then there was a date but I forget it. At the bottom it say: 'Presented by the Y.M.C.A., Jacksonville, Florida.'"

Lee and Tom exchanged a grin. "We are on the track!" said Lee.

This proved to be the extent of the information that Katy could furnish them. "Its worth five dollars to us, Katy," Lee said presenting the astonished woman with a bill. "Keep your mouth shut about this. If anybody comes to the door or calls you on the phone, it will be safest for all of us if you say nothing."

"Faith, I believe you, sir."

Lee and Tom lingered for a moment on the sidewalk. "To Jacksonville?" asked the latter.

Lee nodded. "By plane. Let's not go home to get a bag. Only increase the chance of being spied on. We can buy what we need when we get there."

Tom jerked his head toward the taxi. "What about our watch dogs?"

"We will give them the slip."

CHAPTER SEVENTEEN

IN JACKSONVILLE Lee found his path smoothed for him. Quarter of an hour after he had entered the Y.M.C.A. building he was in possession of Walter Ashley's whole simple story. Born, raised, and schooled in the same city, the son of a commission merchant in modest circumstances, everybody knew Walter and liked him. He was an only child. He had enjoyed considerable local fame as a swimmer and tennis player. Since leaving high school, he had held but the one position, a salesman in the Union Ticket Office.

The bland Y.M.C.A. secretary was terribly distressed by the news which Lee gave him. "I can't understand it," he said shaking his head. "Walt was one of the finest boys we ever had. He had been a member here since he was in short pants! The ideal type of young American."

"Why did he go to New York?" asked Lee.

"Why do they all go to New York?" returned the secretary with some bitterness. "With the idea of bettering himself. If he had stayed with us this would never have happened."

"Was it a sudden decision?"

"Sudden as far as I am concerned. I heard nothing about it until after he had gone."

"Can you give me the name of any close friend he had; one whom he would be likely to confide in?"

"Walt was popular with all the boys. I never noticed that he had one special friend."

"What about girls?"

169

"He was never one for girls. Spent all his spare time playing games or boating on the river. I can't remember ever seeing him with a girl."

He showed Lee several photographs of Walter Ashley as a member of different teams. "One of the best all round athletes the Y. has turned out!"

It was quickly evident that the worthy Y.M.C.A. secretary had never possessed Walter's confidence, and Lee after asking him to say nothing about his visit, went on to the office on Jacksonville's main street where the young man had been employed. Here the manager, himself a brisk young man, told how popular Walter had been both with fellow-clerks and customers. The manager had not been in Walter's confidence either, but he was able to amplify the story in several particulars. When Lee expressed his surprise that such an attractive young man as Walter should never have gone with girls, the manager said:

"There were plenty of girls crazy about him. That was just his trouble. It bored Walter, the way they carried on. Not only the girls he met in a social way, but the women customers who came in here were always falling for him and trying to date him up or sending him presents. He was ashamed of it. It sickened him of the whole sex. I remember at one time the boys started calling Walter 'Beauty.' It got to be a fighting word with him, and they had to drop it."

"How did Walter happen to leave you?" asked Lee.

"That was quite a shock to me," said the manager. "I still miss him. He took his vacation in January this year, and spent it at Miami Beach. He had some extra time coming to him and he was away near a month."

"Do you know where he stopped in Miami Beach?"

"No, sir. Like most of the visitors, he got his mail at the post-office. When he came back to his job I noticed a change in him."

"What kind of change?"

"Well, he was restless sort of, unable to concentrate on his work. Most fellows are like that after a vacation and it passes off. Not with Walter. He was changed. Had no interest in anything."

"Did he tell you anything about his vacation?"

"No. Only that he had a good time."

"Did he have any special friend among the clerks in the office?"

"Not close, sir. Walter never talked much to anybody."

"You think something happened in Miami that changed him."

"Something happened."

"Perhaps he met the one woman for him."

"That would be one explanation."

"And then he left you?"

"Yes. Only a couple of weeks after he got back."

"Had he secured a job in New York?"

"No. But I've been told he had saved a bit of money. He went to look for a job. A fellow like that wouldn't have any trouble; everybody fell for him at sight. He was God's gift to any business that caters to women."

"Did you hear from him after he left?"

"Had a couple of postcards."

"What was on them?"

"Oh, just a colored picture of New York and 'You ought to be here,' or something like that. Walter was no letter writer."

"He got a job?" asked Lee.

"Yes, with the World Tours, Inc., — 5th Avenue." Lee made a note of the address. "Did he cheer up when he left you?"

"Sure. After he made up his mind to go, he was like a new man. There was no holding him. The day he left his eyes were shining like . . . like . . ."

"Like stars?" put in Lee.

"Yes, sir, like stars."

"Please say nothing about my visit to you for the present," said Lee.

Lee was next faced by the task of interviewing Walter's father and mother. It seemed to him gratuitously painful that the news of their son's death should be brought by a stranger. He therefore made inquiries and upon learning the name of their pastor, told him, and asked him to break the news. The pastor was not able to add much to Lee's knowledge of the young man.

In the evening Lee and Tom made their way to the Ashley home. It was a stucco cottage on a quiet street, embowered in semi-tropical flowers and creepers. Lee had never had anything to do that he liked less. Tom waited in the yard. The door was opened by a grave man who looked at Lee as if he had received a mortal wound at his hands. Lee could hardly blame him. Mr. Ashley knew what Lee had come for, and nothing was said. He led the way into an inviting living-room where a little woman in a black dress was sitting with her hands in her lap. Her eyes were big with unshed tears. Lee saw where Walter had got his good looks. Mr. Ashley sat beside his wife and took her hand in his.

"I can't say how sorry I am for you," Lee began. "It would sound impertinent from a stranger. Let us pass over that. I am here to learn whatever I can that may help to solve the mystery of what has happened."

"That won't bring him back to us," whispered Mrs. Ashley.

"No, but justice must be done. It may prevent other tragedies."

"What can we tell you?" asked the man harshly. "We don't know what happened in New York."

"His letters?"

"They didn't say much," put in Mrs. Ashley softly. "Only about his work in the office. He was hiding something from us. I felt it from the beginning, but I didn't say anything about it to him. That wouldn't have done any good."

Lee said: "I believe that this something you speak of started here in Florida."

She nodded. "Yes," she said, very low. "At Miami Beach. He was changed when he came home."

"He gave you no inkling of what had happened?"

She shook her head. "I think he wished to, but it was very difficult for him to speak of his feelings. He was never one to talk. I just waited, hoping it would come out of itself . . . but he went away."

"And his letters gave you no clue to his life in New York?"

"Very little. A boy's letters, matter-of-fact."

"Except his last letter," put in her husband.

She lowered her head. "I felt that he was not telling us the truth in that one—not that I blame him," she added quickly; "a young man is entitled to lead his own life."

"You felt that there was a woman?" suggested Lee.

She nodded. "He was nearly twenty-five. He had never . . . he had never . . ."

"I am not imputing the slightest blame to him," Lee said quickly. "Only when a young man has had no such entanglements, he takes it very hard."

"I know," she whispered. "And nobody could help him. Not even me."

"How often did he write?" asked Lee.

"Once a week, very regularly."

"But now more than two weeks have passed since you heard from him," Lee pointed out. "Did you not find that strange?"

"No. He explained in his last letter that a little time would pass before he could write again."

"May I read the last letter?"

"You can read them all. There is nothing private in them." She went away and fetched her little packet of letters. From the way her eyes dwelt on them, and her hands caressed them, one could see how precious they had become to her.

"Would you prefer to read them to me?" Lee asked.

She quickly shook her head. "I couldn't," she said tremulously.

Lee read the letters. They were, as she had said, a boy's letters, pretty dry fodder for a mother's hungry heart. There was nothing in any of them that was pertinent to Lee's investigation until he came to the last. This had a paragraph that heightened the mystery of Walter Ashley's end.

> I have had a wonderful break. A wealthy old gentleman who bought tickets from us has taken a shine to me. Offered me the job of secretary and traveling companion. He is going around the world. Pretty soft for me, eh? We are leaving for the coast tomorrow. We are going to make several stopovers. After San

Francisco his plans are uncertain. You can drop me
a line at the St. Francis Hotel there, to be called for.
I'll give you a better address as soon as I know it.

"Was that the part that you felt was not true?" asked Lee.

She nodded. "If it had been true, he would have given us more particulars, his new employer's name and so on."

"You see deeply," said Lee.

"Only where he is concerned. . . . He sent me a present," she went on in a mere breath of a voice. "A hat, very pretty and expensive. I think a woman must have chosen it."

She got up and went quickly to the window. Her back was turned towards them. There was a silence in the little room. Mr. Ashley cleared his throat harshly.

"You will please excuse us, Mr. Mappin. I doubt if she can bear any more."

Lee rose. "I am sorry to have intruded on you so far."

Mrs. Ashley came back from the window. "Wait, please," she said. "There is something else I want to say. I don't know what has happened, but I know my boy's heart. If he loved, he loved truly and deeply. There was no sin in his love. Make no mistake about that."

"I'm sure of it," said Lee.

The father walked away to the back of the room.

The tears were flowing fast down Mrs. Ashley's cheeks. "He cleaned his desk out before he left, but I found a clipping under the blotter. It's a poem by George Meredith. I know it by heart. It's about two young people who met in the road.

> "One was a girl with a babe that throve,
>   Her ruin and her bliss;
> One was a youth with a lawless love,
>   Who clasped it the more for this.
>
> The girl for her babe hummed prayerful speech;
>   The youth for his love did pray;

Each cast a wistful look on each,
And either went their way."

When Lee got out of the house he jammed his hat down on his head. He did not feel like talking. Tom, with a side glance, took this in.

"Where away now, Pop?" he asked. "To Miami Beach?"

Lee shook his head. "There is a better lead back in New York."

CHAPTER EIGHTEEN

LEE AND TOM COTTAR alighted from the Florida plane at North Beach airport at the end of the day. As they passed through the barrier, a poorly-dressed woman came pushing up.

"Oh, Mr. Mappin . . ."

Tom, not knowing what to expect, started to thrust himself between them, but Lee held him back. "Why, Mrs. Larkin," he said kindly. "This is a surprise Mrs. Larkin cleans my apartment every day," he explained to Tom. To the woman he said: "Did you come to meet me, Mrs. Larkin?"

"Yes, sir," she said agitatedly. "Oh, I was so afraid I'd be late. It was Mr. Jermyn sent me, sir . . ."

"Wait a minute!" interrupted Lee. He steered her away from possible listeners. "Now, Mrs. Larkin."

"Mr. Jermyn told me to tell you not to come home, sir."

Lee's eyebrows ran up. "Not to come home!"

"He . . . he is not alone there, sir."

"I see! Who is it, Mrs. Larkin?"

"It's a man, sir," she said all in a breath; "I didn't hear him named; a tall, dark-complected man with foxy eyes. He come to the service door this afternoon, and ask for Mr. Jermyn, sir. I didn't like his looks and I left him standing outside. But Mr. Jermyn, he greet him real friendly, and bring him in. I didn't hear anything was said because they went inside, but as I work around the apartment I see them talking real close. The man was all the time watching Mr. Jermyn and following him wherever he went.

"After awhile when the man was telephoning, Mr. Jermyn see his chance and come to me in the dining-room. The man could see us all the time, but Mr. Jermyn while he talk to me was pointing this way and that way, like he was telling me things to do. Mr. Jermyn said to me: 'Mr. Mappin is arriving by plane from Florida at six o'clock. Take a taxi to the North Beach airport and stand by the gate where the passengers come out. Don't let him get by you! Tell him about the man who is here, and not to come home without telephoning first. I'll give you the money when you leave.' So at five o'clock I goes to Mr. Jermyn and I says: 'Will there be anything more tonight, Mr. Jermyn?' And he says: 'No. You may go now, Mrs. Larkin,' and gives me a five dollar note."

"Thank you very much," said Lee. "I shan't forget this, Mrs. Larkin." He stood stroking his chin, and studying over what he had heard.

"You can telephone from here," suggested Tom.

"I'll wait until we get across the river."

"Perhaps Jermyn is in danger."

Lee shook his head. "In that case he would have sent Mrs. Larkin to the police. . . . No, the message means he can take care of the situation, but he doesn't want us butting in unexpectedly. Come on, let's get a cab. You come with us, Mrs. Larkin."

"Oh, no, sir! I can go by subway."

"Nonsense! That would take you an hour."

As they stepped into the taxi, Lee bought an evening paper and was very much put out to discover that the story of his trip to Florida had broken. The murdered man was identified as Walter Ashley and his simple history was related. The dispatch did not give the Jacksonville source of the story, and Lee could not tell who had blabbed. He was very sure it was not the boy's father and mother.

Lee, showing the story to Tom, remarked coolly: "This will make our friend keener than ever to come up with me before I succeed in connecting up the different links."

Tom swore under his breath.

When they got to Manhattan, Lee asked their driver to stop at a drugstore to allow him to telephone.

"What can you say to Jermyn?" said Tom. "If the man is still in the apartment he will force Jermyn to let him overhear both sides of the conversation."

"I have it in mind," said Lee.

The cab stopped. In the telephone booth when Lee heard Jermyn's voice, he said pleasantly: "Well, Jermyn, we're back safe."

Jermyn answered: "I'm glad to hear that, sir." There was no tremor in his voice. "Did you have a successful trip, Mr. Mappin?"

"Very, as you can see from the evening papers. Anything there for me, Jermyn?"

"No, sir. I have referred everything to the office. Only some social letters and invitations."

"They can wait. I have important matters to talk over with Inspector Loasby, and I'm on my way to his office. Mr. Cottar and I will pick up a bite of dinner somewhere, so you needn't prepare anything."

"Very well, sir."

"Jermyn," said Lee—this was the all-important question, "can you take care of the inventory of the furnishings of my apartment by yourself, or will you want help there?"

After the briefest of pauses while this registered, Jermyn answered: "I can take care of it, sir. I should prefer to do it myself, sir, if it's all the same to you."

"Very well," said Lee, "I leave it to you." He went on: "I have a hot tip which will take me up to Connecticut later to-night unless I find something at my office which changes my plans. We'll motor up. So I won't be home until to-morrow, Jermyn."

"Very well, sir."

"You can find me at Police Headquarters or at my office in the meantime."

"Yes, sir."

Lee returned to the cab. "Jermyn appears to have the situation in hand," he said.

After dropping Mrs. Larkin at her home, they went on to Headquarters. Jermyn had already phoned there, and presently he called again.

"The man has left, sir."

"Good. I take it, this was your friend the chauffeur of the Bronx?"

"Yes, sir. He made me hold the receiver away from my ear so he could hear what you said. As soon as he learned that you weren't coming home he went away."

"This suggests that he wanted to see me, eh?"

"Yes, sir. Nothing was said, but I fear that harm was intended."

"Quite! This establishes an important link, Jermyn. You have done well."

"Thank you, sir. But I am afraid, Mr. Mappin, for you, I mean. He may come back. And if he should come to the service door again, I would have to let him in or confess my real character."

"I get you. We three could handle him undoubtedly, but we are not yet ready for a showdown; we need more information."

"That is what was in my mind, sir."

"Very well. This is how we'll proceed. I'll pick up my two plainclothesmen which I meant to do anyhow. Otherwise Mr. Cottar would get no sleep. We'll all be home about ten o'clock. Before coming in, I'll phone you. I'll say: 'We've got to go up to Connecticut, Jermyn.' If your visitor is there you will answer: 'Well, I'm sorry for that, sir. I'm sure you would be more comfortable in your own bed.' But of course if you are alone in the apartment you can say: 'Okay, boss, the coast is clear.'"

Jermyn laughed discreetly. "Very good, sir."

Loasby greeted Lee with relief and reproach. "My God! I was anxious about you until I read the afternoon papers. Why didn't you let me know where you were going?"

Lee merely smiled. They threshed over the situation together. Lee described what he had done in Jacksonville.

"Good work," said the Inspector—a little grudgingly perhaps.

"More good luck than good management," said Lee modestly. "Coming down to the present," he went on, "it is now pretty clear that the murderer of Walter Ashley and Loney Frasca is in league with this mysterious executive of crime that Jermyn has uncovered in the Bronx."

"I have been thinking about this man," said Loasby. "After talking with some of the older officers in the department, I am convinced he is no other than Fingers Claggett."

Lee whistled softly. "Big game!" he murmured.

"One of the cleverest men in the history of crime!" Loasby said impressively; "one of the few who has succeeded in beating the rap. Fingers was before my time. He was the last of the race of great safe-crackers. He didn't require soup to blow a safe. He opened it by listening to the fall of the tumblers in the lock. There was never anybody like him. He got near half a million from the New Netherlands Bank and faded. But I knew he'd turn up some day. I knew it!"

"The clever fingers are warped with arthritis now," murmured Lee, "and he puts the brain to work."

Loasby brought out an old police broadcast sheet with description and photographs of the famous man. "Here he is."

"Let me take that," said Lee. "So I can show it to Jermyn."

"I've discovered his hideout, too," Loasby continued, "from Jermyn's description. I put four men on it. But I wouldn't act in the case without consulting you."

"If any detectives have visited that quiet street in the Bronx," said Lee dryly, "you can depend upon it, Fingers has moved."

"You think my men are all boobs, don't you?" said Loasby sorely.

"By no means," said Lee; "I owe them too much. But in this case we are dealing with a man who has successfully kept out of the hands of the police for— how long is it?"

"Nearly twenty-five years."

"What a feather it will be in your cap when you bring him in at last!" said Lee flatteringly.

It restored the Inspector's good humor.

"As I see it," Lee went on; "Fingers Claggett, if this is he, runs a bureau of crime. He has his lines out wherever they may be expected to attract business. The murderer, needing help, picked up one of his lines and was supplied with Loney Frasca. It was at this moment Jim Costin was hired to spy on me. Ordinarily Fingers would never use so poor a tool. Now they feel that my activities threaten them all, and the whole organization is in motion to get me."

"Exactly," said Loasby. "I wish I could persuade you to stay at home and let me handle the case from now on. You are taking an appalling risk every time you venture into the street."

Lee smiled. "Do you think you could call off the old bloodhound just when the scent is growing strong?"

Loasby spread out his hands. "I'll do my best to protect you," he said, "but . . . !"

Lee and Tom accompanied by their two plainclothesmen drove uptown. Rafferty and McGaha were back on the job. They made a curious contrast these two; Rafferty, elderly, mild of manner with little to say for himself and McGaha, a young giant with a hard boiled front, a voice like a fog horn and an oddly innocent stare. McGaha was a little on the dumb side; there was something about his perpetually surprised look that suggested an overgrown schoolboy.

They stopped at Lüchow's in Fourteenth Street to eat. The detectives took their assignment very seriously, and some of their precautions seemed a little theatrical to Lee. Each of them had a couple of guns concealed on his person. They would always get out of a car first and sharply scrutinize the vicinity before allowing Lee to appear. However, they were good fellows, both of them. In the restaurant they protested that they had eaten their dinner, but Lee insisted on their ordering food and drink.

"Cops can always eat," he said.

At Lee's office the girls had gone home long ago. While the detectives made themselves comfortable with cigars in the outer office, Lee skimmed over his mail. It contained nothing of first-rate importance. He looked eagerly for one of X's derisive letters, but there was none. Evidently for X the matter had now gone beyond a joke.

Jim Costin having heard them come in, sidled into the outer office with his disreputable grin. It was curious to see him trying to make up to the detectives of whom he was secretly afraid. They scorned him. He said he wanted to speak to Mr. Mappin, and Lee called him in. Tom Cottar was sitting in the corner.

"You may speak freely before Mr. Cottar," said Lee. "He is familiar with the situation."

Costin sat down and leaning forward confidentially, said: "I missed you the last three days, Mr. Mappin, but nobody would tell me where you was. Until I read it in the papers."

"Just a little holiday," said Lee dryly. "What did you want to see me about?"

Costin lowered his voice. "Just to report progress, Mr. Mappin. I been continuing my friendship with a certain party. Sometimes I think he's on the level, sometimes not. He's a deep one. I can't say I've got to the bottom of him yet."

There was a good deal more of this, the net result of which was nil. Obviously Costin's object was merely to consolidate his job. Lee, after gravely hearing him out, gave him a little money and dismissed him. Costin went reluctantly. He was smiling still but his shifty eyes turned ugly with balked curiosity.

"Chief, take it from me that guy's crooked," said McGaha hoarsely.

"I believe you," said Lee dryly.

Before leaving the office, Lee telephoned to Jermyn as agreed. Jermyn answered immediately: "It's all right, Mr. Mappin, the coast is clear."

They drove to Lee's apartment.

Jermyn said: "He hasn't been back again, sir."

"We have undoubtedly been watched since leaving Head-quarters," said Lee. "Five men is a little too large a force for them."

"But if he should come to the service door, sir?"

"Warn him as a friend, that I have brought three bodyguards home. If he should insist on entering, which he won't, well, let him come in."

While the detectives regaled themselves with beer in the dining-room, Lee and Jermyn retired to the study for a conference. Jermyn studied the picture of Fingers Claggett that Lee had brought from Headquarters. He said:

"I think I see a likeness, sir, but it's hard to be sure. The nose is the same."

"In my first book I told the story of Fingers Claggett," said Lee. "Fetch it from the library. It is called *Crime*."

This volume contained additional pictures of Fingers Claggett and after a study of them Jermyn pronounced that Claggett and the Bronx paralytic were one and the same. Afterwards Jermyn launched into his story.

"I heard nothing further from those people until yesterday, sir. Costin came up here in the afternoon. After trying to pump me to find out where you were, he told me that the big boss wanted to see me last night. I was to go up there without him this time. I was to get out at the 177th Street station, and he described where I would find the car waiting in a side street. So I went and this time being alone, I got the license number as I came up behind the car."

"I doubt if that will do us any good," put in Lee. "The license plates are undoubtedly stolen or forged."

"Very likely, sir. Anyhow I have the number written down. It was the same driver; they call him Blacky. I was about to sit in beside him, but he told me to get in behind. This was a different car. It was shaped like a sedan but filled in with solid panels behind. It is the type of car that some traveling salesmen use for carrying their samples."

"I know the type," said Lee.

"So I got in behind. There was a chair placed for me. Of course I could see nothing. This time we drove to quite a different place."

"I expected to hear that they had moved," said Lee.

"First we made a circuit back into Third Avenue," Jermyn continued. "That I could recognize from the sound of the elevated overhead. We proceeded North on Third Avenue for seven minutes then turned to the left which would be West, and after four minutes to the right, which would be to the North again. I had my watch and a small flashlight. We traveled North at increased speed for eleven minutes, which must have taken us well beyond the city line. We then slowed down and turning to the right traveled very slowly over a bumpy road for fifty yards or so, made another right turn and over a piece so rough it was not like a road at all but a ploughed field. Then a little smooth bit and we stopped. When Blacky opened the door for me I found we had driven directly into a garage. From the garage there was a door into the basement of a house, so that I did not see the outside at all. Blacky had a key to this door. He frisked me in the garage and took my gun. He said:

"'Everybody who comes into this house has to give up his gun. It isn't because we suspect you of meaning anything bad, but we don't want any trouble or quarrelling here.'

"I judged from its style that it was a fairly modern house, but everything was dusty, indicating that it had been vacant for some time. There was no furniture in the rooms that I saw, and the electric current had not been turned on. Nobody lives in this house. My guess is that they only use it for meetings at night. Blacky led the way with an electric torch. In a room on the ground floor the old man in the wheel chair was sitting at a folding table with a small portable electric lamp on it. There was a folding chair for me. Rugs had been tacked up inside the windows so that no light could show outside.

"Blacky went away and left me with old Fingers. I am certain now that he is Fingers Claggett. I didn't see anybody but these two, but I judged from sounds I heard, that there were others up-stairs. It would have been easy for me to strangle the old man, but even if I had wished to do so, I doubt if I would have had the nerve—and he knew that. Broken as he is, there is an awful power in him. His eyes beat you down. As on the first time, he started in by flattering me in an oily voice, telling me what a clever fellow I was, and how he wanted me to work for him, and would make my fortune and so on.

"In spite of all this beating around the bush, I soon understood why I had been sent for. He wanted to know where you were, sir. They had lost you for two days and were badly worried. They must have some connection at Headquarters because they knew that you had given the plainclothesmen the slip also. All that about wanting to steal your papers was just a stall. It is not your papers they are after, but you. The old man had me sweating there, because there was a hidden threat in every question. All I could say was I didn't know where you were. It's a good thing you didn't tell me, because I was able to answer more convincingly.

"I told him you had called me and told me you were going out of town for two or three days, and if you were kept longer you would let me know. I told him I had asked you if you didn't want me to pack a bag and bring it to you, and you said no, that there was a certain danger of my being followed, and that he would pick up what he needed wherever he happened to be. It was a long time before the old man would let it drop. He asked me a hundred questions about your habits and customs all of which I answered truthfully as you advised. Finally he appeared to be satisfied that I really didn't know any more than I had told him.

"I then went on to tell him about the papers and notes relating to the two murders, that were in your desk at home. He was interested, but not as much interested as he was in finding out where you had gone. He asked me why I hadn't brought the papers along to show him. I said it was because I was afraid you might come home before I got back. Then why hadn't I copied them, he asked. Because I didn't know if they would be of any value to him, I answered.

"Well, he said, that was all right; he'd send Blacky down to the apartment to look them over. Blacky was not to remove them, because he didn't want your suspicions aroused as yet. Blacky would just read the papers and make notes of anything new. I said, 'Suppose my master is in the house when Blacky comes?' He said: 'Well, he doesn't go out in the kitchen does be? Make out that Blacky is a man delivering something, or a personal friend of yours.' He asked me where my bedroom was, and when I said alongside the kitchen, he said: 'Put Blacky in there until your master goes out.'

"Well, that is about all that is worth repeating, sir. I omitted to say that there was no telephone connection in the house, but they had some way of receiving messages, for three times while the old man was questioning me, Blacky came in with a slip of paper on which something was written. Each time my heart squeezed up in a tight knot because I thought it might be: 'This man is a spy.' But as yet they do not appear to suspect me. On one occasion the old man scribbled an answer on the paper; the other two times he tore it up. Blacky drove me back the same way we had come."

"Did he return your gun?"

"Yes, sir. . . . There is not much to say about Blacky's visit here this afternoon. His first act was to shoot the bolt on the front door so that you would be forced to ring if you came. He came about four-thirty. By that time the news of your trip to Florida was out. It has thrown a bad scare into their camp. They feel that you are drawing too close to them. They didn't know what time you were returning, but I had your telegram giving the hour.

"Blacky showed only a cursory interest in the papers you left out for a decoy. He was listening for your ring at the door. He made me show him over the whole apartment and he made a sketch plan of it with every closet, every window and door marked on it. If you had come, I would have found a way to warn you, of course, but it would have been the end of my usefulness as an undercover man. Luckily I had Mrs. Larkin to send to the airport."

Lee asked: "Do you think it likely they will be sending for you again, Jermyn?"

"Undoubtedly, sir. As long as they think they can use me."

"With every visit the danger is greater," suggested Lee. "I should be just as well pleased if you didn't go again."

A faint, unaccustomed flush appeared in Jermyn's leathery cheeks. "If you please, sir, I would wish to follow wherever the trail may lead. I am not in so great a danger as you are, sir."

"Very well," said Lee. "You're a man, Jermyn."

"Thank you, sir."

Lee after spreading Jermyn's map of the Bronx on the desk, made his man repeat the story of his ride with Blacky. Jermyn had a remarkable memory; he could even tell Lee how often the car had been stopped by traffic lights. Lee studied the map and figured.

"You said seven minutes North on Third Avenue, then four minutes East. The usual rate of travel in town is thirty-five miles an hour, say forty in the Bronx. The westbound street was Smallwood Parkway and that would bring you in four minutes to Fern Avenue. This is an old thoroughfare not much used since the new Parkways have been opened. Here you traveled faster, say fifty miles an hour."

"No traffic lights on that street, sir."

"Right. You are over the city limits now. Say, nine miles." Lee made two pencil marks on the map. "The house we are looking for is just off Fern Avenue somewhere between those two points. In the middle of the space I see a road to the eastward called Beaver Lane. I shouldn't be surprised if Fingers Claggett's hideaway fronted on Beaver Lane."

"Very likely, sir."

Lee made a memo of his conclusions and enclosed it with the map in a note to Stan Oberry.

> Dear Stan:
>
> Somewhere between the two points marked on the map lies a house that I am anxious to visit. Put Seventeen on this job. That lad has a head on him. Warn him that I expect him to fool some of the cleverest crooks in the world. They may not use this house in the daytime, but I am certain they keep an eye on it. Let Seventeen hire a couple of bicycles in the morning and take a girl and a lunch box. If they act like lovers no one will suspect them as they ride up Fern Avenue and through Beaver Lane.
>
> Yours,
>
> L. M

Before going home, Rafferty and McGaha insisted on searching every corner of Lee's apartment for a possible hidden assassin. Lee pointed out that it was hardly necessary since nobody had entered the place but one man, and Jermyn had seen him out. The windows were two hundred feet above the street. However, he let them have their way and afterwards invited them to go home, and have a good sleep.

CHAPTER NINETEEN

N<small>EXT MORNING</small> shortly before nine the four men set off from Lee's apartment. Lee had good reason to suppose that they would be followed, and as he wished to keep his present errand a secret if possible, he ordered their driver to take them to the Hotel Biltmore. He and his friends entered an elevator and, getting out at the mezzanine floor, returned to the basement by a stairway invisible from the lobby. From here they entered the long underground corridor that leads to the concourse of the Grand Central Station. Midway in the corridor they halted as if for a brief conference, thus allowing those who were behind them to pass.

"If we are being followed," said Lee, "our trailers will have to stop at the end of the corridor to see which way we turn."

There was nobody waiting at the end of the corridor. They ascended the steps to Vanderbilt Avenue and hailed another taxi.

"One may hope," said Lee, "that our friends are still waiting in the lobby of the Biltmore for us to come down."

They now had themselves driven to the address of World Tours, Inc., on Fifth Avenue. The firm occupied a second-floor suite in one of the older buildings with a display window at the right level to catch the eyes of those riding on the upper deck of the buses. The exigencies of war had worked havoc with the tourist business, and they were obviously only hanging on in the hope of better days.

Lee left a part of his guard waiting in the corridor.

Without giving his name, he asked for the manager and was shown into a private office. A well-fed gentleman, rather dandified in his attire, arose to meet him with some eagerness, for Lee had the look of a prosperous traveler, accompanied by his son. The manager's name was Morison. In his mind's eye Lee could see him conducting a party through the halls of Europe with great éclat. Unfortunately when Lee gave his name, Mr. Morison stopped short; his ruddy face paled and then became redder. This before Lee had even stated his business. Lee said:

"I came to obtain what information you could give me about the unfortunate Walter Ashley, Mr. Morison."

Fear leaped from the other man's eyes. "I have read the young man's story," he said; "unfortunate indeed! But why do you come to me, Mr. Mappin?"

"Walter Ashley worked here," said Lee dryly.

"I don't know who could have told you that, sir. Your information is erroneous."

Lee, nettled, drew a long breath for patience. "I see you have been frightened," he said. "Probably by an anonymous letter signed with the letter X. I have had a good many of them myself. By withholding information, you understand, you are constituting yourself an accomplice in his murder."

"I don't like your language, sir," blustered Mr. Morison.

"Sorry," said Lee, "it's no more than the truth."

"Do you presume to call me a liar, sir?"

"I'm not calling you anything, sir. I'm asking you for information."

"Which I haven't got."

"I know he worked here, Mr. Morison. I have seen his letters home written on your firm's paper."

"We keep a desk in the outer office for the convenience of our clients. It is stocked with our note-paper. Anybody could write a letter there, and if he wished, take a few sheets away with him."

"His letters described his work here, day by day."

"Then for reasons of his own he was lying."

"He is dead, sir."

Mr. Morison raised his voice. "As I said before, I don't like your tone, sir. I must ask you to leave my premises."

"There are two detectives out in the hall," said Lee blandly. "Would you rather receive them?"

Mr. Morison's jaw dropped. He fussed among the objects on his desk without seeing any of them. He finally recovered himself sufficiently to say: "I couldn't tell the detectives any more than I can tell you, sir."

"And that is nothing?"

"Nothing, sir! I never saw Walter Ashley in my life!"

Lee shook his head. "I am sorry to see how low fear will bring a man! . . . It is foolish of you, sir, because it can easily be proved that Walter Ashley worked here."

"Prove it then! Prove it!" cried Mr. Morison excitedly.

"I shall be under the necessity of questioning your employees."

"By all means! I should have insisted upon it in any case." He pressed a button on his desk and a woman entered as promptly as if she had been listening at the door, a woman no longer young with a bleak face and a self-controlled air. "My secretary, Miss Simpson," said Morison.

Lee said: "What can you tell me about Walter Ashley, Miss Simpson?"

"Walter Ashley?" she echoed with well-simulated surprise. "I don't know anything about him. I never saw him to my knowledge."

Lee perceived at once that he would not get anything out of her. This type of woman gives first loyalty to her employer. "Thank you very much," he said; "that's all."

A little disappointed, she went out. Morison said, to her: "Please ask Miss Emmart to step in." To Lee he explained: "My office force is reduced to a skeleton this year."

The second clerk was younger than the other, not a bad looking girl, with medium brown hair and greenish eyes, but emotionally unstable; she frowned and bit her lip; her eyes shifted from side to side. Lee saw that he could easily break this one down, if she were separated from her employer. She denied knowing Walter Ashley, and Lee let her go.

"I am sorry I cannot be of more help to you," said Morison hypocritically.

"So am I," said Lee pleasantly. "Principally for your sake. When the truth comes out this will redound very greatly to your disadvantage, Mr. Morison." Without more ado he and Tom got out.

From his own office, a few minutes later, Lee rang up Stan Oberry. "Stan," he said, "take down this address. World Tours, Inc., — 5th Avenue. A tourist agency. They have a woman clerk called Miss Emmart." Here Lee gave Stan a description of her appearance. "I want you to find out where she lives and what her circumstances are. I suggest that you have a man call at the office to make some inquiry about travel. He can look the girl over and later at the close of business, follow her home."

"Okay, Mr. Mappin."

As Lee hung up, McGaha entered his office. "Excuse me, Mr. Mappin," he said hoarsely, "but they're back on the job. There's a hard-faced guy walking up and down the other side of the street watching all who come out of this building."

"That's to be expected," said Lee.

"Why don't I go out and run him in?" suggested McGaha.

"What charge could you bring against him?"

"Charge? I don't need no charge. Suspicious character is enough. The guy's got a nerve to tail the police to their faces!"

Lee shook his head. "Wouldn't do any good. You can be sure there are others watching the watcher, and ready to take his place. It's better to let them think we're not on guard."

McGaha was as disappointed as a child. "Just as you say, Mr. Mappin, but I sure don't like it. It's defiance of law and order."

In the course of the morning Inspector Loasby called Lee on the phone. "Mr. Mappin," he said, "I'm putting a bullet-proof sedan at your disposal, if you will take the risk of riding around town. It's waiting at the Acme Garage in East 33rd Street. The chauffeur is a police officer, in plain clothes, name of Riordan. Just phone the garage when you want him. He can then draw up in front of your office door, and you won't have to expose yourself unnecessarily."

Lee smiled into the transmitter. "I certainly am obliged to you, Inspector. But don't you think I'd lose as much in one way, as I'd gain in another?"

"How do you mean?"

"Well, they will soon recognize this car as mine, and be able to pick me up at any time, whereas I could change from taxi to taxi."

"Mr. Mappin," said Loasby earnestly, "I am responsible for your safety; I ask you as a personal favor to use the bullet-proof car."

"If you put it that way how can I refuse?" said Lee good-humoredly. "I will, and many thanks to you."

Lee obeyed the dictates of prudence insofar as not to go out to lunch. Instead, he telephoned to the Vanderbilt for what the old writers used to call a superb collation—including champagne. When it came, they locked the office door and all six of them sat down to do it justice; Lee, Tom Cottar, Fanny, Judy and the two Headquarters men. Banishing thoughts of crime and danger, they determined to have a good time. Rafferty and McGaha were enormously impressed by the honor of eating with two such beautiful girls. The innocent heavy McGaha was a perpetual source of amusement to them. He didn't mind being laughed at.

In the middle of the afternoon Stan Oberry called up to say that his operative Seventeen had returned with full particulars of the hide-out in Westchester County. Stan thought the young man ought to make his report to Lee in person so that Lee could question him.

"Right," said Lee, "but don't send him down here. This building is watched. Let him take a roundabout route to my apartment. I'll meet him there in half an hour."

Lee telephoned for the bullet-proof car and it presently drew up in front of the door. It was a black sedan outwardly no different from any other car, except, perhaps, that the keen-faced chauffeur had the indefinable look of an officer. Lee, telling the girls they might lock up and go home, went downstairs with Tom and the two detectives. Rafferty rode beside the chauffeur, while Tom, McGaha and Lee sat in the back seat in that order, left to right.

McGaha immediately leaned over Lee, then Tom, to screw up the rear windows. "Bullet-proof glass ain't no good to us if it's not there," he remarked. Rafferty likewise rolled up the glass on his right.

They sped through East Forty-second Street, through the tunnel under Tudor City, and turned north in First Avenue. First Avenue, having little or no cross traffic, was the main motor thoroughfare on the East Side, with a roaring traffic of trucks and cars up and down all day. Their chauffeur drove with a nonchalant assurance even more pronounced than that of a taxi-driver, for he had no fear of the police. He had to keep the window beside him open in order to signal the following cars, but Lee noted with what care he kept to the outside lane of the northward moving cars, so that no car could pass him on the left.

Below Forty-ninth Street, a shabby, powerful limousine on their right took advantage of a break ahead to draw alongside. "Look out!" yelled McGaha, and instantly a hail of bullets splashed against the closed windows on that side. The glass splintered but did not break. McGaha and Tom dropped to the floor of the car; Lee pressed himself into his corner. It all happened too quickly for him to have any sensation of fear. In front Rafferty slid out of his seat, but the police chauffeur, knowing the quality of his car, remained scornfully upright at the wheel.

Lee could see nothing through the splintered windows. As the limousine endeavored to shoot ahead, the police chauffeur whirled his wheel around in an attempt to pin the gangsters' car against the parked cars at the curb. The limousine escaped by inches and the police car unable to turn back, smashed against a parked car and stalled. At that moment the traffic lights turned red and everything stopped. But through the windshield Lee saw the gangsters' car turn left on screaming tires and speed away west out of sight in Forty-ninth Street.

Nobody was hurt except Rafferty who cut his head against the instrument board when the cars came together. Instantly a crowd gathered. The owner of the parked car appeared, screaming objurgations at the police chauffeur. The latter coolly displayed his badge saying: "Present your claim to Inspector Loasby at Headquarters, and it will be paid." Almost immediately a patrol car with two uniformed officers drew up on the other side. Hasty explanations were

made, and the patrol car, wheeling left, raced away through Forty-
ninth Street—just a little too late.

The bullet-proof car was not damaged beyond a bent radiator
grill and a couple of smashed lamps. Backing out of the wreck, they
proceeded up First Avenue, and around the corner to the door of
Lee's apartment. All the way McGaha was muttering to the accom-
paniment of heartfelt curses: "The nerve of them! The nerve of
them! Daring to fire on the police!"

The chauffeur, entirely unruffled, said to Lee: "I'll have to roll
this job in for repairs, Mr. Mappin. If you'll call up the Inspector,
he'll assign you another car."

"I'll report to him," said Lee.

Over the telephone Loasby's reaction was similar to McGaha's.
"My God, Lee! They dared to attack a prominent citizen in the open
street! By heaven! I'll get this gang if it's my last act on earth!" His
voice broke. "Aren't you thankful . . . aren't you thankful you had
the bullet-proof car?"

Lee grinned. "Sure! But if I'd been in a taxi I might have fooled
them in the traffic."

"I'm coming up there," said Loasby.

Lee when he hung up, saw by Jermyn's face that his servant
had a private communication to make. Leaving Tom and the two
detectives excitedly discussing the attack in the street—it had only
lasted a few seconds but it gave them plenty to talk about, Lee preceded Jermyn into the study.

"Blacky called me up this afternoon," Jermyn said. "The boss
wants me to come up there tonight. Blacky will meet me near the 177th
Street station. I told him I couldn't get there until nine. That was to
give you time to prepare something after dark if you wanted to."

"You did right," said Lee. He stroked his chin and studied.

"Is it your wish that I should keep the appointment?" asked
Jermyn.

Lee shook his head. "Too dangerous. I don't know what they
want you for when Blacky can come here at any time. They may
suspect that you are playing them false. If all goes well, I'll spring
a surprise on them first."

"Can I go with you, sir?" Jermyn asked.

"Sure. I'm counting on you."

A ring at the door announced the coming of Stan Oberry's operative, Seventeen. Jermyn brought the good-looking young man into the study. In the secure privacy of that little room his dead pan broke up in a grin. Seventeen made no secret of the fact that Amos Lee Mappin was his admired model. Lee said:

"You may remain, Jermyn. You will be interested in this."

"Thank you, sir."

To make a long story short, the ruse of the girl and the two bicycles and the lunch box had been a complete success. Seventeen found the empty house facing Beaver Lane where Lee had figured it would be. Seventeen said that the house must have been vacant for several years. As there was no For Rent or For Sale sign displayed, he judged that the place was in litigation. The grounds were completely overgrown and neglected. The main entrance was closed by a pair of rusty iron gates which obviously had not been opened in some time. By making a wide detour on the bicycles, Seventeen came upon the farm road in the rear by which the gang was accustomed to enter. Making a right turn from this road and passing through a gap in a stone fence, you could enter the garage from behind the house.

Seventeen and the girl friend had eaten their lunch under a tree outside the stone fence. They had seen nobody moving. They had taken care to display no curiosity about the place, making out to be completely absorbed in each other. Seventeen, without having actually entered the grounds, was able to give Lee a good description of the place as seen from front and back.

"Good!" said Lee when he had finished. "With the aid of the police, we'll raid them at nine-thirty tonight. Will you come along and show the way? I'll fix it up with Stan Oberry."

"You bet your life!" said Seventeen.

The next person to arrive at Lee's apartment was Inspector Loasby. "Don't tell me anything about the attack on you!" he said, waving his hands. "I've already had six reports on it!"

"They got away?" asked Lee, knowing what the answer would be.

"They got away—for the moment. But I'll get them! I promise you results within twenty-four hours."

Lee smiled.

"What I came up here for," said Loasby, "was to beg you to remain in your apartment until these thugs are caught. Up here two hundred feet above the street, protected by a couple of steel doors and two or three dependable men, you are safe. In the street no matter what precautions I take, I can't tell where they may strike. The attackers enjoy too great an advantage."

"I'm sorry," said Lee. "I can't promise to stay in the house. If I let this gang bluff me, I could never look myself in the face again. I expect to go out again early this evening."

"I was afraid you'd say that," said Loasby heavily. "Well, there's another car for you at the Acme garage if you must have it."

Lee called on Rafferty and McGaha. "What about it, men? Do you want to take another drive with me this evening, or shall I ask the Inspector to relieve you?"

"I stay on the job," said Rafferty shortly.

"Me too," said McGaha. "If we can have tommy guns. An automatic is no defense against a tommy gun."

"You can have all the tommy guns you want," said Loasby. "I'll order them put in the car."

Lee producing his snuffbox, offered it to the Inspector. Loasby hastily waved it away, whereupon Lee took two leisurely sniffs and tapped the box shut. "Inspector," he said, "what say if you and I make a raid tonight on the hideaway of the gang?"

"Hey?" cried Loasby, opening his eyes very wide.

Lee relayed the information he had obtained from Jermyn and Stan Oberry's operative, Seventeen. Loasby's face while he listened was a study; gratification mixed with chagrin because Lee had got so far without any aid from him.

"You don't think much of my men, do you?" he growled.

"There are none braver or more persistent," said Lee. "It is only in certain delicate operations that I prefer to act independently."

The Inspector's soreness soon vanished, and joint plans were formed. Lee was to take the five men with him and Loasby to bring as many more as he considered necessary. The two parties were to proceed by separate routes to the first scene of action near the 177th Street station and join forces at nine o'clock.

CHAPTER TWENTY

BEFORE INSPECTOR LOASBY left the apartment, Lee was again called to the telephone by Stan Oberry. Stan said:

"Mr. Mappin, the full name of the young woman who works for World Tours is Adele Emmart. She rents a furnished room in the apartment of Mrs. Sanders at — West 20th Street in the Chelsea neighborhood. The number of the apartment is 6A. Miss Emmart at the present moment is eating her dinner in the Parkside cafeteria at number — Ninth Avenue. One of my men is watching the place."

"You may call him off," said Lee. "I'll pick up the girl myself, directly." After explaining to Stan that he would keep Seventeen with him for the evening, Lee hung up. To Loasby he said:

"This is a very important lead, Inspector. I'll have time to follow it up before we start on the main business of the evening."

Loasby shrugged somewhat sourly. "All right. Just give me time to order a couple of tommy guns stowed in the car."

"Okay," said Lee. "Let Miss Emmart finish her dinner in peace. I couldn't talk to her in a cafeteria anyhow. Well take a bite ourselves before starting out."

Jermyn made haste to put cold food and beer before the men.

Lee said to Loasby: "I expect to be back here in plenty of time for our expedition, Inspector. But if I should be delayed, Jermyn will call you up at Headquarters at eight-twenty and you can bring what additional men you think necessary to take our places. After telephoning you, Jermyn and Seventeen will proceed by taxi to the agreed meeting place in the Bronx. You will need them for guides."

Inspector Loasby then left the apartment.

Later, when Lee and his bodyguard got downstairs, Riordan was waiting in a car precisely similar in appearance to the one he had smashed in the afternoon. He saluted smartly. The four of them disposed themselves in the car as they had done before. In the dead-end street before Lee's door, there was no sign of spies or watchers but you never could be sure. Though it was a warm evening all the windows of the car were closed. The windshield was raised a couple of inches to give them air. McGaha was delighted to find a couple of submachine guns hidden under a lap robe in the back.

They proceeded directly west to Ninth Avenue, then south under the elevated railway. There was very little traffic over here at this hour. If they were followed, it was Lee's intention to make a rapid zigzag around many corners before reaching their destination. However, McGaha, watching through the rear window, swore that they were not followed. There were times, he said, when there was no car visible for blocks behind them.

"All right," said Lee. "But don't let's be overconfident. These fellows are so darn clever it is possible they may have known where I was going beforehand."

They drew up in Twentieth Street (an eastbound street) before a tall narrow apartment house of the older type. A house still respectable but somewhat rundown, where rents would be low. Lee said:

"The young lady I am calling on here is of a somewhat nervous type. If I took my whole gang upstairs she would certainly have hysterics and I could do nothing with her. Rafferty and McGaha will wait in the car. Note you two, that the main door and the service entrance to the house are both right in front of you. Nobody can get in the house after me without your seeing them."

"Okay, chief."

Lee and Tom entered the building. There was a single elevator of the grilled ironwork type run by a sleepy negro. He let them off at the sixth floor and went down again. There were only two apartments to a floor, A and B. Lee rang the bell at A, and the door was presently opened by a woman with an expression of chronic suspicion, obviously the landlady. Lee raised his hat.

"I would like to see Miss Emmart, if you please."

Little Lee, so beautifully dressed in his own quaint fashion, so polite, could not fail to make a good impression; red-headed Tom too, as has been noted, had a way with the sex. The woman's expression softened. Perhaps she did not often have such gentlemanly visitors. She hastily rolled up her apron as if to hide it.

"Please to come this way, gentlemen."

They stepped into a long narrow hall running from front to rear. At their left was a living room. Along the hall were a number of doors. The landlady knocked on the nearest door, saying: "Gentlemen to see you, Miss Emmart." She opened the door and after sticking her head around it to make sure that her lodger was presentable, threw it wide. So Lee and Tom walked in.

It was what the English call a bed-sitting-room, rather shabby. The narrow bed had a green denim cover, and the more intimate bedroom features were hidden behind a screen in the corner. There was a bumpy armchair and a single window looking east over the roofs of lower buildings. In the armchair sat the tenant of the room staring at them; medium brown hair, green eyes, a sullen expression; a plain girl, highly emotional. Touched with happiness, she might have been lovely.

She recognized Lee and rose. "How . . . how did you get here?" she stammered.

Lee ignored the question. "Sit down," he said easily. "I won't take but a minute or two of your time."

"I don't want to talk to you. I've got nothing to tell you!" she said stormily.

"About Walter Ashley . . ."

"I told you today I never knew the man! He means less than nothing to me!"

Pinned to the wall above a table on the left, Lee had spotted a newspaper reproduction of the portrait of Walter. He silently pointed to it.

With three swift steps she snatched it down and crumpled it in her hand. "That's nothing! It was a sad story. My curiosity was aroused." She tossed the paper in a waste-basket with pretended indifference.

Lee had not much time to spare and he ventured on a white lie, hoping thereby to break her down quicker. "What's the use?" he said with a regretful air. "His mother allowed me to read his letters home. You were mentioned in them."

Her head flashed back, her cheeks crimson, then very pale. "What did he say about me?" she demanded breathlessly.

Lee did not smile at the success of his trick. "I can't repeat the exact words. He was telling his mother how friendly and helpful Adele had been."

She hung her head murmuring: "I didn't think he ever noticed me." Suddenly realizing how she had betrayed herself, she broke out harshly: "I don't care! I'm not going to tell you anything. I don't want to lose my job. Jobs are too hard to get . . ."

"I want to find out who murdered Walter," said Lee mildly. "I should think any friend of the boy's would wish to help me. After working beside him for two months you must know something. Listen, if you can give me a new lead, a clue, anything to help me on in this case, neither Morison nor anybody else need ever know where I got it."

"I can tell you nothing," she murmured. "He never paid any attention to me."

Lee took a new tack. "I learned quite a lot about him in Jacksonville," he said simply. "Nobody could help being fond of Walter. In addition to his extraordinary good looks he was so honest and kind and decent."

Tears started to rim down Adele's cheeks but she remained obstinately silent.

"Weren't you fond of him yourself?" asked Lee casually.

Adele nodded towards Tom. "Send him away," she murmured in a strangled voice.

Tom stood up. "Sure, I'll wait outside." He left the room.

Adele dropped her face on her arm, and wept unrestrainedly. Lee gave her time. "Oh, I wish I'd never seen him! I wish I'd never seen him! He has spoiled me for other men. My life is so empty!"

"He loved you?" suggested Lee.

"No! No! No! I was nothing to him. His eyes skated over me. He was the same to everybody. He did his work, he was polite to the customers, friendly with the staff, but he lived in a different world from us!"

Lee was struck by the repetition of this phrase. "Then there was another woman?" he asked.

The girl nodded.

"Who was she?"

"I can't tell you. He got a letter from her nearly every day, generally in the afternoon. Although he saw her often, too. I could always tell when he had been with her by his expression and his voice. His voice was gentled. . . It drove me wild! . . . wild! Nobody knows what I suffered!"

"Did she ever come to the office?"

"No."

"The clue to the murder lies through this woman," said Lee. "If you suffered so you must have thought about her a lot. You must be able to tell me something."

She shook her head.

"Didn't you try to find out something?"

Hanging her head she murmured: "Yes. I used to get down to the office early and go through his desk, but he never left any of her letters there," she sneered painfully. "Maybe he put them in his safe deposit box. I used to see a safe deposit key in his drawer. Once when I was alone in the office a letter from her came in the morning mail. I . . . I couldn't resist the temptation. I steamed the envelope open at the radiator and read it. It didn't do me any good. I sealed it up again, and put it on his desk and he never knew."

"No clue to her identity in the letter?"

Adele shook her head.

"Signed?"

"Just a pet name; Lollie."

"Can you tell me in a general way what the letter said?"

"I can repeat it word for word," she said bitterly. "Mushy! 'My beloved: I am broken-hearted about last night. He never went out, so I couldn't come. I went to bed and dreamed about you, darling. Not happy dreams because I was separated from you. I'll try again tonight, but don't wait for me longer than a quarter of an hour. I love you! I love you! I love you! Lollie."

"What kind of paper?"

"Plain white paper; thick and expensive-looking."

"Perfumed?"

"No."

"What was the postmark?"

"New York City."

"Sure. But what post office or station?"

"I didn't notice."

"You haven't given me much to go on," said Lee.

"I told you I knew nothing."

"What other letters did he get?"

"Not many. Letters from Jacksonville; I didn't bother about them. That's all."

"Think back," urged Lee. "No other letters? Anything might furnish a clue."

"Well, he traded on the street in a small way. Once in a while he got a letter from his brokers."

"Ha!" cried Lee. "That's something! Who were his brokers?"

"Warner, Mills and Company."

"I know the house," said Lee. ". . . Now about his leaving the office. Did you know beforehand that he was going?"

"Only two days. He told Mr. Morison on Tuesday and he left on Thursday. Mr. Morison didn't mind, because he was paying Walter a good salary and business had fallen away to almost nothing. He was glad to save his salary. He refused to pay Walter for the four days he had worked but Walter didn't care."

"Did Walter say where he was going?"

"Said he was going to San Francisco to take a position with his uncle."

Lee reflected that for an honest fellow, young Walter's lies were many and varied. "He seemed happy about going?"

"Oh, sure!" Adele said bitterly. "It was perfectly clear that he was going with her."

"He left on Thursday," said Lee softly; "and on Friday he was killed."

"He came into the office on Friday morning, but only to get his letter," said Adele.

This was the sum total of the information that she could supply. There was no doubt that she was speaking the truth now. Lee assured her that Morison should never know what she had told him. He offered the girl what words of sympathy he could, and rose to leave. He promised Adele that if she lost her job at Morison's he'd get her another. He looked at his watch. It lacked a few minutes of 8 o'clock and he had just about sufficient time to make his apartment before setting out for the Bronx.

Outside in the narrow hall Tom Cottar was leaning against the wall, smoking a cigarette. "What about it?" he asked.

"Okay," said Lee. "Let's go."

Tom, who was nearest the entrance door, opened it, and instantly slammed it shut again. The cigarette dropped from his lips; automatically he rubbed out the fire with his foot. "Six men waiting on the landing," he said curtly. "Masked. Each has a gun in his hand."

"Six?" said Lee. "They respect us!"

A man threw himself against the other side of the door and an ugly voice said: "Open up or we'll shoot it down."

Lee and Tom backed away. Two men flung themselves against the door together. It creaked dangerously; obviously it would not hold for long. Attracted by the sounds, Adele Emmart appeared from one side and the landlady from the other.

"What's the matter?" gasped Adele.

"Six armed men laying for us," said Lee.

The landlady wrung her hands together. "Oh, why did you bring this trouble on us!"

"They won't hurt you," said Lee. "Is there a service stairway?"

"No. No other stairway."

"Fire escape?"

"This way," gasped the landlady. She flung open another door in the hall. There was a woman in this room. She screamed and ran behind a screen. Lee and Tom could not stop to look at her. Tom locked the door into the hall, while Lee flung up the window. They climbed out on the fire escape in the dark. At that moment the entrance door of the apartment was burst in. Lee and Tom started down the iron ladder.

The window of the apartment below was closed; they went on down. The window of the fourth floor apartment was open. They now heard the window through which they had come, being thrown up; men were climbing out on the fire escape over their heads. They went through the open window and softly pulling down the sash, locked it. Crossing a small dark bedroom, they came out in a narrow hall like the one upstairs. Here they faced a frightened man and woman.

"What . . . what are you doing here?" stammered the man.

Lee raised his hat politely. "Sorry to intrude. Chased by gangsters. I'd be obliged if you'd telephone for the police. Please mention my name: Amos Lee Mappin."

Without stopping, Lee and Tom were making their way to the entrance door. Opening it, they paused to listen. They heard feet clattering down the stairs below them.

"Cut off below," said Tom.

The door of apartment B across the landing opened and a man appeared there with a look of astonished inquiry.

Lee raised his hat. "We are pursued by gangsters. Will you give me shelter for a moment or two?"

The door was slammed in his face, and they heard a bolt shoot across. Lee with a shrug pointed upward. "They wouldn't expect us to go that way. If we can gain a few minutes time, the police will be here."

Yanking off their shoes, they ran noiselessly upstairs; passed the fifth, sixth, and seventh floors, and up the final flight to a door opening on the roof. As they stepped out under the dark sky, two flash-lights were thrown into their faces.

Lee sensed that Tom was drawing his gun. "Don't shoot!" he ordered peremptorily.

Tom lowered his gun. Two dim figures faced them. One seized Lee and threw him down, while the other, with a flashlight in one hand and gun in the other, kept Tom blinded and covered. With astonishing quickness and efficiency, the first man threw a rope around Lee, pinning his arms to his sides and his legs together. The two of them together then did the same to Tom.

"Why did you stop me?" groaned Tom. "I could have got one of them anyway."

"What good if they had got you?" Lee answered calmly.

The two men were tall and brawny specimens. After making sure that Lee and Tom were firmly bound, they half carried, half dragged them down the stairs to the top floor of the house. One of the doors on the landing was cautiously opened and quickly slammed again. Here with perfect effrontery one rang for the elevator. The two were so insolently sure of themselves they no longer troubled to mask. A hard, vicious pair; Lee had never seen either man before. Looking contemptuously down at their prisoners lying on the floor, they lighted cigarettes while they waited. When the car rose into view, one drew his gun and presented it at the operator. The negro turned ashy with terror. The man with the gun said:

"Open the door, nigger. If you make a sound it will be your last."

He was obeyed, of course. Lee and Tom were dragged into the car. "Take us down to the basement," ordered the man with the gun, "and don't stop on the way." As they descended through the house, they heard the distant sounds of approaching sirens. The two gunmen yanked Lee and Tom to their feet and held them in front of them while the car descended past the ground floor. The two prisoners caught a glimpse of Rafferty and McGaha running in from the street, tommy guns in hand. The detectives stopped, helplessly staring.

The other four men of the gang were waiting in the cellar. Lee and Tom were dragged out of the elevator, lifted by shoulders and feet, and rushed down a passage and through a door into the open air. The door was locked behind them. They were carried across a paved yard, through another door, likewise locked behind them, and through another long passage. Lee thought: This is how they came.

At the end of the passage they issued into the open air again, and were carried up a steep stair to the street. There were people in the street, but all shrank away in terror. A sedan waited at the curb with engine running. This was 19th Street, a westbound street. Lee and Tom were flung into the back of the car; two of the men piled in on top of them, a third climbed in alongside the driver; the car sped west. Three men were left in the street.

In 9th Avenue they turned to the left, then presently to the right, to the left, to the right again, always making west. These streets were completely deserted. Satisfied that there was to be no pursuit, the driver presently slowed down and they rolled through old Greenwich at an easy rate. From cobblestones they passed on to a smoother pavement; planks creaked under the wheels of the car. They stopped, letting the engine run, and the gunmen piling out, went into a huddle beside the car. The whistle of a tugboat sounded startlingly near.

"North River," Lee whispered to Tom. "We have stopped on a pier. I can hear the water lapping."

Tom struggled vainly in his bonds. "The river!" he groaned.

They heard one of the men standing alongside say: "Here they come." Another car rolled softly up behind them and stopped. The balance of the gunmen joined their companions. A voice said: "Let in your clutch, Zack, and give her the gun. . . . Mind you don't go over with it," he added, laughing.

"God! . . . like rats!" muttered Tom.

As the car started to move forward, quickly gathering speed, the driver dropped off the running board on the left hand side. Lee, knowing what was coming, contrived with a violent exertion to knock down the handle of the rear door with his head. The door opened a little. As the car leaped over the string-piece, Lee with a further effort got head and shoulders through the door, thus holding it open. The car dropped, headforemost, parting the water with a tremendous splash. As it poured in, Tom, heaving up under Lee, forced him all the way through the door. While he still had air, Lee filled his lungs. He rose to the surface and floated quietly. A second or two later, to his inexpressible relief, Tom rose beside him and floated.

Presently Lee felt Tom's teeth closing in the shoulder of his jacket. The next thing he knew, they were floating under the pier. Lee's head struck against a submerged cross-piece. He heard Tom muttering tensely: "Get your head over it and let it support you."

Lee did so, and rested. Tom was beside him. Overhead they heard the two cars turning on the pier and driving off. The knot which fastened the ropes around Lee's arms was upon his stomach. He felt Tom's teeth pulling at it. It was a long business because Tom frequently had to leave off to get air. The rope loosened at last, and Lee found his arms free. The rest was comparatively easy. Supporting himself with one arm over the cross-piece, Lee untied the ropes which bound Tom. Tom then freed Lee's feet.

"Can you swim?" asked Tom.

"Surely."

They swam out from underneath the pier and headed for the shore, feeling their way along by the piles. They found a rough ladder fixed to one of the piles and clung to it.

"Have you got the strength to draw yourself up?" asked Tom.

"Sure," said Lee. "I'm not a cripple."

"You go first," said Tom.

A minute later they were sitting on the string-piece; water streaming from their clothes. It was a short pier. At the shore end were several rows of quaint little brick buildings with big chimneys. To the north and to the south of them stretched out steamship piers, covered with sheds. No light showed anywhere and no creature moved. Lee's extraordinary knowledge of the town was of service to him now.

"West Washington market," he said. "This little pier was built years ago for the market boats. Now that everything is brought by truck, it is no longer used. There is not another spot in town that could have served their purpose so well."

They were shivering violently. Not until that moment had they realized how bitter cold the water was.

"We must keep moving," said Tom.

"You saved my life," said Lee.

"It would be just as true to say that you saved mine," said Tom. "My struggles in the car had freed my legs just enough so I could strike out a little."

They made their way towards the shore. Passing between the rows of little brick buildings, they came out on 11th Avenue. Cars were purring up and down on the express highway overhead, but nothing moved at street level.

"We'll have to go some distance to find a cab," said Lee.

As they started walking through the silent streets, they heard the clock in the distant Metropolitan tower start to strike. "Nine o'clock," said Lee. "We're too late for the party in the Bronx."

"I hope the guys who attacked us don't escape Loasby," growled Tom.

"They won't, if they drove up to report to the boss," said Lee. "Loasby was not to strike until 9:30."

At the end of 14th Street they hailed a taxicab. Their clothes were still dripping; they had lost their hats; Lee was bleeding from a cut on his forehead. The driver looked them over dubiously.

"Yes," said Lee calmly, "we've been in the river. This fellow saved my life. Five dollars if you take us where we want to go, and no questions asked."

It was sufficient for the driver. Lee gave the address of his apartment and they climbed in.

The apartment was empty, of course. As they had plenty of time, they took hot baths before changing to dry clothes. Lee made a pot of coffee.

They got to Headquarters about 10:30. Inspector Loasby had not yet returned, and they sat down in his office to wait. Half an hour later the Inspector came in looking pretty well done up. When he saw Lee and Tom, the change in his face was magical.

"Thank God . . . Thank God!" he stammered, pumping their arms up and down. "You're all right?"

"Right as rain," said Lee.

"Rafferty and McGaha joined me," said Loasby. "They thought maybe you'd be taken to the hideaway. When we didn't find you there, we were near crazy. What happened?"

"Tell us your story first," said Lee. "Did you get Fingers Claggett?"

"I got him," said Loasby grimly. "Everything passed off like clockwork. Fingers and eleven of his gang. That's pretty near the lot, I reckon."

"Did they put up a fight?"

"No. It was a complete surprise. First we took Blacky near the 177th Street Station. Blacky had the sedan with the closed panels. We left our car some distance short of the vacant house, and I loaded my men in the back of Blacky's car. It was quite a squeeze. We drove right into the place and into the garage. They were expecting Blacky, of course, and if they had an outside man we looked all right to him. I had taken the key off Blacky, and we were in the house and had 'em covered before they knew what was up. If there was a lookout, he escaped; but some of these guys downstairs are ready to sing. I promise you we'll wipe out the gang complete."

"Splendid," said Lee. "But we haven't laid hands on the actual murderer of Walter Ashley."

"We've linked him up with Fingers," said Loasby. "Look what I found in the old man's wallet." He unfolded and handed Lee a sheet of plain white paper, typewritten, signed with an X. The sight of it affected Lee with a slight feeling of sickness. He read:

> Lee Mappin as you see by the newspapers, has discovered the identity of Walter Ashley. This damn snooper is so smart it's unhealthy. He'll get me now, and he'll get you through Loney Frasca's girl if he's not stopped. There's no time for me to plan anything singlehanded. You've got the organization; you must strike and strike swiftly. I will pay fifty thousand dollars if Lee Mappin is liquidated within 24 hours. You don't know me, but you know that I paid on the nail before, and I'll pay again. You've got to do it anyhow to save your own skins.

Lee handed back the letter. "We still have work to do," he said.

"Do you want to question Fingers?" asked Loasby. "He's down-stairs, wheel-chair and all."

Lee shook his head. "He'll keep. I've had enough for one day."

CHAPTER TWENTY-ONE

ON THE FOLLOWING MORNING Lee drove downtown to the office of Warner, Mills and Co. He was still accompanied by his bodyguard, since Loasby feared that the principal in the affair, made desperate by the capture of Fingers Claggett and his gang, might venture to take a shot at Lee himself. At the stockbrokers Lee's name provided an immediate passport to the private office of the senior partner.

"I have called in reference to the unfortunate Walter Ashley," said Lee. "I am told that he had an account with your firm."

"Walter Ashley, the young fellow who was murdered?" said the astonished Mr. Warner. "I know nothing about it."

He made an inquiry over the phone, and a clerk presently entered bringing a loose-leaf ledger.

"It is so," said Mr. Warner, consulting the ledger. "Why wasn't I told of this?" he demanded of the clerk. "Mr. Mappin ought to have been notified immediately."

"The account was closed two weeks ago, sir. Such a small account nobody happened to remember it."

"That's right," said Mr. Warner, returning to the ledger. "Closed out two weeks ago Tuesday. I see by this that Ashley was lucky enough to call a turn on American Can. The balance in his favor was three thousand and some dollars."

"That's important," said Lee. "Would your check to Ashley have been returned as yet from the bank?"

"Surely. We get a weekly statement from the bank."

The clerk was dispatched to find the check. While they waited Lee and Mr. Warner discussed some of the aspects of the extraordinary case. In due course the check was brought in, and Lee looked eagerly at the endorsements.

"This was deposited in the 96th Street branch of the Grain Exchange bank," he said. "An important clue, and I am very much obliged to you, sir."

"Not at all," said Mr. Warner. "Always happy to be of assistance in a matter of this kind."

Lee and his bodyguard immediately made the long drive up to 96th Street. The branch bank was not far from where Walter Ashley had lived. It did not take long to discover that Ashley had cashed his check the same day he received it, and had closed his account.

"The check was certified," explained the teller.

Lee thought glumly: Another dead end! However, he had one more lead. "Do you have safe deposit boxes in this building?" he asked.

"Yes, sir."

Lee was directed to the manager, sitting in a little enclosure nearby. A book was consulted and it was discovered that Walter Ashley had rented a safe deposit box. Moreover, he had not given it up when he closed his account; it still stood in his name. Lee's spirits rose.

"Must I go to Police Headquarters to obtain a written order to have the box opened?" asked Lee. "Or could it be arranged by telephone? I have two men of Inspector Loasby's force with me, if that makes any difference."

"I think it can be arranged by telephone, Mr. Mappin," said the manager affably. "It will save you such a long wait."

Having been assured by the Inspector that a written order would be on the way in five minutes, the manager led Lee and his guard down to the safe deposit boxes in the basement. The small box rented by Walter Ashley was forced open. It contained nothing but two packets of letters in square white envelopes addressed in a woman's hand.

Lee's face became very grave. "With these letters I shall solve his murder," he said.

He would not read the letters until he was alone in his little office. There were about thirty of them, all arranged according to the date of the postmark. Lee's face was heavy as he unfolded the first sheet. He recognized the handwriting. He felt a sense of sacrilege in reading these pitiful love letters to a dead boy, but he could not evade that duty.

> My darling boy:
> Your presence is still with me. I have only to close my eyes to see your face, to hear your voice. All my life I waited for you and when you came I lost myself. You asked me tonight if I were happy and I could not answer. I don't seem to know whether I am happy or not. It doesn't seem to matter. But this I know, for the first time since I was a child life seems to have meaning. I am living—living in you! And Oh! the world is so beautiful! Perhaps this is happiness, but it seems to me to be more than happiness, I have no word to express it . . .

Many letters in the same vein. Lee skimmed over them hurriedly. They had all been written after meetings between the lovers during which practical matters had been thoroughly discussed. Consequently it was not necessary to speak of them in the letters. They were full of references to which Lee possessed no clue.

Midway in the series, there began to be hints of the intention of the two to go away together.

> . . . I cannot honestly feel as you do about my jewels. After all, they are mine, legally mine, whoever gave them to me. I don't see why I shouldn't take them. I would never have any feeling of guilt in taking them. From the beginning I have never had one moment's

feeling of guilt in connection with you. You are my light, my life, my good angel. Before you came I led a hideous existence. I was often on the point of ending it. I shouldn't have had any feeling of guilt about that either. I shouldn't mind poverty for myself; I could starve cheerfully with you. But it would nearly break my heart to see you suffer, or to see you idle and feeling useless. However, my beloved, it shall be as you wish. I guess your sense of honor is higher than mine. I will leave the jewels behind. I will take nothing with me but a change of clothing . . .

In a letter mailed a few days later Lee found this significant reference.

. . . Yesterday was a blank day, a lost day, a dead day. I did not see you. Last night after dinner I heard the men talking about American Can. They said that owing to a deal which has not yet been published, there would be an advance of 10 points in the stock within the next week or two. These men know what they are talking about; they are on the inside; they are buying the stock themselves. Isn't this worth taking a chance on? . . .

The next to the last letter had been written on Wednesday, two days before Walter was killed. It was brief.

. . . I am so happy, so happy that you actually have the money in hand. Friday it shall be. I feel like a life-prisoner who unexpectedly sees release two days ahead.

The final letter had been posted on the following day, Thursday.

My darling, soon to be my very own:

It seems best to change our arrangements. There is
a possibility that I am watched, that I might be followed to the railway station. Tomorrow night I am
invited to a dance given by the Holland Society at
the Waldorf-Astoria. I shall proceed to the hotel in
my own car, driven by our chauffeur. After entering
the hotel I shall come out by another door where my
maid's husband will be waiting for me in his car. She
describes it as a faded blue sedan. My maid and her
husband are under great obligations to me and I can
rely on them absolutely. My maid will see that the
suitcase I am taking is waiting for me in this car.
Her husband will then drive into the transverse road
which enters the Park just north of the Menagerie.
They tell me this road is very little used after night-
fall. We will get there about 10 minutes past 10 and
will wait about 300 yards in from 5th Avenue. I will
be wearing my green net dress and the white evening
coat with white fox collar that you are familiar with
and will have a green scarf over my head. When you
come, my maid's husband will drive us up to Harmon
where we can get on one of the late trains for the
west without showing ourselves in the city station.
You must not try to communicate with me after getting this. It would be too dangerous. Just be on hand
in the Park and you'll find me there. . . .

Lee's face turned hard upon reading the reference to the faded
blue sedan, the green dress, the white evening coat. Placing this
last letter beside another of the series, he studied them through a
magnifying glass. It was soon clear that the last letter was a forgery. It was a clever forgery and an eager lover would easily have
been deceived. The details of the plot were now only too clear.
Walter Ashley, hastening into the transverse road that Friday night
and finding the faded blue sedan waiting, had seen in the dim light

the green dress, the white coat, the green scarf in the rear, and had opened the door. Loney Frasca had received him with a blow from the neat silencer, and Walter had then been carried down to East Second Street. How devilish and how simple!

Lee's heart was heavy. In order to make assurance doubly sure, he now got from his personal file a brief note written on different paper, and compared it with the others. The handwriting was the same.

He had not the heart to tell his office force what he had discovered. He merely gave the word for Headquarters, and his bodyguard accompanied him downstairs. They hailed the first taxi. At Headquarters, leaving his guard outside Inspector Loasby's private office, he laid the letters before his friend and told his story. Loasby was transfixed with amazement and a kind of horror.

"Good God, Mappin! This will blow the town sky high!"

Lee was silent for a moment before replying. "It is too horrible, Loasby. I cannot bear to feed the sensation-loving public such a story. Consider what the woman has suffered already. I put it to you, wouldn't it be better to warn the man that the police are coming for him?"

"What!" cried Loasby. "Give him a chance to escape! A brutal, crafty killer like that! A double murderer!"

"You misunderstand me," said Lee. "Before warning him, find out where he is, and have the place surrounded so that, if he should try to make a getaway, he will be taken. He won't try to escape."

"You believe then . . ." Loasby left his sentence in the air. After a moment he added slowly: "I get you." He considered for awhile. "All right, Mr. Mappin. I'll take that responsibility."

They quickly established the fact that the man they wanted was at home. Loasby dispatched a sufficient number of men, and after giving them time to take their places, caused a telephone message to be sent to the man in question. Loasby, Lee, Tom Collar, Rafferty and McGaha then started uptown in the Inspector's own scarlet sedan. Loasby, on account of some ceremony that was to take place later in the day, was in uniform. In a few minutes they reached the magnificent apartment house overhanging the bank of the East

River. Several plainclothesmen were visible in the vicinity. They went up in an elevator. As the button was pressed at the door of the penthouse apartment, there was the sound of a shot inside. Lee and Loasby exchanged a somber glance without speaking.

They had to ring repeatedly. Finally the door was opened by a terrified manservant. "Police!" he gasped at sight of Loasby's uniform. "I . . . suppose you have to know! I suppose you have to be admitted! . . . A terrible thing has just happened . . . My master has shot himself!"

The servant led them to the magnificent library with its heavy oaken furniture and its line of casements looking out over the river. Tyrrell Blair, sitting in his chair, had sprawled forward on his desk. A wide crimson stain was spreading in the desk blotter. The gun had fallen to the floor.

At the door of the room, Tom Cottar, et al., understood the significance of what had happened without the necessity of any explanations.

"But Mappin," muttered the perplexed Inspector, "we had evidence that Mr. Blair remained here at home on the night of the first murder."

Lee shook his head. "Our evidence was only that he did not go out by either of the doors of this house. There is the yacht landing, remember. Blair always protested that he hated the water and never owned a boat. He could have hired a hundred boats if he had need of them. . . . I have been in this room many times," he went on, "and have used my eyes as well as I could." He pointed to a handsome carved chest under the windows. "I have always been curious about that piece of furniture. It is locked."

"Probably the key is on him," said Loasby.

A bunch of keys was found in Blair's pocket. One of them fitted the carved chest. When the cover was thrown back they saw a typewriter of a well-known make, together with a supply of plain white paper and envelopes. The typewriter was lifted out and placed on the table. Lee inserted a piece of paper and wrote a few lines. Handing the paper to Loasby, he said:

"If you compare that under a magnifying glass with the anonymous letters, you will have conclusive evidence."

Lee left the police in charge of the Blair apartment. Rafferty and McGaha remained to assist the Inspector, and Tom Cottar stayed in his ordinary capacity of newspaper reporter. Lee telephoned for his own car and when it came, ordered his chauffeur to drive to Old Westbury. He had no further need of a bodyguard. Crossing the high-flung Queensboro Bridge he had plenty to think about. A painful task still lay ahead of him, yet for better or worse the matter was ended and he experienced a profound relief. He vowed to himself that hereafter he would stick to his writing and avoid contacts with the raw material of crime. It was not the first time that he had made such a resolution.

The Blair country house, in deference to the modern manner, was not in the least magnificent, but supremely comfortable and inviting. One of the perfect Blair menservants opened the door. Lee saw from the man's face even before he spoke, that he would be denied admission.

"Madam is not at home, sir."

"Can you tell me when she will return? I have driven all the way from town to see her."

"I do not know when she will return, Sir. I might say, however, that Madam is not seeing anybody at present." "Anybody" was delicately underlined.

By this, Lee knew that Mary was at home. "Lovely afternoon," he said. "I'll just take a little look around the grounds, before I go back."

He strolled along a path that would lead him around the house. He was known to be a family friend, and they were hardly likely to throw him out, he thought. He knew the place well. It was the inferior part of the house that faced the drive; the best rooms and the garden were at the back. He was pretty sure that he would find Mary in the garden. It was a secret garden hidden within a tall enclosure of arbor vitae. The two trees which flanked the entrance were trained into the form of an arch.

She was sitting on a bench inside. She had a pair of shears in her hand, but they hung down listlessly. He was shocked by the change in her. Gaunt and thin as from long illness, she was nevertheless still beautiful. There was a noble quality in her grief. The garden was full of delphiniums and she was wearing a cotton dress of delphinium blue. She was glad to see him.

"Lee!" she cried rising. "What a surprise!"

He silently took her hand.

She dropped on the bench as if her knees had suddenly failed her; tears started from her eyes. "Don't mind me," she faltered. "I'm not usually a cry baby. But . . . it's so long since I have seen a friendly face!"

Lee sat beside her, retaining her hand in his. "Mary, dear, you must brace yourself to hear serious news." She looked at him questioningly, without alarm. "Your husband is dead. He shot himself."

Her expression scarcely changed. For some moments she continued to look at Lee without speaking. At last she said: "I can't make pretenses with you, Lee. What is it to me if he's dead? He was a bad man. I am relieved because I shall see him no more. He's been coming out here just to taunt me." A shiver went through her thin frame. "It was hard to bear."

"To taunt you!"

"Somehow he had learned what happened . . . I'm going to tell you now."

"Dearest," said Lee, "I already know it." He took the packet of letters from his pocket and dropped it into her lap.

"My letters!" she exclaimed opening her eyes wide. "Did *he* have them?"

Lee shook his head. "I got them out of Walter's safe deposit box."

"I wonder why Walter kept them," she said with a look of bitter pain.

Lee was astonished. "Mary! you don't know what happened, then!"

"I know that Walter was faithless."

"Walter? No! Haven't you been reading the newspapers?"

"No," she said indifferently. "Newspapers no longer mean anything to me."

"Well, I'm glad I came," Lee said grimly. "I can cure at least a part of your hurt. Why do you say Walter was faithless?"

"His last letter," she said with twisted lips. "He said it was all a mistake. He said that he did not love me well enough to ask me to share his life, and that he was going away alone."

"Have you got that letter?"

"No. I destroyed all his letters."

"The last one was a forgery," said Lee.

Turning she seized his arm. "What do you mean? What do you mean?" she cried wildly.

Lee drew the bottom letter from the packet in Mary's lap. "Read the last letter that Walter received from you," he said.

Her eyes flew from line to line. "But . . . but I never wrote this," she cried wildly.

"Of course you didn't. This letter is a forgery, and so was the last letter that you got from Walter."

Mary stared at him piteously. Moments passed before she could take in the significance of his words. "He . . . *he* did it? My husband?"

"I doubt if he had the skill himself. But he had it done."

"And what happened?" she whispered.

"Blair was privy to the whole correspondence. I have no doubt he planted the tip on American Can. Walter kept the appointment that he thought you had made. Blair killed him."

Mary wavered on the bench. Lee caught her in his arms and held her close. When she was capable of taking it in, he said: "Dearest, it's better than what you thought, isn't it? Isn't it?"

"Oh, yes!" she whispered. "Anything is better than to feel oneself betrayed. . . . Now I can keep his memory sweet always, always!"

CHAPTER TWENTY-TWO

ON THE FOLLOWING DAY at his office Lee found some reports from Stan Oberry which had been overlooked during the excitement. Stan, having received no orders to the contrary, was still having Rafe Deshon followed. Two nights before, Rafe had started out from his home, carrying a suitcase. When he proceeded to the Pennsylvania terminal and, as on a previous occasion, disappeared in one of the dressing rooms in the basement, the operative who was trailing him, expecting that he would try to repeat his former trick, made hasty arrangements over the telephone to have all the exits from the Times Square Station watched. Rafe, therefore, now dressed as a shabby underworld character, was picked up when he came out in Times Square and followed over to Hoboken. He entered a dive frequented by low characters of both sexes. It appeared that he was well known in the place. Thus his boast of liking low company was in fact true, and there was no more to it than that. The details of his activities made unpleasant reading, but they were not indictable, and were therefore of no interest to Lee or to the police. His wife, Lee had reason to know, was familiar with the nature of his amusements, and if she did not wish to sue him for divorce, that was her lookout.

Upon the death of Tyrrell Blair, Deshon succeeded to the control of Blair and Middlebrook. The Middlebrook interest had retired long before. The firm continued to prosper, and the Deshons, Rafe and Peggy, to shine in the glittering circle of society that they led. To a hard-working man like Tom Cottar this seemed like an injustice. "The so-and-so ought to be shown up," he grumbled. But Lee, older and more philosophic, merely shrugged. "You have no cause to envy the Deshons," he said. "I doubt if there is an unhappier pair in New York. They won't last long."

Lee, in pursuance of his resolve to have nothing further to do with criminals in the flesh, left Fingers Claggett and his gang to the police. Fingers was convicted under the old indictment for robbery and sentenced to Sing Sing for a long term. The old man was dead within three months, and there was no person on earth who regretted his passing. Lee and Tom Cottar were able to identify the six men who had tried to drown them, and these also received long sentences. Jermyn identified others; all the members of the gang were had under one charge or another, and were put out of the way of doing further harm.

With old Jim Costin, the case was somewhat different. Lee had proof that Costin had stolen papers from his file which he had subsequently sold to Fingers through Blacky. However, since this appeared to be Jim's first criminal offense, Lee, for the sake of his hard-working wife, forebore to prosecute. The fright that Jim received, Lee thought, would be sufficient to keep him out of such dangerous courses in future. Mrs. Costin continued to be the caretaker of the little office building on Madison Avenue and Jim pursued a completely worthless but harmless existence between the Public Library and Hymie's Saloon.

The man known to the public as Boris Fanton received the limit of the law. Everybody felt that he ought to have gone to the chair, but that was impossible since his victim had been saved from death by a hair's breadth. The sorrows of this unfortunate young woman made her a kind of public heroine. One of the detectives who had assisted in the arrest of her husband fell in love with her out of pity and married her. It turned out all right.

The other bereaved woman, Marta Corioli, found no man to take Loney Frasca's place in her heart. She was the one-man type. But the publicity attending the case brought her friends and helpers. She received the offer of a position in a better dress shop than she had ever known before. It subsequently transpired that she

had a real talent for design which attracted the attention of no less
a person than Madame Hattie Carnegie. Marta rose fast in her pro-
fession and was not dependent on any man.

Judy Bowles' wound, though painful, was not a deep one. It
healed quickly and Lee was much relieved to see her adopt the
maxim that there is safety in numbers. She soon acquired a round
dozen of admirers.

The red-headed Tom Cottar did his best to use his narrow escape from death as a lever to bring Fanny Parran to the point. When
she first heard of the danger he had been in, Fanny surrendered
completely, and Tom had a glimpse of Paradise. But only a glimpse,
for Fanny quickly recovered herself.

"Why marry?" she said. "We have good times as it is."

"We don't," said Tom. "We scrap all the time."

"Well, that's stimulating. Marriage seems so flat. Like the inevitable last chapter of a novel. I hate to finish a good book."

"Why shouldn't it be the first chapter of a better novel?"

"A novel is no good without suspense."

"No man who lived with you would ever be without suspense,"
said Tom grimly.

Fanny clasped her hands demurely. "I would do my best."

"Have you no heart?"

"Frankly, I don't know," said Fanny innocently. "What would
you say?"

"I can't talk to you," said Tom, waving his hands. "I'd like to
beat you."

"Really?" said Fanny. "And you ask me to many you!"

Tom climbed down. "I wouldn't beat you if we were married,"
he said, reaching for her hand. "I would only love you."

Fanny let him keep her hand for a moment. "So you say. It
would be an awful risk to take, with a redheaded man."

"Suppose I had drowned in the North River?"

Fanny's eyes softened. "Then I would have been sorry I hadn't
married you. I would have regretted it to my dying day!"

"Well then?" he said eagerly.

"But you didn't drown," she said provokingly, "and you're not likely to drown any more. You're a husky specimen. You ought to be good for eighty years. You might turn out to be a horrible old man."

"How about you? I'd be taking the same chance."

"I know I'll be a horrible old woman," said Fanny. "I want to save you from that."

Tom surrendered. He was no match for Fanny in these verbal set-tos. "I've done talking," he said. "I'm going to kiss you when we get out in the hall."

"What a treat for the little woman!" said Fanny.

WHEN THE EXCITEMENT attendant upon the arrests died down, Lee, with a thankful heart, resumed work on his big book, "The Psychology of Murder." This, he told himself, was his true metier, an intellectual examination of crime, without this running around the streets to shoot and be shot at. Leaving Fanny Parran and Judy Bowles to take care of the vast mail and the endless telephone calls resulting from the latest glare of publicity, he spent his working hours quietly in his library studying the crimes of long ago and taking notes.

For relaxation he continued to accept such invitations to dinner as promised good food and interesting company. This was supplemented by his long walks through unexplored New York dressed in old clothes, and the conversations he had with odd characters he picked up. Lee held firmly to the maxim that the proper study of mankind is man. He liked to give dinners himself, too. The food might not be as good as that provided by the late Tyrrell Blair because Lee could not give his whole time to food, but the company was of the best. Lee did not accept the world's judgment on men but formed his own. You met all kinds at his table except one; archbishops, actresses famous or obscure, Salvation Army officers, young writers—Lee did not run much to famous authors because he said they were asked out too much. Also aviators, seafarers, models, in fact anybody who was supremely good at his or her job. Only the stuffed shirts were left out.

COACHWHIP PUBLICATIONS

ALSO AVAILABLE

1

HULBERT FOOTNER
THE ADVENTURES OF
MADAME STOREY

ISBN 978-1-61646-236-9

THE
DEATH
OF A
CELEBRITY

HULBERT
FOOTNER

AN AMOS LEE MAPPIN MYSTERY

ISBN 978-1-61646-263-5

COACHWHIP PUBLICATIONS

COACHWHIPBOOKS.COM

THE
MYSTERY
OF THE
FOLDED
PAPER

HULBERT
FOOTNER

ISBN 978-1-61646-255-8

ORCHIDS
TO MURDER

HULBERT
FOOTNER

ISBN 978-1-61646-262-8

COACHWHIP PUBLICATIONS

COACHWHIPBOOKS.COM

WHO KILLED THE
HUSBAND?

HULBERT FOOTNER

ISBN 978-1-61646-256-6

COACHWHIP PUBLICATIONS

COACHWHIPBOOKS.COM

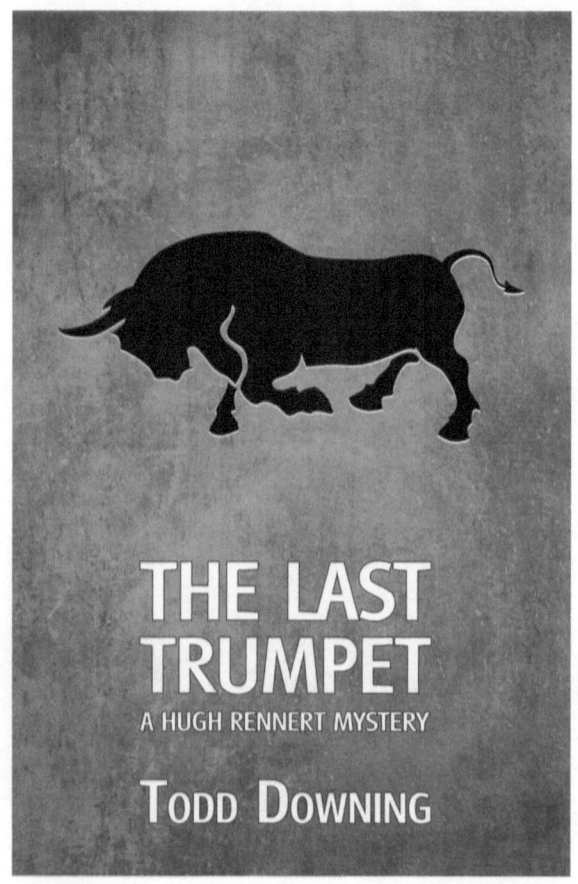

THE LAST
TRUMPET
A HUGH RENNERT MYSTERY

TODD DOWNING

ISBN 978-1-61646-152-2

THE QUINNY HITE
MYSTERIES

CHINESE RED · HERE LIES THE BODY

RICHARD BURKE

ISBN 978-1-61646-247-5

COACHWHIP PUBLICATIONS

COACHWHIPBOOKS.COM

MURDER OF
THE HONEST BROKER

WILLOUGHBY SHARP

ISBN 978-1-61646-211-6

THERE IS
NO RETURN
THE ADELAIDE ADAMS MYSTERIES
ANITA BLACKMON

ISBN 978-1-61646-223-9

www.ingramcontent.com/pod-product-compliance
Lightning Source LLC
Chambersburg PA
CBHW020553020726
47494CB00006B/2053